To everyone who has felt as if life is too much, as if there is no reason to go on, as if merely waking up each day is an impossible feat: take one more step, take one more breath, take it one day at a time and know that you are not alone;

"No man is an island, entire of himself."
~ John Donne, Meditation XVII

One: Drifting
Ben

I HAVE NO IDEA WHERE THE HELL I AM. AND, HONESTLY, I don't even care. I'm still headed west on the I-80 as I have been for like…shit, like a month. I mean, yeah, I know you can make it from coast to coast in like three days nonstop, but I'm not in a rush. I'm not going anywhere. I'm just…going. So I drive until I get sick of driving, and then I find a cheap motel to crash in, and I'll just stay there for a while. A day, sometimes more if I like the place. A few times I've swung off the 80 on a detour, just to meander and go wherever I feel like going.

I've always known I was a very, very lucky guy to have the parents I do. I mean, I've never wanted for anything. Not a damned thing. But they still made me work for things, one way or another. I had to keep my grades up and help out around the house and shit, but that's to be expected anyway. But to have the financial freedom to do what I'm doing, to just drive and not worry about money? It's incredibly freeing. I've got money of my own I've been saving. Once I turned sixteen I started working part-time at the coffee shop near school, just to have my own savings. I worked there for five years, staying on when I started college. I never really spent much of what I made, so I've got some cash banked up. Plus, if I ever need more, I could just call Dad...but I won't.

So...I drift.

And I try not to think about Kylie.

Which, not having much to do but drive and listen to music is...nearly impossible.

So I make a game out of it. If I can make it ten miles without missing her, or wondering what she's doing, or thinking about calling her, I get to wallow in my own misery for five whole minutes. It's a bargain with the devil, and it's fucking pathetic, and I hate myself for it.

But it gets the job done.

Ten miles. Hey, look at the cow. How many cows are there in that field? God, it's only been a mile, shit. Change the radio station to the Liquid Metal station on the XM, crank it, and see if I can decipher all the lyrics to three songs in a row. Hey, it's been ten miles.

Fuck, I miss her. I miss her strawberry blonde hair and her blue eyes and her laugh. I miss the easy way we could spend an entire day hanging out and doing homework and watching TV and driving around and exchange maybe a hundred words the entire time, because we just *got* each other. And then I'll indulge in memories until my heart aches and my eyes burn and I want to drive off the fucking road. I try to force my thoughts away.

After a month of traveling this way I make it to Iowa. By then I'm bored of my own company and the inside of my truck, and sick of my own thoughts, so I rent a room on a month-by-month basis and get a job at a bar, bussing tables. It's a tiny dirty place just off the freeway and I work for cash under the table, giving the owner only my first name. It feels exciting, in a way, like I'm on the lam or something. I make friends with the line cook, Dion, and we get wasted after the bar closes, playing poker for quarters. I mess around with the waitress, a woman seven years older than me named Abby, who has lived in the same shitty little nowhere town her whole life. She's the daughter of a cocktail waitress who had drifted into town years ago, got herself knocked up and never left. Then

Abby had gotten knocked up at nineteen and the pattern continued.

It's sad.

But Abby is kind and doesn't ask any questions about who I am, or where I came from, or where I'm going. She's content to drink cheap whisky with me in my hotel room, watch reruns of M*A*S*H and *Cheers* and make out, play wandering hands. That is, until she pushes me to go further and I can't...she doesn't get that. Apparently "I just can't" isn't explanation enough when I—*ahem*—very clearly and obviously and physically seem to *want* to go further with her.

So I pack my clothes in my duffel bag, toss the bag in my truck, and I take off right then, at 4:19 in the morning.

I drive north, up into South Dakota, and end up in another one-stoplight town a few miles off the freeway. I land a job splitting logs, which then turns into digging postholes for a fence that ends up running around a thousand-acre ranch. I stay there doing that for two and a half months, chopping firewood and digging holes and planting posts and running fence. It's hard physical work, and it keeps my mind occupied.

Eventually, though, the work is done and I'm back in the truck. West again, through Montana, where I discover that herding cattle is a lot more boring than I thought it would be. After that I head south through the corner of Idaho, and do a three-month stint in a restaurant as a line cook.

By this time it's winter, so I point my truck west and aim for the coast. In a little industrial town on the coast of Oregon I unload pallets of I-have-no-clue-what off a boat and load them onto a semi. I do this for a while and then head south along PCH, following the Pacific, finding work where I can in bars and restaurants, doing temporary unskilled labor for cash.

In time, it gets easier to pass entire days without thinking about Kylie. And then days turn into weeks, and then I only think about her late at night, right before I fall asleep.

Eventually, I stop thinking about her almost entirely.

Almost.

I faithfully call my parents once a week, 'cause I'm a momma's boy, deep down.

I follow Dad's games on TV, watch him lead the league in TDs and take the Titans to the Superbowl, which is exciting, even though they ended up losing to the fucking Patriots again.

Eventually, after spending most of the winter in San Diego working on the docks, I head eastward once again through the Southwest, this time driving through the desert with my windows open, stopping to flip burgers or pour beer or wash dishes for a week or two here and there.

I'm restless.

Not unhappy, just...sick of traveling. Sick of driving.

Sick of myself.

So when I hit the Texas border, I discover I have an affinity for the wide open spaces and the huge sky. I make my way through Texas, meandering and exploring, not in a hurry, not headed anywhere in particular. After a month or two of drifting around Texas, I end up in San Antonio. I like the city, and decide to stick around for a while. I apply for an actual job in a bar downtown, with a W-2 and everything. A month later, I'm leaning against a wall in Starbucks, waiting for my mocha, when I see the ad:

Football players wanted for an experimental minor league team. Serious, experienced players over eighteen. Open tryouts, May 9th at noon, Alamodome.

Boom.

After three seasons starting as a wide receiver for Vanderbilt, making university records for rushing and TD receptions...I make the team easy.

God, it's good to be playing ball again. I'm fucking hungry for it. I play harder than I've ever played in my life—run faster, jump higher, make catches I didn't think were possible. It doesn't pay much, so I keep my day job at the bar working from nine to four, then practice, then home. It becomes a routine. I make friends with the guys on the team, drink with 'em, hang with 'em, go to keggers after games, big bonfire parties in the country outside the city with dozens of people getting wasted and having a great time. I get in drunken brawls, make out with wasted girls in the shadows...

But making out never goes anywhere.

I can't.

I just can't.

I don't think about Kylie much anymore and I sure don't ask Mom or Dad how she's doing. I don't want to know. I mean, I do, but I don't. If things start to get hot and heavy with a girl I can only see Kylie, and I think about how long I waited for her, how I saved my first kiss for her, saved it until I was seventeen, at which point I got drunk and wasted it by accident on Allie Mercer.

My brain has gone haywire. I want to move on, but I can't. I freeze up. And I can't even explain it—I can't get the words out.

Eventually, I stop bothering with girls. It never goes anywhere, and it's not fair to them to lead them on, make them think it's going somewhere it's not.

My self-loathing is a great motivator. I turn the gut-churning hatred of my own failings into insane rushing and reception stats, which get me noticed by scouts. I mean, that's the entire point of the experimental league, after all—to get a place, other than at a university, which grooms raw talent and discovers untapped potential.

Halfway through the season, we're in a game, in the third quarter, playing Los Angeles.

We're up by fourteen, both TDs mine. We're on our own forty, second down. Timo Jeffries, the QB, calls the play, feints a hand-off, which gives me time to cut through the lines and sprint downfield. I slice left…BAM, the ball hits me dead center and I'm gone, blasting toward their end zone.

Only, I'm not alone. Their defense has been double teaming me the last three drives, and it's fucking effective, goddamn them. So there are two defenders on me, and though they couldn't stop me from making the catch, they're fucking fast and they're on me like white on rice. I try a fake right, one of them buys it and I lunge left, but the other has me around the waist, dragging me down. I lean into the tackle and push forward, straining for one more yard or two.

More defenders are rushing up the field, catching up. I'm seconds from letting myself hit the turf when I see it happen in slow motion.

A big-ass dude with dreads hanging around his shoulders, a fierce grin on his face, is coming straight for me. I put a hand out and start to go down, but he flies at me anyway, and he hits me on an angle.

I feel it; it's like a fucking Mack truck smashing into me. But he missed his tackle. Instead of nailing my midsection, he misjudges and his shoulder drives into my right knee.

I hear the *crack* of bone snapping; feel an explosion of raw agony. I'm down, and no one knows what just happened except me and the guy who hit me. A body drives me into the dirt, and another hits my knee, and I hear someone screaming.

It's me.

I don't hear the whistle; don't feel anything but the pain in my knee.

"Shit, man, you okay?" It's the guy who hit me, his helmet off, dreads dangling around his worried face. "I didn't mean it, man, I'm sorry, you okay?"

I can't breathe from the pain.

Someone is kneeling beside me, and I feel hands on my knee, and then I'm being lifted onto a stretcher. They set me down too hard and I feel dizziness wash over me, darkness rushes up and I'm out cold.

Two: Now What?

I'M IN A HOSPITAL BED. MY KNEE IS WRAPPED AND elevated, and I'm alone.

I just woke up from surgery. I remember agreeing to whatever they had to do. I remember saying I'd call my family afterward. I remember the mask and the anesthesia floating through me.

And now I'm alone, and my knee hurts, and I don't know what's next.

Fuck. This isn't good. Not good. I don't know how bad my knee is, but I'll probably miss the rest of the season, at least.

A nurse comes in. "Oh, you're awake. How do you feel, Mr. Dorsey?"

I shrug. "Okay, I guess. It aches." That's an under-statement. It fucking kills.

"Need something for the pain?" she asks. The nurse is a pretty middle-aged woman with brown hair and brown eyes.

I nod. "Sure."

I want to ask, but I don't.

So I wait until she returns thirty minutes later with a paper cup containing two pills and a half-can of ginger ale. I take the pills and settle back, then finally get the courage. The nurse's name tag identifies her as Pam.

"Pam?" I touch the bandage around my knee. "How bad is it? When can I play again?"

Her expression goes carefully blank and she doesn't answer right away. "Um, I think maybe you should talk to Dr. Lane, Mr. Dorsey."

"Shit." I lean back and squeeze my eyes shut. "That's not good."

She tries to smile, but it doesn't reach her eyes. "You'll be all right, sweetie. I'll page Dr. Lane for you."

Two hours later, a tall, thin, balding man in a lab coat sweeps into the room and pulls up a seat beside the bed. "Ben, how are you, son?"

I shrug. "Depends on what you're about to tell me, Doc."

He's quiet for a minute, and then he leans back in the red plastic visitor's chair, letting out a long sigh. "Well, then...I'm not gonna bullshit you, son. You messed up your knee pretty bad."

"How bad?"

His eyes meet mine, and I see pity in them. Fucking pity. "Pretty bad. The hit you took...that was a career-ender, Ben. I'm sorry."

"Career—" I have to clear my throat and blink hard several times. "Career-ender. You're kidding. Tell me you're—you've got to be fucking kidding me."

Dr. Lane shakes his head. "I'm sorry, Ben. You'll need intensive physical therapy just to be able to walk on it again. With months of work, you *may* be able to jog short distances. But competitive football? That's over for you, son."

How many times is this guy going to call me *son* in one conversation?

I nod and stare at my knee rather than at him. He's just the bearer of bad news; it's not his fault. Smashing his nose in would be bad form, I'm guessing.

"Can I have...a minute, please?" I ask.

He stands up, but doesn't leave right away. "You got family to call?"

I nod. "Yeah."

But even after he's gone and I have my phone, I don't call home. I'm not sure why.

That's a lie, though. They'll make me come home, and I'll have to see Kylie and Oz. Mom let it slip a few weeks ago that they got married recently. So now she's Kylie Hyde. She married him. I got wasted when I found out. Missed work the next day, and skipped practice.

I can't go back.

Dad bought me my own health insurance policy before I left, so this'll be covered by the deductible, and what's not I can take care of on my own. I don't need them to visit me. I don't want them to.

They'll be sad and tell me it'll be fine.

It's not fine.

I'll never play football again.

I nearly cry, sitting there alone in the hospital bed. But I don't.

A taxi takes me home. Timo swings by and gets my keys and then brings my truck back for me. I thank him, and he leaves, even though he clearly wants to stay and hang out. But he's a football buddy, and I can't handle that right now.

I flip through the folder of instructions I got when I checked out of the hospital. Primarily, I look through the list of outpatient physical therapists in the area. I settle on the closest one. It's a mile and half away, so I can take a taxi there until I figure out a better way to get from place to place. Driving is out of the question for the immediate future.

At home, there'd be Mom and Dad to drive me to therapy. Or even Colt and Nell. Here? It's just me. But I'm determined to do this on my own. It's fucking stupid, even I know that. I should call Dad and tell him what happened, let him come get me and bring me home. But what then? Back to Vanderbilt? Where everyone will know me, where the pity over my ruined football career will be the talk of the whole college. It was bad enough when I dropped out at the end of my junior year and vanished, but if I were to show up a year and half later, in a fucking wheelchair? Fuck no.

Next morning, woozy from pain, I hobble with the help of crutches into the kitchen of my rented apartment and make coffee. It's easier to drink it standing up than to lower myself onto a chair only to have to stand back up again. I call a cab and give the driver the address of the physical therapist.

It's a storefront in a strip mall, sandwiched between a Supercuts and a dry-cleaner. *Leveaux Physical Therapy and Fitness Training.* I pay the small fare, grip my crutches in both hands, lean on them and lever myself to my feet. I find my balance, and then adjust my crutches and make my way to the appointment. It's hot as hell outside, and I'm sweating by the time I reach the door.

Alan Jackson is playing from the overhead speakers, and it's blessedly cool inside, the way Texans like it. It's a fairly small space, filled to the max with weight machines of all kinds, free weights, treadmills, stair-steppers, and a space cleared around the perimeter of the room for a small walking track. I scan the gym: there's an older man working a leg-lift machine, an overweight woman sweating buckets and puffing and gamely limping along on a Stairmaster. A woman with blonde, braided hair stands beside a young black guy with an athletic prosthetic from the knee down, encouraging him as he squats, lifts a free-weight bar, and stands up with it, lifts it over his head, and then bends, squats, and sets it down again.

A bell dings as I walk in, and the blonde woman pats the young man on the back. "Keep going, Nick. You're doing great. Six more reps, okay? I'll be right back."

She approaches me, a bright, warm smile on her face. She's gorgeous. Not real tall, maybe five-six or so, but she's clearly fit as hell. She extends her hand to me, and I take it and shake, squeezing gently.

"Hey there," she says. "I'm Cheyenne Leveaux. How can I help you?"

My gaze wants to roam down, take in her body, but I keep my eyes on hers. "Hi. I'm Ben Dorsey. I had a knee injury recently, and the hospital referred you as a physical therapist."

Cheyenne nods. "Sure. Why don't you come on back to the office and we'll set things up." She nods at a door in the back. We pass by the guy with the prosthetic. "That's great, Nick. I saw that set. I think that's good for today. See you Wednesday, right?"

"See you Wednesday, Cheyenne." Nick waves.

Her office is clearly a converted storage closet, containing no more than a tiny desk with an ancient laptop, a filing cabinet, and a medicine ball rather than a desk chair. There's a folding chair leaning against one wall. Cheyenne unfolds it and waits while I lower myself carefully onto the chair.

It's interesting: she watches me like a hawk as I sit, watching the way I do it, but she makes no move to help me. When I'm arranged with my crutches between my legs, she takes a seat on the medicine ball, bouncing gently.

"So, Ben. Tell me what happened."

I shrug. "Football. Took a hit to the knee, needed surgery…now no more football."

"Doesn't seem fair, does it?" She leans with her back to the wall, crosses her ankles and props them on her desk.

Now that I have a moment to examine her in the context of conversation, I realize she's older than my initial estimation. Originally, I'd pegged her to be a handful of years older than me, but now I'm realizing it's more than that. She's insanely fit, dressed in skin-tight yoga pants and sports bra, showing off ab definition I know a lot of guys would be jealous of, toned arms, powerful legs. But there are wrinkles around the corners of her eyes, a hardness in her gaze, a world-weary wisdom that only comes with age.

"What doesn't seem fair?" I ask.

"How quickly a dream can be snatched."

I shake my head. "It doesn't seem real, yet. I keep thinking I should be able to work it out and go back to playing next season."

"The doctor was firm on the prognosis, huh?"

I nod. "Yeah, Dr. Lane was pretty clear. He said it'd take months to even be able to walk without a cane, and even longer before I'll be able to jog short distances. Competitive ball will never happen again for me, he was very clear on that."

She blows out a breath of commiseration. "I know Dr. Lane very well. He's a great doctor. But I'm sure we'll have you mobile quicker than expected, especially if you're determined. I can't promise miracles, meaning your career playing football is over for sure, but I can get you walking in no time." Her gaze pins me. "As long as you're dedicated, and determined. Your success depends on you."

"Sounds like you know what you're talking about."

Cheyenne shrugs. "I've been a physical therapist for eight years, and I was an ER nurse for ten years before that. And, yeah, I also know from experience."

"What experience, if you don't mind me asking?"

She smiles, and god, that smile of hers is an expression of pure warmth. "Well, I was a dancer. Ballet and contemporary. My mom started me in ballet when I was four, and I was competing with a troupe by the time I was seven. I got into Juilliard. I spent two amazing, glorious years there. Then…god, it was so stupid. I was ice-skating at the Rockefeller Center with my boyfriend, I slipped, and fell. Snapped my ankle. I tripped, and when I hit the ice, my boyfriend's skate sliced across my Achilles tendon as he tried to get out of the way, so he didn't land on me.

"I healed fine, and I can run and walk and I'm totally normal, but competitive, professional dance was out. My ankle and the tendon just couldn't take the strain. I tried. I toughed it out a whole 'nother year, but my advisor eventually was just like, Cheyenne, I think you need to face facts." She shrugs, but I can tell it's still hard for her. "I probably could have kept dancing, could have gone easy on myself, taken some time off and rested it longer, maybe joined a troupe and taken it slow. But I was competitive, you know? I had to be the best, and if I couldn't…well, why bother? So I quit, left New York…eventually had my daughter and studied to be a nurse."

"You've got a daughter, huh?" This is an oddly personal conversation to have with a potential therapist. I'm not at all sure this is how things usually go.

Cheyenne smiles. "Yeah. About your age, off at college."

I'm not sure where to go with that, so I let a silence hang briefly and then change the subject. "So. Where do we start?"

She takes her feet off the desk, opens a drawer of the filing cabinet, and withdraws a folder, handing me a stack of papers. "Well, with paperwork of course. Fill these out, and I'll be right back. I need to check on my clients."

She disappears out the door, and I can't help appreciating how well she fills out her yoga pants. But then I feel oddly guilty about that thought, considering she mentioned having a daughter my age. But jeez, however old she is, she's beautiful, and I can't help noticing it.

I turn my focus to the paperwork. At least physical therapy will be something to look forward to, what with having such a lovely piece of eye candy as my therapist.

We agree to start with three appointments a week, evenings, seven o'clock. It seems late to me, but Cheyenne claims she works weird hours, especially since a lot of her clients are fitting in their therapy appointments around their own work schedules.

I end up quitting the bar, since there's no way I can manage a full shift on my feet any time soon, and they can't exactly hold a position open for me indefinitely. I've got enough money put aside that I can afford to take some time off. The biggest enemy at this point, for me, is boredom.

I discover the bus stops not far from my apartment, and it stops near both the library and the gym, so I spend a lot of time at the library, reading. I can settle in a corner with a book and stay there as long as I want, which ends up being from open to close a lot of days. Once it was clear football was over for me, I distanced myself from my former teammates, which wasn't that hard, honestly. We were football buddies, workout buddies, drinking buddies. None of them knew where I came from, or why I'm in San Antonio alone, so it's easy to withdraw and retreat back into myself.

Therapy is fucking hard.

For a sweet, warm woman, Cheyenne is a fierce motivator, unrelenting in her determination to push me to my limits, while still managing to be encouraging and unfailingly kind.

But Cheyenne, even though she doesn't ask me very many personal questions, has a way of drawing things out of me while she works on me. I tell her about growing up as the son of a famous football star, about Mom and her work with people with speech impediments. I even manage to casually mention my best friend Kylie without totally losing it, although the way Cheyenne quickly pushed our conversation past that topic tells me I might have sounded a little *too* casual.

Slowly, quietly, Cheyenne becomes my only friend. I find myself looking forward to Monday, Wednesday, and Friday evenings. We end up sitting on the weight machines after my session, the door to the gym locked, and we talk. She tells me about dancing in New York, how she and her friends would go to

Central Park or Bryant Park and dance together, just for the fun of it, and how they'd draw crowds even when they were just goofing around. She tells me about how angry she was when she was faced with the decision to quit dance, how she was so angry for so long, angry at life for taking her dream away.

I understand that, perfectly well. I'm pissed off. I want to hate the motherfucker who drilled my knee. I want to hate life. I want to wallow in self-pity. What the fuck am I going to do? Another season or two in San Antonio and I could've gone to the draft, gone pro. My coach told me as much, and I had a few talks with scouts about it. They told me to spend another season or two here, hone my skills, put up more stats, and I'd be in good position.

So now I've got useless football stats, a fucked knee, a fucked career. I've got three years toward a political science degree, and now I'm wondering what the fuck I thought I was going to ever do with that degree. I didn't think, that's the point. It was always football. Just get a degree, Dad insisted. You can still play ball, you can still pursue the pros, he said, but get a degree. You won't regret it.

Now? Fuck political science. I'm not a goddamn politician. I'm a shitty liar, and I have no patience for self-serving assholes. So, clearly, D.C. or a state capital are out for me.

So now what?

I have no clue.

But Cheyenne encourages me to put all my anger and frustration into therapy, use my anger and my confusion and my doubt and channel it into getting my mobility back. Get walking with crutches again, and then figure out the next step.

In the meantime, I keep the conversations with my parents short and I avoid sharing any details. Dad asks about the season, and I always act like I've got to go, trying to avoid his questions as best I can. I can't lie to him, but I can't tell him the truth either.

I need to do this on my own.

Why?

Maybe because I'm a stubborn son of a bitch.

Three: 2:36 a.m.

I PUSH THE WEIGHT UP WITH MY LEGS, STRAINING, aching, and fighting the agony in my right knee. I manage to straighten my legs, and I desperately want to lower them and release the strain. I start to do just that…

"Hold it there for me, Ben," Cheyenne says. "For ten seconds. That's all. Ten seconds. You can do it, I know you can."

But I can't. I'm a fucking pussy, and it hurts. I try, though. I shake all over, sweat sluicing down my face. I strain, and a growl escapes me as I fight the urge to let the weight go.

"…nine…eight…seven…six! Keep it up, Ben! Five more seconds, come on!" She's kneeling beside me, her voice patient and encouraging as always.

My leg trembles, and the pain in my ruined knee is so bad I could almost cry. "I can't—fuck, I can't. I gotta let it go."

I start to lower the leg press, but my knee gives out. And Cheyenne is there, catching the weight and lowering it. I slide to a sitting position, grab my right leg near the knee and lift it over the bench, and then collapse forward, elbows on my thighs, gasping.

The most pathetic thing about this? The press only has a hundred pounds on it. And I only managed two sets of ten. I used to be able to press over twice my body weight, six or eight reps of twenty each. Now, a hundred measly fucking pounds pushed twenty times and I'm out of breath, sweating, and my knee hurts so bad I don't dare speak in case the tremor in my voice shows.

I feel her hand on my shoulder, and a white towel appears in front of my face. I take the towel and wipe my face, neck, and chest, and then accept the bottle of water she hands to me.

"That was great, Ben. You're making excellent progress." She sips from her own bottle of water, another towel slung over her slim shoulder. She toys with her hair, a sleek blond braid hanging down her back. "Next time we'll try for three sets, huh?"

"I barely managed two today, Cheyenne. Gonna take awhile to get to three." I hate how defeated I sound.

She crouches in front of me, and my eyes go involuntarily to her gray-and-pink sports bra, visible beneath the white tank top, and then to her muscular thighs, encased in black knee-length stretch pants. I force my eyes back to her hazel-green gaze. If she noticed me checking her out, she doesn't give anything away.

"Ben, you're too hard on yourself. It's only been a month. It's going to take some time, okay? You have to be patient with yourself."

"I know," I sigh, and roll my head around my shoulders to loosen the tension. "It's just frustrating to be so limited."

She smiles, warm and understanding. Only the slight wrinkles in the corners of her eyes give away the fact that she's older than me by quite a bit. I don't know how much, but enough. She has a daughter in college, so she's got to be at least forty. But, Jesus, what a gorgeous forty.

"I get it, Ben. I do." She pats my knee, the good one. Is it me, or do her fingers linger a few seconds too long? "I went through it too, remember? I know what you're going through, how hard it is. You can do this. You just have to be patient and stay the course." She stands up, turns away and grabs two ten-pound hand weights from a rack.

She's facing away, so I let myself eye her ass. Taut, all toned muscle.

Fuck, what's wrong with me? She's got a daughter in college, for fuck's sake. She's my physical therapist. I should *not* be checking her out. But yet, every time I've been here since being injured in the game that ended my chances at a football career, I check her out. I struggle to keep my eyes off her, especially when she's looking my way.

Like she is now. Shit. She totally caught me staring. But she doesn't turn cold, doesn't scold me, or glare at me. She just offers me the same kind, warm, patient smile she always has for me.

"Come on. Time to walk that knee out, mister. Come on. Up, up, up." She grabs me by the hand and pulls me up to my feet.

Her hands linger in mine, just for a moment, but it's enough to make me wonder. And then she hands me the weights and gestures to the track that leads around the perimeter of the gym. She walks beside me, twenty-pound weights in her hands, and sets the pace. She ignores the fact that I'm fighting to keep up, that I'm hobbling so bad it can barely be called walking.

And then a ripple in the carpet catches the toe of my cross trainer, and I trip. I lurch forward, hobble, and my bad knee twists and goes out from under me. I fall, the weights dropping from my hands. My knee crashes into the floor, and pure agony lances through my leg, shooting from toe to hip, throbbing so hard my gut tightens. I roll off my knee, clutching it, gasping, fighting the urge to curse a blue streak.

"Ben! Shit! Are you okay?" She's kneeling beside me, helping me sit up.

Her hand goes to my knee, and she rips open the snaps of my track pants up past my knee, baring my hairy thigh. Her hands are warm and strong, flexing my knee, straightening my leg until I yelp.

"Fuck!" I pull free of her hold on my leg and lie back. "Fuck, that hurt."

"I think we'd better call it a day," Cheyenne says, a concerned expression on her face. "I'm worried that's going to swell."

"Yeah, no shit." My voice is hoarse with the effort needed to breathe through the pain.

"Can you stand up?" She's taking my hand, pulling.

"Yeah, I can fucking stand, okay?" I snap, jerking my hand away.

"Fine then, stand up." She backs away, not quite hiding the hurt before I see it.

I scrub my hand through my hair. "God, Cheyenne, I'm sorry. I'm being an asshole and you don't deserve it."

And just like that, the smile is back. She holds her hand out to me, and this time I take it and let her help me to my feet.

"Okay, see if you can put any weight on it," she tells me, not letting go of me.

I hobble, get my balance, and gingerly put weight on my knee. "Nope, nope, nope. Not happening," I grunt, hopping as my knee gives, wincing.

"Okay. Lean on me." She slides her slim shoulder under my arm and supports me.

She's a lithe little thing, barely five-five to my six-two, and I outweigh her by at least seventy pounds, but she still manages to support my weight and help me limp out of the gym and into the locker room. I lower myself to the bench and straighten my leg, closing my eyes as the motion sends pain shooting through me.

"That set us back, didn't it?" Cheyenne asks.

I nod. "Yeah, I think it did."

She sits down next to me and buttons the snaps of my pants leg. When she's done, she's sitting just a little too close to me. "You need ice on that."

"Yeah, I'll ice it when I get home."

"You have a ride?"

I shrug. "No, I'll just take the bus, then walk, same as always."

She frowns. "Ben, you can't. You'll hurt yourself worse."

"Well, I can't drive with my knee fucked up, and I'm still working on teleportation."

She snorts and smacks my shoulder. "Smart ass."

"Better than being a dumbass," I retort.

"Well, you'd be a dumbass not to just ask me if I can drive you home, then, wouldn't you?"

I swallow my pride. "Cheyenne, would you mind driving me home?"

She smiles brightly. "Why sure, Ben, I'd be happy to."

So I wait, leaning against the frame of the door as she wipes down the machines, shuts off the lights, and then locks the door behind us. She hikes her gym bag higher on her shoulder, and I, out of the instinct drilled into me by my mom and dad, take it from her.

"Ben, I can—" she starts to protest.

"And so can I. I have a shit knee, but I'm not useless." I hang the bag from my right shoulder and lean on the cane.

She lets me carry her bag, shooting me a smile that's somehow different from the ones she usually gives me. This one is...more personal, somehow. Less politely professional, containing a note of...I don't know what. I can't read Cheyenne, most of the time.

She opens the back door of her F-150, takes the bag from me, and tosses it onto the backbench, then climbs up into the driver's seat. It's not a big truck, not jacked up as high as my Silverado, but the step up and in is still going to be hellishly difficult. I set my cane—my stupid fucking cane—inside, grab the handle and the seat and lift myself into the seat using only my upper body.

"Clearly nothing wrong with your core muscles," Cheyenne says, a strange note in her voice.

I glance at her, surprised by the comment, but she focuses on putting the truck in gear and backing out. I have to be crazy, because it almost looked like she was blushing there for a moment. But that's stupid. There's no way a forty-year-old fox of a woman with a grown daughter would be blushing over a twenty-two-year-old kid.

I give her directions to my apartment, and the ride is surprisingly comfortable, no awkwardness. She tunes the radio to The Highway, an XM country music station, and "Cowboy Side of You" by Clare Dunn comes on. I surprise myself by knowing the lyrics. But then, you don't grow up in Nashville, and then live in Texas, without hearing some country music, even if it's not really your thing.

We pull up to my apartment, and she hops out, circles around and hovers near me as I slide out. God, I hate being a damned invalid, having her hover over me in case I fall. But a part of me, *way* deep down, kind of likes having her close, having her hover. Because it means she cares.

And shit, I've been lonely for a long fucking time.

I have to lean on the cane more than I'd like on the way up to the front door of my apartment, which, fortunately for me, is on the ground floor. Cheyenne is beside me, not really hovering now, more just... there. In case. I unlock the door, shove it open and let it bang against the inner wall. I hobble through, and glance back at Cheyenne, who hasn't crossed the threshold.

"Hey, so...you want to come in for a second?" I ask.

She hesitates. "I..." Her eyes go to mine, and then she smiles. And it's that *other* smile. Still bright and warm and genuine, but...intimate. I don't know how else to describe it. "Sure, for a few minutes."

I flick a switch to turn on the lights in the kitchen, and then the lamp in the living room. And that's the apartment. Kitchen, living room, a bedroom. Tiny, but mine. Well, Dad's. He's been subsidizing me while I got started in the FXFL, the experimental minor football league. Except now...I'm not sure what's going to happen. I didn't tell him about the hit I took, or what it means. I've been avoiding it.

And fuck, my place is messy. Dishes in the sink, clothes on the floor in the doorway to my room, unmade bed, a pizza box on the counter.

I grimace and glance sheepishly at Cheyenne. "This place is kind of a mess. Sorry."

She just grins. "You're a bachelor. I'd be worried if it wasn't." She lifts the lid of the pizza box with a thumb and forefinger, glances in and closes it again quickly; it's been there a while. "And you should see my place. It's not much better."

See her place. Huh. I'm not sure I'm entirely comfortable with the thoughts that inspires. I think of a cute little two-bedroom house in the 'burbs some-where, and then I think of a king-size bed, maybe a blue quilt, and a bra hanging on the bathroom door-knob. I feel my cheeks heat and turn away from her before she sees.

"I do have some pizza that's only from yester-day," I tell her, grabbing the box from the fridge. "And some Killian's."

Her eyes light up. "Now that's the best idea I've heard all day."

So that's how I end up sitting on my couch, finishing off a large pepperoni pizza and a six-pack with my physical therapist, watching *Die Hard 2*.

More confusing, though, is our arrangement on the couch. I'm in the corner, feet propped up on the coffee table, and she's sitting right up against my side, body twisted to face the end of the couch, legs curled up under her, watching the movie. And my arm…it's along the back of the couch. Not around her, per se, but close. Very close. And my pulse thunders in my veins, my hand itches to go lower, to curl around her shoulders. I mean, that's crazy talk, right there. But the desire is there.

And I can't help but wonder what she'd do if I did let my arm slide down onto her shoulders. Maybe nothing, maybe she'd welcome it, maybe she'd get upset. But no, she's not that kind of person. She'd find a way to let me down gently, and that'd be that.

Halfway through the movie, she gets up to visit the bathroom, and with my nerves jangling, I let my arm slide just a bit lower on the couch back. She comes back, her eyes flicking to me, to my arm. But she sits down anyway, and she settles in close once more. And now…my arm is around her. She sinks lower in the couch, and actually leans in closer to me.

My mouth is dry.

The exhaustion of the day catches up to me, and I find myself blinking to stay awake. Beside me, Cheyenne is fighting sleep as well, drifting closer and closer to me so that, by the time the movie is over, she's fully propped up against me. For a woman who's fit and taut and muscular, she's also soft. My hand slides down as the credits roll, and it comes to rest against her waist, my fingertips brushing the upper swell of her hip.

I'm nearly asleep, but her proximity, the feel of her against me is heady.

But eventually I can't fight sleep any longer, and I drift off.

I start, blink, and realize I've fallen asleep. The TV has turned off on its own to conserve energy. I crane my neck and glance at the red numbers of the microwave: 2:23 am.

Shit. We slept for a long time. I quickly re-cap the last several hours—my therapy appointment was at seven, it lasted for an hour and a half, and then Cheyenne drove me home, and then the movie…

Cheyenne stirs against me, stretches, making a sound in the back of her throat that has my heart clenching for some odd reason, something to do with how cute it is, how intimate a sound it is.

"Time's it?" she asks.

"Two-thirty."

She jerks upright. "Shit. I've got a client at nine, I've gotta go."

I lever myself to my feet, leaning on my cane. But I forget how weak my knee is and put too much weight on it and stumble. And she's there, catching me. Close. So close. She's looking up at me, hazel-green eyes full of things I don't know how to interpret.

"Okay?" she asks, her voice barely above a whisper.

And she hasn't moved away, and somehow, for some reason, her arms are around my waist…or one is, the other resting on my chest. My breath comes slowly, deeply, because my arms are around her too, resting on her back and sliding lower, and she's not doing a damned thing to stop me.

She blinks, and her tongue slides across her lips, and my eyes follow that movement.

I refuse to think, just let whatever is going to happen happen.

She smells like shampoo and faintly of sweat, and she's small and soft in my arms, and her chest is pressed up against mine, breasts that even a sports bra can't hide despite her svelte, athletic build.

Fuck me, I want to kiss her so bad. I've been so lonely, dealing with such wrenching heartbreak for so long. I held myself back from making a move too soon with Kylie, wanting the time to be right. I waited, and I waited too long. I don't want to make that mistake again. I'm not going to let fear hold me back any longer.

So I lean in and I feel her breath on my lips, feel her fingers curling in my Under Armour shirt...and I feel her lips, soft, damp, warm, against mine...

But then she's backing away slowly and carefully, but decisively. "Ben...god, I can't. We can't." She waits until she's sure of my balance, thinking of me even now.

Embarrassment, hurt, and disappointment all war within me. "No, I'm sorry, I don't know what I was thinking."

She reaches toward me, but doesn't touch me. "Don't apologize, Ben. It was as much me as you. But I just… I can't." She lets out a long, shaky sigh. "I have a daughter your age, Ben. And I'm your therapist. You're my client. I just can't let this…I just can't."

I nod. "I get it." I shutter my emotions, shove them down, forcing a casualness into my voice that I don't feel. "You're a great therapist, Cheyenne. For real. You've helped me a lot over the last month. I just hope…I hope this doesn't affect our working relationship."

She smiles, but it's strained and slightly closed, now. "It'll be fine." She lets out another breath, and then rubs her eyes. "I have to go. It's late and I live on the other side of town."

And now that I'm paying attention to anything other than how I feel, I see how tired she is. There are dark circles under her eyes. She seems to sag for a moment, and then gathers her strength and straightens up.

"Cheyenne, maybe you should…" I hesitate to offer, considering what just happened. "Are you sure you're okay to drive?"

She smiles and shrugs. "Oh, sure. I was an ER nurse for a long time, remember. I'm used to it."

I gesture at the couch. "You can stay here, you know."

She shakes her head and moves toward the door. "No, I should go. But thank you."

I follow her to the front door, leaning on my cane. She pauses with the door open, and I wasn't expecting it, intending to follow her through and watch her go from the front step. So when she stops and turns back, I'm right there, and she bumps into me. And now my arms are around her again, and I don't know what the fuck I'm thinking, but I'm milliseconds away from trying to kiss her again.

She stumbles away from me, less carefully this time. Her eyes seem pained, haunted, as if pulling away is difficult for her. "Ben, stop. Please don't."

I back away. "Jesus, I'm sorry, Cheyenne. I'm sorry."

She stays in place, hands over her face. She suddenly seems so tired, so small. "You don't know how I wish I could…it's been so long, and—" She shakes her head. "But I can't. Not with you, not now. I just can't. I'm sorry, I really am."

She walks away then, and her feet drag. Her shoulders are bowed, as if the pressure of refusing my kiss, twice, is too much.

"Cheyenne?" I call. She stops with one foot in the cab, holding on to the roof. "Are you sure you're okay to drive? You seem really tired."

She smiles faintly. "I'm fine, Ben. I didn't sleep well last night is all. But thank you."

She climbs into the truck, closes the door, and starts the engine. Backs out. I stand in the doorway, the warm San Antonio night wrapped around me like a blanket. I watch her as she turns onto the main road, and I watch as she waits to make a left turn. There is no traffic and the streets are quiet. I'm about to go back inside when the light turns green and she steps on the gas.

And then I see it. I see the oncoming older model red Mustang run the light.

She doesn't see him. She's too tired to check for traffic, probably focused on the light ahead of her.

Her white truck is halfway through the intersection when the Mustang slams into her driver's side door, going forty or fifty miles per hour.

"CHEYENNE!" I shout and hobble forward.

Her truck rocks with the impact and jolts to the side, topples, and then momentum and weight take over and the vehicle rolls over onto the roof. I watch the cab crumple. Smoke rises from the hood.

I can see that her driver's door is smashed in, crumpled.

"CHEYENNE!" I'm trying to run, but I can't. I can barely walk, but I somehow make it out into the street, knee throbbing and protesting.

The Mustang is a few feet away, the hood accordioned, smoking.

I get to her overturned truck, just now remembering my cell phone is in my pocket. I dial 911, my heart hammering, fear ramming my pulse into overdrive.

"Nine-one-one, what's your emergency?"

"A car...it ran the light and slammed into her." I don't know how to make sense. "The truck...I think she's hurt..."

"Sir, can you tell me your location?" Her voice is calm, smooth, emotionless.

I glance at the street names and relay them, and then I'm awkwardly, painfully lowering myself to one knee at the driver's side window, which is smashed out.

There's blood on the road.

She's not moving. Her head hangs; her braid is dangling over her shoulder.

"Cheyenne. Talk to me. Hey. Come on. You're okay. Talk to me." I reach in and tap her shoulder hesitantly. She doesn't respond. "No. No. Cheyenne? Come on. Fuck. Fuck."

"Sir?" I'd forgotten about the 911 operator. "Sir, are you there?"

"She's not moving, she's not—she's not—"

"Help is on the way, sir. We have your location and paramedics are en route. Just stay calm and don't try to move her…"

But it's no good. I can tell.

They won't be able to help.

And when they show up and check her pulse and vital signs I know from the minute shake of a head…

She's gone.

My gaze falls upon the lock screen of my phone: 2:36 a.m.

Four: Whiskey Lullaby

"DEARLY BELOVED, WE ARE GATHERED HERE TODAY to mourn the tragic passing of our dear friend, Cheyenne Leveaux." The minister is a big, bearded bear of a guy wearing a black suit and white collar despite the Texas heat. "She was taken from us too soon, much too soon indeed. A beautiful life was cut short by a tragic accident, and I know we who are left behind are so often wont to ask God why. Why? Why do these things happen, God? We cannot know the mind of God. We cannot know His will, or foretell His plan. But we can know that He is with us, especially in times of heartache such as these."

I'm leaning back against a headstone, at the back of the tiny crowd gathered around Cheyenne's grave.

There's her mother and father, frail, hunched, tear-stained eyes. Half a dozen friends, Dr. Lane and a few other former co-workers from the hospital, and three women about Cheyenne's age, beautiful, lithe, dancers for sure. They are mothers now, but are clearly Cheyenne's friends from her days as a dancer.

And me.

In the back, hoping my guilt doesn't show on my face.

There's one other person here, a young woman about my age, standing nearest the grave. I can't see her very well, since she's got her head down, her shoulders shaking now and then. Black dress, blonde hair falling in a loose cascade around her slim shoulders. In profile, at least, she is the spitting image of her mother.

Cheyenne's daughter.

"I knew Cheyenne, actually," the minister says, his voice shifting from preacher to friend. "She was...a beautiful person, in every way. I suffered a heart attack some years ago, a very sudden one. I thought I was healthy, but apparently my body thought otherwise. And Cheyenne? She helped me get in shape, helped me find a healthier lifestyle. She was...the kindest woman I ever knew. Patient, encouraging. But she never gave up, and never let me give up, even when I wanted to."

Everyone is nodding, including me.

"So...I don't know God's reason for taking Cheyenne from us so unexpectedly. I'm sorry if that's...if that's not what a man of God in my place is supposed to say. But I can't and I won't spout the usual clichés about God's plan, or about celebrating her life rather than mourning her death." He pauses, lets out a harsh breath. "Those are true, though. God *does* have a plan; we just don't know what it is. And she did live a wonderful life, touching many, many lives in her forty-three years. So we *should* celebrate her life, remember the beauty of her soul, and we *will*. But I also believe we who are left behind are granted the right to mourn the loss of someone we loved. We have that right. We must give ourselves permission to be sad about her death. We are here, and she isn't, and that's hard. But let us not lose ourselves in mourning, for God isn't done with us, any of us. Let us pray."

Cheyenne's daughter is sobbing, now. Her grandmother wraps a thin arm around her shoulders, and they cry together.

I'm sorry, I want to say. *It's my fault. I let her drive away. I'm so sorry.*

But I can't move, and I know the words won't come out.

And I couldn't tell them anyway. Even though nothing happened, the circumstances would lead to questions I don't know how to answer. Why was she there so late?

I tune out the prayer, feeling only anger toward a God who may or may not exist, and if He does, how *does* He get off letting shit like this happen? Cheyenne's death, or my leg, or any of the horrible shit that occurs every day.

"Excuse me?" I hear a soft voice, and a small, feminine hand touches my shoulder.

I realize I've got my eyes closed, and I'm fighting my emotions. Cheyenne should be alive, but she's not and it's my fault, and…now what?

I blink, startled, and look down at the person who just spoke to me. My heart seizes, and my guilt is almost too hot and hard and thick inside me to bear. It's her, Cheyenne's daughter. And fuck…she looks *just like* her: blonde, perfect ripe-wheat blond hair, the color of honey and sunlight. Wide eyes somewhere between gray and brown and green, slices of stone and streaks of rich soil and patches of moss. She's an inch or two taller than her mother was, and curvier in build, not as tautly toned.

Guilt strikes even harder, now, because I'm checking her out. I mean, no, it's not checking out per se. It's noticing her beauty, but in these circumstances it feels like one more ton of guilt on the pile.

"Do I know you?" she asks, and her voice is low, musical.

I shake my head. "No—" My voice catches, and I have to clear my throat and try again. "No. I was...I was a client of Cheyenne's."

"Oh." But her eyes are on me, like she sees something in me that doesn't jive with my brush-off answer. "It's just...she had so many clients over the years and..."

Why am I here? That's what she's getting at.

I move to my feet, keep my cane planted in the grass so I don't pitch forward. "Sorry to intrude, and I'm sorry for your loss."

I move past her, take a rose from the vase and toss it onto the casket, stand there for a moment wondering if I should say something or just have a moment of silence, and then I shake my head and limp back through the cemetery where a taxi is waiting for me, the meter running.

I'm climbing into the taxi, cane between my knees, when I hear feet approach on the gravel drive, and then the girl is in the taxi with me, shutting the door.

"Nearest bar, please," she says, her voice choking.

I'm at a loss. Her shoulders shake, and she's clearly crying, and I have absolutely not a single fucking clue as to what to say or do, especially with this girl, the daughter of the woman whose death can be laid at my feet.

She takes a deep breath, then wipes at her eyes. "Sorry. Sorry. I just couldn't take it anymore, Grandma and Grandpa hovering, Father Mike hovering, everyone hovering."

"I—" Words fail me, but I've got to say something. Something, anything, damn it. "It's fine."

Wow. I mean *really? It's fine?* Is anything fine anymore? But she doesn't reply, just puts her elbows on her knees and her face in her hands.

I feel an odd compulsion to comfort her, but I don't know how.

The taxi pulls into a parking lot. It's a dingy dive bar, only three cars in the lot, an open sign flashing, red letters lit one by one—*O...P...E...N.* "Thirty-nine fifty," the driver says.

I hand him two twenties and a five, and then I'm hobbling after the girl, who's already in the bar, sitting on a stool with two pints of beer in front of her, and two shots of whiskey. I take the stool beside her, lean my cane against the bar, and look around as I take the first sip of my beer. This place is a shithole. The bar is sticky, scratched, and pockmarked. There are a few small square tables covered in shitty plastic red-and-white checkered tablecloths surrounding a make-shift stage with cheap in-house karaoke equipment. A dartboard on one wall, a pool table with ripped felt and only three sticks, a pinball machine, a TV tuned to poker on ESPN 3, and an electronic poker and lotto machine on the far end of the bar.

The girl's got half her beer gone already, her shoulders hunched, her hair pulled over one shoulder. She's got her high heels and a small clutch purse sitting on the stool beside her. Her cheeks are streaked with black.

She glances at me, grabs the shot glass with her left hand and holds it up to me. "To Mom."

I clink with my own shot glass. "To Cheyenne."

We down the whiskey, Jack Daniel's I'm pretty sure.

"I'm Echo," the girl says, glancing at me.

"Ben." I'm a little impressed: she didn't make a face after downing the shot. Clearly she's no novice at shooting whiskey.

We drink our beer in silence for a few minutes and, strangely, it's not at all awkward. I'm loath to break the silence, to start a conversation, lest it turn into telling her how I knew her mother, why I was compelled to go to the funeral even though I'd only known her for a month. I'm sipping my beer, Echo is guzzling hers. She lifts a hand and the bartender—a wiry, greasy-haired old guy with an untrimmed goatee—silently pours another pair of Coors and sets them in front of us, and then goes back to staring at the TV.

"So. Ben. Let's try this again. How'd you know my mom?" Echo pivots on the stool, angled toward me.

I shrug. "I told you. I was her client."

"But out of all the clients she's had over the years, even the ones she was currently working with, why are you the only one at the funeral?"

I almost shrug again, but don't. I move my nearly empty pint glass in circles on the slick yet sticky wood of the bar top. "She was a friend when I needed one."

Echo nods. "That's Mom for you."

"Yeah, seems like it."

"You work with her for long?"

I shake my head. "No. Just over a month, not quite six weeks, I think."

"So you barely knew her."

"Guess so."

Echo wipes at her right eye with a finger and sniffs. "She made everyone she worked with feel like they were important. It was what made her so good at her job. You always had her full attention." She lifts the empty shot glass and the bartender refills it, and mine. "I can't believe she's gone." She knocks back the shot without warning, and I follow suit.

"She was patient," I say. "But she had this core of...I don't know. Hardness. She wouldn't give up. Like the priest said."

"Father Mike. I grew up calling him Uncle Mike, actually. He was one of Mom's first clients, and he was a friend before that. I think he was a little in love with her, to tell you the truth. I mean, he couldn't and wouldn't do anything about it, and didn't as far as I know, but the way he looked at her, I knew he always wanted to help her however he could."

I nod. "Sounded that way, the way he talked about her."

"It was hard *not* to love my mom, though. She just had that way." Echo's voice breaks, and she puts her face in her hands and breathes deep several times, and then blows out a harsh breath and shakes her hands.

Watching her struggle with her emotions is hellish. "I'm sorry," I can't help saying.

She shakes her head. "Why? You didn't have anything to do with it."

Ouch. That cuts. Because I very much did, only… how do I say that? Answer is: I don't. I don't dare.

"I just mean—"

"I know what you meant," she interrupts, not looking at me. She lifts her shot glass again, and as soon as the whiskey fills the glass she tips it back. "I'm sorry if I'm being a bitch. I'm just…I don't know what to do…how to handle this."

"There isn't any way to handle it. And you're not being a bitch. It's fine." I need to get out of here, away from this girl. I stand up, leaning on the bar, and fish for my wallet in my back pocket. "I'll go. Let you— have your space, I guess."

A small hand—thin, elegant, strong fingers, unpainted but manicured nails—wraps around my wrist. "Don't. I don't want to be alone right now."

I settle back down onto my stool, feeling unstable emotionally and physically. I don't know how to interact with this girl. How to comfort her, how to keep up a conversation when all that runs through my head is *I'm sorry! I'm sorry! It's my fault!*

"What's your story, Ben?"

I tip back the pint glass and finish it, and start on the second one. "Not much to tell. I was playing football; a tackle went wrong and took out my knee. Your mom was helping me get my mobility back."

Echo looks at me, eyes red-rimmed with sorrow and yet still piercing, knowing, sharp. "There's more than that to it. I can smell it on you. You don't go to the funeral of a woman you just met. You maybe stop by the visitation and pay your respects, but you don't show up at the burial. And you don't—" she waves at my face with her shot glass, which is somehow full again, and then shoots the whiskey, making a face as she swallows and keeps talking, "you don't have that look on your face for someone you just met."

"What look?"

She shrugs and wipes her mouth with the back of her wrist, then takes a swallow of beer. "I don't know. But there's something. You look...distraught? Upset? I mean, me? She was my mom. My one and only parent. My best friend. So I get to be distraught. But you? No disrespect, dude, but you knew her a month. Why do you get to be upset?"

"I told you. She was a friend to me when I needed one." I blow out a breath, resigned to giving at least some of the truth. "The tackle that took out my knee, it ended my football career. I could've gone pro. Would have. There were scouts…but that's over, now. Permanently. And Cheyenne told me about how her dance career ended and I guess we…I don't know… bonded over it, to some degree. That's all."

But that's not all. Not even close. But I can't say any of that.

Echo nods. She's now on her third beer, and there's another full shot waiting for her, and I'm getting worried about her. She's starting to look like she's feeling the booze, and I'm wondering how far she's going to take this. She lost her mother, so I mean, god, she's got the right to this bender, but we're in a shithole bar on the outskirts of San Antonio. I don't have a car, and neither does she as far as I know, and she's on her way to shitfaced, and I'm responsible for her mother's death, and what the *fuck* am I supposed to do?

She knocks back the shot, and I've officially lost count of how many that is. Five? Six? Echo finishes her third beer, chugs it, drains it like pro, and then presses her knees together and spins on the stool, stands up.

"Gotta visit the girls' room. Be right back." But then after two steps she wobbles, stumbles, and has to catch herself on the bar. "Whoa. That caught up fast."

I stand up, snag my cane and limp to her side. Ignoring the screaming multitude of things in my heart and head and body—the pain in my knee, worry for this girl I just met, the undeniable attraction I feel to her because holy shit, she's even more beautiful than her mother, the guilt I feel over that very fact piled on top of the guilt already there—I put my arm under her shoulder, around her waist, support her and help her walk to the bathroom. I shove the door to the ladies' room open with my cane and help her through it, to a stall. She grabs the sides of the stall door.

"Thanks," she says, her voice small and wobbly.

"No problem," I tell her.

Seemingly oblivious or uncaring of my presence, she lifts her dress up around her hips, baring black panties and long strong pale legs. I feel myself blush and turn around, start toward the door.

"Just wait. I'll probably need your help again, so just wait." I hear the stall door bang closed and then the sound of her urinating, and then the flush of the toilet. My cheeks burn hotter.

I don't hear the stall door open; don't feel her approach behind me, so I'm startled when I feel her hand on my shoulder. Her fingers tighten in my trapezius muscles, and I turn to see her swaying on her bare feet, blinking, taking deep breaths.

"Okay?" I ask. God, what a stupid question.

She seems to think so too, because she snorts gently and shakes her head. "No. I'm not even remotely okay. But thanks." She peers at me, and her fingertips touch my cheek. My skin tingles where she made contact. "Oh my god. You're blushing. Jesus. What, have you never heard a girl take a piss before? So fucking cute. Lemme wash my hands and then we can get back to the drinking."

"Should you maybe slow down a bit? I mean, I don't really know you and I'm not trying to tell you what to do, but I just—" I don't know what else to say, so I leave it there.

Echo rinses her hands, dries them on a wad of paper towel, and then turns away from the sink, squaring her shoulders and trying gamely to walk a straight line on her own. And damn, she does, too. Slowly, carefully, but she does it. I follow her back to the bar, wait until she's perched on her stool and then take my own seat.

She takes a long pull off her beer, and then turns to me. "No, I don't think I should slow down. If I slow down, I'll have to start feeling shit, and I'm in no shape for that. It's not real yet, and I don't want it to be real. I want to drink myself into oblivion. Which is exactly what I'm going to do. I'm going to drink until I pass out."

"Ah. I get that," I say. "Well, at least tell me where you're staying. Do you have a car here somewhere, or what?"

"Nope, no car. I took the bus here from school. I'm staying with Grandma and Grandpa, about an hour outside the city." She glances at me. "Is my drunk ass going to be a burden to you, Ben?"

I shake my head slowly. "No. Not at all."

So that's what happens. I sip my beer and we make small talk. She likes a wide variety of music, as do I, so music becomes the focus of our conversation.

"So, Ben. Favorite song of all time." She's drunk as hell, but holding her liquor a lot better than I'd have ever thought a girl her size could.

I shrug. "A single favorite song of all time? I don't even know. I'm not sure I could pick one."

"Sure you can. Just close your eyes, clear your mind, and think of music, think of your favorite song. What's the first song to come to mind?"

I try it. The answer comes immediately, but it takes me a few beats to get the words out. "'Let Her

Go' by Passenger."

She looks up at me, wobbly gaze speculative. "Ooh. I hear a story there."

I shrug. "An old story, and a long one."

"How 'bout you just say it's a story you don't want to tell?" She leans toward me and bumps me with her shoulder. "We've all got stories like that."

I laugh despite myself. "All right, then. It's a story I can't tell. Not now, anyway. Maybe another time." I glance at her. "You? Favorite song?"

Her answer is immediate. "'Better Dig Two', The Band Perry."

"Why?"

This time her answer is longer in coming. "You ever hear the song?" she finally asks.

I lift a shoulder. "A couple times, maybe, but not recently."

She reaches to the stool beside her, unzips her purse, and withdraws her phone. Taps at it, and then sets it on the bar between us. A familiar melody emerges from the phone, a banjo picking out a simple count. The bartender glances at us, and then mutes the TV. We listen to the song, and I pay attention to the lyrics. When it's over, I glance at Echo, who has a faraway expression on her face.

"So. Now you get it?"

"I guess."

She puts a forefinger on the screen of her phone and spins it in circles. "I guess it's like a vow, for me. A promise to myself. With what Mom went through and how that affected me, I just…it's like the song says, 'this is the first and last time I'll wear white.' You know?"

"I hear a story there," I say.

She shoots a grin and a sideways glance at me. "A story I don't feel like telling right now. Besides, not much new about it, but it's my story."

"Heard that," I say, sliding off my stool and grabbing my cane. "My turn for the bathroom."

She tosses back the shot she'd asked for and forgotten about, and then carefully lowers herself to her feet. "Me, too." And this time she grabs my elbow, her hand slipping around my arm easily. She leans into me for balance, and still manages to trip a few times. We both go into the men's room, and I make sure she's in a stall before heading for a urinal.

I'm washing my hands when I hear the stall door bang open. I turn to see Echo stumbling out, fumbling with the hem of her dress, which is caught in the waistband of her underwear. I laugh and try to keep my eyes in appropriate places, but it's a lost cause. She's got killer legs, long and strong and curvy.

I tug the hem of her dress free and let it float down around her ankles once more, and look up to see that she's staring at me.

The tensions and the questions and the sorrow and the doubt and the desire and the heat and the intoxication all mix, hers and mine and both and neither, and I can't look away from her, those eyes, so many shades and colors all mixed together.

"Think I'm...think I'm done," Echo says, ripping her gaze from mine and lurching past me.

I follow her, and when she stumbles again, I grab her arm with my free hand and keep her upright. She snags her shoes and purse, withdraws a wallet and peers into it, sorting through what seems to be mostly fives and tens and a couple twenties.

"What's the damage, boss?" she asks the bartender. Without a word, the bartender prints out a ticket and sets it on the bar in front of Echo. I reach for it, but she slaps my hand. "No. I got it. You just get us a cab." She hands him a debit card, gets it back and signs the slip.

"To where?" I ask, glancing at the bartender, who is already on the phone, mumbling into it and hanging up.

"I dunno. Anywhere."

"What's your grandparents' address?" I ask.

Echo ignores me, weaving an unsteady line toward the door, and then she walks outside, blinking in the sunlight. It's late evening, the sunlight a golden-orange, the heat fading to something less oppressive. She leans against the wall beside the door, heels dangling from two fingers, purse tucked under her arm. She's staring at the street, watching cars pass but not seeing them, I don't think. I glance down. Her feet are bare, and the ground outside the bar is dirty, bits of glass and old cigarette butts and oil stains.

"Not going back there," she mumbles. "Can't. I can't—I can't handle Grandma and Grandpa right now. I just can't."

"Then where?"

"I don't care!" she yells. "I don't care. I don't fucking care."

Are these drunk emotions, or she-just-buried-her-mother emotions? Both, probably, and I don't know what to do, what to say. I don't know her. I barely knew her mother. So I don't say anything. We wait in silence until a white older model Dodge Caravan with the name of a taxi service printed across the side pulls up. I hobble past Echo and slide open the door, then extend my hand to her. She fits her palm in mine but doesn't look at me as she climbs in, slides to the seat on the far side. I hop in after her and close the door. The driver pulls out of the parking lot.

When he's waiting at a red light, he glances at me in the rear-view mirror. "Where to?"

I glance at Echo, but she's staring out the window, head against the glass. Her breath comes slowly, deeply, as if she's fighting for each breath. Holding back vomit, maybe, or holding back sobs. Can't tell which.

"Just drive for now," I tell him.

He nods, and turns up the radio. "Give Me Back My Hometown" by Eric Church comes on.

And, of course, it's followed by "What Hurts the Most" by Rascal Flatts.

"You've got to be kidding me," Echo says when Rascal Flatts comes on. "Mom loved this song." The driver moves to change it, but she shakes her head. "Leave it on. Just…leave it." Her voice sounds faint, distant.

I look over, and I see her eyes flutter, close once or twice, and then she's asleep. "Shit," I mumble. I glance at the reflection of the driver's eyes in the mirror. "Now what do I do?" I rub my forehead with the back of a knuckle, and then give him my address.

Her head wobbles and bobs with the turns and the bumps in the road. Even passed out, she looks troubled, eyebrows pinched and drawn.

Twenty minutes later, the cab squeals to a stop outside my apartment. I pay the driver, and then nudge Echo's shoulder with my hand. "Echo. Echo. Wake up."

She moans, and her eyes flutter, flicker open. "What? Where am I?"

"Come on. We're going in, okay?" I tell her.

She nods sloppily and sits up straighter. I get out of the cab and move around to the driver's side, open the sliding door, and she topples out, into me. I catch her; help her find her feet. She wraps an arm over my neck, clinging to me. I lean heavily on my cane and hobble carefully toward the door. I've been on my feet too much today, and my knee burns, throbs, and I know I can't make it much farther on my own, much less support Echo as well. But I don't have much choice, it seems. She's not even really awake or aware, more just holding onto me instinctively.

I refuse to acknowledge the press of her body against mine, or the feel of her breath on my neck. I'm an asshole for even thinking about it, for having to stop myself from dwelling on it.

I'm not sure how I make it to the door, or how I get it unlocked and open, but I do. Barely, though. I get her to the doorway to my room, and then my knee gives out, leaving me clinging to the doorway, an arm slung around Echo's waist holding her upright as I hop on one foot and fight for balance, gritting my teeth. She's groaning, head lolling, and I'm about to drop her.

"Echo. Can you stand up for me for a second?"

She murmurs something unintelligible, and then peers at me. "I know you. We just met. Hi."

"Hi there, yeah, you know me. I'm Ben, remember? I need you to stand up for me. Can you do that?"

She blinks, closes one eye and then the other, and then widens them both. "Maybe. Possibly." She grabs my arm and hauls herself upright. "There."

I let her go and get my foot under me, gingerly stepping on it and leaning on my cane. And then she sways and starts to fall backward, and I have to catch her, hobbling forward as she stumbles away from me as she tries to find her own balance. I grab her, catch her around the waist again, and then we're both falling, hitting the bed, thankfully.

"You caught me." She peers at me, grinning. "Good job, Benny. Benny. Is that short for Benjamin? Bennnnn…jamin…" She draws the middle sound of my name out, and then grins again. "Bennnnjaminnnn. Benj…amin. Benji? Benji. Maybe I'll call you Benji."

My heart lurches. Only one person ever called

me Benji. "How about you just call me Ben?" I say.

She tries to wriggle onto the bed, turns onto her stomach and crawls army-style. And then she waves at me. "Come on. Up here. Come up here with me, Benji."

"Ben," I say through clenched teeth, my heart cracking as I force down the hurt and the thoughts and the memories I've tried to bury. "My name is Ben."

She blinks at me. "But I like Benji. It's cute, and you're cute." Her gaze narrows. "You've got a lot of stories, don't you...Benji? Ha. I hear the story there too, you know? I may be wasted, but I remember. I remember."

"Yeah, I guess I do." I move to a sitting position on the edge of the bed and watch her as she kicks the blankets down and tucks her feet under them, making herself comfortable in my bed.

"I need a drink, Benji." She leans against the wall, head lolling and eyes narrowed and watching me.

"I've got some water bottles and some Gatorade," I tell her.

She shakes her head. "No, Benji. A *drink*. A fucking drink. I still remember, and I want...I want to forget. I need to forget."

"I don't think that's a good idea—" I start.

"You're not my fucking mother!" she snarls, darting forward and jabbing the air with her finger. "You're not my fucking mother, and I need a drink, goddammit." She flops back against the wall, head smacking the drywall. "Ow. Please. Please, Benji."

Every time she says that nickname, something inside me clenches, stings.

I push to my feet and limp into the kitchen, hating that I'm doing this. But I don't know this girl, and her pain is bright in her eyes. So I grab a nearly empty bottle of Jim Beam from the cupboard over the fridge. I snag two juice glasses from a different cupboard, and a bottle of water from the fridge. When I make it back into my room, Echo is standing up, unsteadily at best, reaching awkwardly behind her back for the zipper of her dress.

"Fuck this dress," she mumbles. "Done with this stupid dress."

She's facing away from me so I know she doesn't see me, which makes it almost funny. It would be funny if this were any other circumstance. She finds the zipper and pulls it down, shrugs her shoulders, and the black material falls to pool around her feet. I swallow hard. She's wearing a black dress, black underwear, and I can't breathe, can't look away, can't avoid the desire and the guilt raging inside me.

"Um. Hi." I clear my throat, duck my head.

"Oh. Benji-boy." Echo turns, wobbles, and topples into the bed, then pushes herself upright. "Couldn't handle that fucking dress anymore." Her eyes go to mine, and I see an odd note of something I can't decipher in her expression. "Hope you don't mind, Benji. I just can't wear that dress anymore. You don't mind, right?"

"No...I mean..." I don't know what to say. This feels wrong. She shouldn't be practically naked, and I shouldn't be struggling with my instincts. Not like this. Not her. "You want a T-shirt or something?"

"Yes! A T-shirt. What a great idea. There's nothing as comfy as a boy's T-shirt." She points at me. "Shirt me, Benji." And then she giggles, like she's said something funny.

I move to my dresser and set the bottle and glasses on top of it, and then rummage in my drawer for a shirt. When I turn to hand it to her, she's somehow moved to stand right behind me, and she's lost her bra in the process. Breathing, swallowing, looking away, guilt...the list of impossible things grows by the second.

"Like what you see, Benji-boy?" She's just standing there, two feet away, topless, in nothing but her panties.

My zipper tightens, and I've got to clench my fists to keep them at my sides.

I squeeze my eyes shut, breathing hard, and duck my head. I've got the T-shirt wadded in my fist, and I crush it with every ounce of strength I possess as she sidles toward me.

"Echo…" I move backward, but there's nowhere to go except into the dresser. I'd be willing to climb in a drawer and close it over me, if only to get away from the burning knot of desire and guilt lodged in my chest. "Stop."

She doesn't, and I put a hand up, only…she walks right into it, and I feel the soft squish of her breast. I hurriedly drop my hand and slide sideways.

She's just trying a different tactic, I know. Trying to forget.

It's not about me.

Not about me.

I shake the T-shirt loose and find the neck hole, reach out and fit it over Echo's head, which works to cover her from my gaze and pinion her hands at the same time.

"What's the matter, Benji?" she says, a sultry pout on her face.

"You're drunk, and I'm not doing that."

"But I want to. Don't you?" She's still shifting closer to me even as she slides her arms through the sleeves.

"No you don't, Echo. That's not going to help you forget."

"Yeah, it will."

I shake my head and grab her wrist as she reaches for me. "No, Echo. It really won't."

Except...how would I know?

She jerks her wrist out of my grip, eyes blazing. "Fine. Fuck you, then." She grabs the bottle of Jim off the dresser, unscrews the cap and puts it to her mouth, takes three long swallows, hissing as it burns down her throat. "Or don't, whatever. You could've, but no. Too damned...*chivalrous*, aren't you? Benji, my honorable knight in shining armor, is that it?"

She turns away and misses a step, catches herself with a hand on the bed, the bottle clutched in her other hand. I just watch from across the room, not daring to speak or move. Echo makes it to the side of the bed, sits down and scoots back, tucks her legs under the blankets and settles with her back to the wall. The bottle goes to her mouth and she tips it back and gulps a big mouthful, and then sets it down with a loud *thud* on the bedside table.

"Put on music, Benji. Something Mom would like. Country music."

I fish my phone from my pocket and bring up Pandora, then dock the phone in the Bose alarm clock on my bedside table.

When the first song comes on, Echo lets out a sound that's half-sob, half-laugh. "Are you for fucking real?"

It's "Whiskey Lullaby" by Brad Paisley and Alison Krauss.

"Should I change it?"

She shakes her head floppily. "Don't you fucking dare. It's perfect." She pats the bed beside her. "Sit down, Benji. I won't test your virtue again, I promise."

If only she knew how deeply that cuts.

We listen to music for a long time. She doesn't say a word, and neither do I.

"Henry Lee" by Crooked Still comes on, and Echo is horizontal now, scrunching a pillow under her head and a cheek under her hand, long eyelashes fluttering against her skin.

She's snoring in moments.

I watch her sleep and can't help wondering what I've gotten myself into.

Five: Ease the Ache
Echo

OH...OH JESUS. IT FEELS LIKE THE SUN IS EXPLODING inside my skull.

Throb...throb...throb...

I blink my eyes open, and thank god the blinds are closed.

Shit, I'm not at home. Where am I?

I sit up, look around. I don't recognize the room. It's a dude's room, spartan and messy and male. A six-drawer bureau, piles of clothes on the floor, a white laundry basket with folded clothes. Boxer-briefs, jeans, gym shorts, T-shirts.

I look down, and...yep. I'm wearing a guy's Mumford and Sons concert shirt. It smells of him, and that worries me a little, because it smells good, familiar and comforting somehow. There's a bottle of Jim Beam on the nightstand to my left, empty but for maybe a shot's-worth. Beside that is a Bose alarm clock/iPhone dock with a black iPhone connected to it.

I grab the bottle of Jim, uncap it, and finish it off, as in my experience hair of the dog is the best way to negate a hangover. That and lots of water and aspirin and greasy food. But first...my clothes.

And that's when it all hits me: I see my dress on the floor. The black dress, the one I bought before leaving school.

The one I bought for the funeral. Mom's funeral.

Mom.

Oh god, Mom.

It's instantaneous. I go from zero to hyperventilating sobs in a split second. My chest is being torn open. My heart is in pieces.

It all comes back. The call from a police officer in San Antonio, informing me of my mother's death. A car accident. She was dead before the paramedics even showed up.

The funeral. Father Mike...Grandma and Grandpa...

And him.

Ben.

Flashes of last night flicker in my head, but I push them away. I can't deal with whatever I may have done to embarrass myself last night. Not now.

Mom.

She's dead. She's gone.

I feel the bed dip, and I smell him before I see him or feel him. He smells just like the T-shirt I'm wearing, deodorant, and something spicy and citrusy, like cologne maybe, and those other faint scent-elements that can't be defined. And then his arms are around me, lifting me, cradling me.

He's a perfect stranger. I remember only bits and pieces of what happened after the burial, and even less about him. But here he is, holding me as I sob for my mother. He doesn't say anything, doesn't shush me, just feathers his fingers into my hair and presses my cheek to his chest and holds me.

I hear his heart beating, and it's hammering as if he's nervous.

"She's gone." My voice is hoarse, and the words are barely intelligible through the gasps and the sobs. "She's—Mom…Mom is dead."

"I'm so sorry, Echo. I'm so sorry."

"I never—I never even got to say goodbye. The last time I talked to her we argued. We fucking *argued*.

And now she's gone and I can't ever—I won't ever be able to tell her—" I can't even finish.

"She knew, Echo. I promise you, she knew." His voice is low and smooth and soothing.

"You don't know that." My voice breaks, cracks.

God, what am I doing? Clinging to this guy, crying on him? What the fuck. I barely even remember what he looks like. I shift off him and he lets me sit up. I twist to look at him and I'm struck breathless.

He's gorgeous.

Tanned olive skin hinting at Mediterranean heritage, wide brown eyes so dark they're almost black, and thick messy black hair cut close on the sides and longer on the top. I felt it when he held me, but now seeing him, I realize he's powerfully built, broad through the shoulders and chest. He's wearing a sleeveless black Under Armour shirt which is stretched across his chest, leaving his arms bare, long and thick and bulging with muscle.

My gaze rakes over him, and then goes back to his eyes, and something inside me clenches. His expression is shuttered, but I can see through it. I can see worry and pain and doubt and strength and self-assurance. Such expressive brown eyes, even when he's trying to keep from showing his feelings.

Or maybe I can just read him.

Fuck. I'm checking this guy out, and I just buried my mom yesterday. What the hell is wrong with me?

He clears his throat and swings his legs off the bed, scoots forward, and stands up, hopping a little as he grabs a cheap black drugstore cane from where it was propped against the bed. I remember flashes of him from last night—that cane, a limp. Something about a football injury?

"Want some coffee?" he asks.

"Maybe some water and aspirin first?"

He nods. "Sure. Stay put." He turns away, but not before I notice his gaze flicking to my legs and then quickly away.

I realize then that the T-shirt I'm wearing has hiked up, giving him a nice view of my entire lower half from the waist down. At least I wore panties with the dress yesterday. I pull the sheet over my waist and stuff the pillows behind my back, lean against the wall and ignore the pounding in my head as I reluctantly try to summon memories of last night.

Nothing good comes to mind.

Ben returns with a bottle of water, a mug of coffee, two aspirins, and a toasted cinnamon raisin bagel slathered generously with cream cheese. He's got his cane hooked over his arm so he can carry everything.

I feel immediately guilty, letting him hobble around bringing me breakfast in bed.

Jesus. This is nuts. I've known the guy for like five seconds and he's treating me better than anyone I've ever dated. Which, honestly, isn't that hard, but it's worrisome.

"You didn't have to bring it to me—" I start.

He waves me off, handing me the pills first and then the bottle of water, then setting everything else down on the bedside table. "It's fine. You've got to have the mother of all hangovers—" He cuts off abruptly. "I mean, a hell of a hangover."

The shitty thing is, I really do feel that fragile, that even the word 'mother' has the power to make me choke up.

"God, Echo. I'm sorry." He winces, rubbing at his forehead. "I'm an idiot. I'm sorry."

"It's fine. Thank you." I swallow the pills and force myself to drink the entire bottle of water slowly, sip by sip, until it's gone.

He starts to turn away. "I…I'll—let me know if you need anything. You're welcome to stay here as long as you need."

The idea of being alone right now scares me. I'll lose it if I have to be on my own. "Ben, wait." I scoot over to the other side of the bed and then reach out for the coffee mug and the paper plate with the bagel. I pat the bed beside me. "Sit. It's your room. And...I wouldn't mind the company."

He seems reluctant, oddly, but then lets out a breath and takes the spot on the bed beside me, lifting his injured leg onto the bed with obvious relief. He snags his phone from the dock and scrolls through his FB feed while I eat my bagel. It's strangely comfortable, the silence between us. I'm not given to idle chatter, and neither is he, it seems.

When I'm done, and my stomach is less tumultuous—a little, at least—I set the plate aside and sip at the coffee, which is strong and lightly creamed, which is how I happen to like it.

I let out a sigh, knowing it's time to bite the bullet. "So. My memory of last night is...hazy." I can't quite look at him. "But knowing myself and how I get when I drink as much as I did, I probably embarrassed myself. So...fill me in, would you?"

He clicks the top button of his phone, putting it to sleep, and sets it aside. His gaze goes to mine, serious and compassionate. "Nothing to be embarrassed about, Echo. I think...under the circumstances..."

I groan at the hesitancy in his voice. "Just tell me what I did."

He shrugs. "You hopped in my cab as I was leaving the cemetery, and you had the driver take us to the nearest bar. Which, by the way, was one of the nastiest shithole dive bars I've ever been to. You must've had…oh man, like four or five pints and at least six shots in maybe an hour and a half at most."

I thunk my head against the wall. "Jesus."

"So, yeah. That hit you pretty quick. We left the bar and just drove around for a while. You ended up passing out in the cab, so I brought you back here."

I close my eyes and try to remember. I have flashes of memory: the cab ride, hearing one of Mom's favorite songs, seeing the outskirts of San Antonio through the window, wishing I could fall asleep and never wake up. Ben helping me walk, a strong arm around me, holding me up.

"I remember some of that." I try again, and recall a memory of fighting with my dress, and calling Ben "Benji." I remember him not liking it, but not fighting me on it. But then, I was probably pretty belligerent. "I remember calling you Benji, for some reason. And I also remember trying to get my dress off."

The fact that I'm in nothing but his T-shirt worries me. What did I do? And what do I not remember doing? I'm scared to ask.

Ben's lips quirk. "Yeah, you…I was getting you a drink. You demanded a drink after we got here, and I guess maybe I shouldn't have given you anything else, but I did. So when I came back in with the whiskey, you were trying to unzip your dress and you were all like 'fuck this dress, I'm done with this stupid dress.'"

"Anything else?" I ask, not daring to even look at him. "I didn't…I mean…did we…?"

"No," he answers immediately. "You were beyond wasted, and there's no way in hell I'd ever take advantage like that. No fucking way."

"So I took my dress off and passed out?"

He makes a face. "Not…quite."

"Fuck."

He won't look at me directly, and I'm pretty sure he's blushing hard. "You…took your bra off, too. And you…"

"I threw myself at you, didn't I?"

He shrugs. "Sort of. Yeah." He finally looks at me, and I see a welter of emotions in his gaze. "So I got a shirt on you, and got you in bed. You asked me to put on music, so I did, and then you fell asleep."

"God, Ben. I'm sorry—"

He cuts in over me. "Don't. Please don't apologize. You have nothing to apologize for."

I take a long sip of hot coffee. "I guess I'm lucky you're an honorable guy. Most guys wouldn't have hesitated."

Ben doesn't answer right away. "I'd like to think there are more decent guys out there than that. How could anyone have even considered it? You were drunk and hurting. You just wanted to forget—that's what you said. And I get it. It was…a defense mechanism. Just forget it. It's okay."

"I can't forget it. How can you?"

"Do you remember doing it?" he asks.

I think back. I do, sort of. I have a memory of thinking he was sexy and that his kindness was sexy. He was taking care of me, he was there for me, and that was sexy. That's what scares me about this situation. I may have been shitty wasted last night and, like he said, throwing myself at him was a defense mechanism, a reflexive act of desperation to not have to think or feel, even for a minute. But that sense of desperation is there, still, even now. Especially now. Sober, it's even worse. And Ben isn't making it any easier. He's insanely hot, those big expressive dark eyes, that powerful athlete's body, and the fact that he didn't take advantage of me, that he listened and held me and let me cut loose, and understood what I needed.

"I do, a little. I remember…" I close my eyes and summon the memory. "I remember you backing away from me. I remember you putting your hand out to stop me, and accidentally touching my breast." I look up at him as I say this, watching for his reaction.

He's looking down, rubbing his hand on the fabric of his gym shorts. "Yeah, that was an accident. You walked into me. I didn't mean to—" He's blushing hard. Even with the shade of his skin, it's easy to tell.

I can't help grinning. "It's fine, Ben." The humor is gone immediately, though. "For real, Ben. Thank you. For…everything. For putting up with me. You don't know me, and you don't…you didn't have to do any of this."

He shrugs. "You clearly needed someone. What else was I supposed to do?" My coffee is gone, and Ben nods at the empty mug. "More?"

I shake my head. "I'm still hungry, actually."

He starts to get off the bed. "I've got—"

I interrupt him. "How about we go somewhere for breakfast? I know a couple good diners." I glance at the clock, and I'm glad to see it's only ten in the morning.

He shrugs. "Sure. Let me change, then." He points to the other side of the bed. "Your dress and bra are over there." He flushes again as he mentions my bra. How cute is that? Why is he so easily embarrassed by such simple things?

I don't really relish the thought of going to breakfast in my funeral dress, but my bag with my things is at my grandparents' house, which is a good hour away. I should probably call them, just to let them know I'm okay; after breakfast, I decide. Maybe I can stop at a Kohl's or something and buy a new outfit.

Ben slides off the bed and rummages in his bureau, withdraws a pair of khaki cargo shorts and a blue-and-white striped polo shirt. "I'll change in the bathroom real quick. You can take a shower, if you want. I don't have any girly shower stuff, but you could rinse off if you want."

"Girly shower stuff?" I laugh.

He shrugs, grinning. "Yeah, you know, all that shit girls have in their bathrooms."

"Like…shampoo and conditioner?" I tease.

"Well, how the hell am I supposed to know? I'm not a girl. I use two-in-one shampoo and conditioner and a bar of soap. What else would I need?"

Now why the hell does my mind bring up a visual of Ben taking a shower? I can almost see him running a bar of soap over his tan skin…I force the errant thought away.

"I could stand to rinse off, I guess. Thanks."

Seconds later, Ben tosses his old clothes on a pile in the corner. "Bathroom is all yours. I put a clean towel on the sink."

"Thanks."

I fish a hair tie out of my purse and knot my hair on top of my head, and then take a quick shower. He wasn't kidding. The shower literally has a single bottle of shampoo, a bar of soap, and a washcloth. My bathroom at home has easily a dozen different bottles, since my roommates and I each have our own shower supplies. I leave my hair and wash off, and then get out, tying the towel around my torso.

Ben is in the kitchen, and I glance at him as I move back into his room. His eyes go to mine, to the towel and my cleavage, and then away. I can't help a little smile from crossing my lips at the way he quickly looks away, as if embarrassed to be caught looking at me. I close his door behind me and put on my bra and the dress, not bothering with underwear, which I stuff into my purse; I'd rather go commando than put on dirty underwear after a shower.

I slip my feet into my heels and join Ben in the kitchen, where he waits with his phone and wallet in his hand. "So. I'm ready," I say.

He smiles at me. "I can call a cab."

I frown. "Don't you have a car?"

He nods. "Yeah, but I still can't drive yet, not with my knee. Shouldn't be too much longer, but…"

"Well, then, I can drive your car, if you don't mind."

He grabs a pair of keys from off the microwave and hands them to me. "Not at all. Let's go."

Ben drives a massive black truck, a three- or four-year-old Silverado with huge, knobby, off-road tires and a lift-kit. I glance at him, and the step up. "You gonna be able to get in okay?" I ask. He pulls open the passenger door, tosses his cane in, grabs the oh-shit bar with both hands and pulls himself up and in. "All right, then. Guess that's a yes," I say with a grin, climbing up.

"You gonna be able to drive this big ol' monster of a truck?"

I snort at him. "I'm from Texas, Ben. What do you think?"

"All right, then," he says, grinning. "Guess that's a yes."

Once again, I'm struck by how oddly comfortable I am, being around Ben. We don't need to talk much as we drive to the nearest department store, and it's easy to browse the aisles with him, picking out a pair of jeans, a T-shirt, a new bra and underwear, and a pair of sandals. The funniest part is when he opts to wait in the main aisle rather than going into the lingerie department with me. I pay for the items and change in the bathroom, call grandpa real quick and let him know I'm fine and not to worry about me, and then we're off again, heading across town to a greasy spoon my high school friends and I used to go to all the time.

And it was just that easy. We sit and drink cup after cup of deliciously shitty coffee while we wait for our food, talking about movies and music and anything and everything. I can almost forget why I'm back in San Antonio.

Eventually, there's nothing left to do but pay the bill, and Ben insists on paying for it. Which is cool. The last date I went on, the guy not only didn't offer to pay for mine, but he didn't even pay for his half, so I picked up the tab and blocked his number in my phone when I got home. I don't expect chivalry or whatever, but it sure is nice when it happens.

"So, you got anything to do?" I ask. "After this, I mean?"

He shrugs. "Not really. I need to find a gym at some point, because I've still gotta work out my knee."

It takes a lot for me to sound casual. "Mom was your therapist. I'd almost forgotten." I tap at the table with a spoon. "There's a good clinic near the hospital, Mom knows—*knew*, I mean—a couple of the thera-pists there. I can take you, if you want."

"Fuck. I'm sorry, Echo." He closes his eyes and rubs at the bridge of his nose with the knuckle of his forefinger. "I should've just kept my mouth shut."

"It's fine." My voice catches, though, and I'm dangerously close to coming apart right here in the diner. "I need to—I need some air."

I slide out of the booth and hurry outside, around the corner of the building. I breathe deeply and try to keep the tears at bay, try to keep it in, keep it down. But I can't. My knees give out, and I slide down the wall until I'm sitting on the concrete. Ben finds me there, face in my hands, tears wetting my cheeks. He lowers himself to the ground, extending his leg out straight. His arm extends behind me, and it's the most natural thing in the world for me to lean into him.

"I'm fine for a few minutes, an hour or two, and then it hits me all over again," I tell him, when I can breathe and speak again. "It's like…I forget, and then I remember. And…part of me likes it when I forget, because it doesn't hurt as bad. But then I hate myself for wanting to forget, you know? Because she…she's my mom. And she's—she's gone."

Ben's arms tighten around me. He doesn't say anything, doesn't try to tell me it's okay or offer any meaningless explanations. After a few minutes, I stand up and wipe at my eyes, then breathe and try push down the emotions.

"I have an idea," Ben says.

"What's that?"

"Let's go to a movie." He stands up too, near me but not too close. "We can just stay there all day, watch movie after movie. Eat too much popcorn and drink too much Coke."

"Sounds perfect," I say, grateful that he's not ready to part ways just yet.

"That's how I used to spend the long summer days when there wasn't much to do. Me and...a friend. We'd just stay in the theater all day. Eventually our parents discovered what we were doing and they made us start buying tickets for every movie we saw."

Something in the way he hesitated a bit tells a story, but I'm not sure I know him well enough to ask about it.

So that's what we do. We buy a ticket to an action movie, and when it's over we slip into the next theater and watch a romantic comedy. The hours pass, and it's easy to spend them all sitting next to Ben. He's laid back, he doesn't treat me like I'm as fragile as I really am, but he's always mindful of what he says, careful not to say anything that would break the spell.

Eventually it's evening, and we're both hungry, so I drive us to a bar-and-grill near the cinema. We drink beer and eat burgers, and the conversation stays light and easy. There are as many comfortable silences between us as there are conversations.

And then it's night, the clock inching closer and closer to midnight, and we're parked at his apartment building, just sitting outside on a bench in a courtyard behind his building, drinking a beer from his fridge and talking about the movies we watched, which ones we liked and which ones we didn't.

Silence floats between us, and I know that he's thinking about something…or someone. I want to ask but I don't intrude.

"Thanks for today, Ben," I say.

"It's been one of the best days I've ever had," he says. "I just wish we'd met under better circumstances."

"Me, too," I tell him, trying not to notice how, over the course of the minutes we've spent on this bench, we've somehow inched closer to each other, until our thighs and knees and hips touch, and how I tingle all over at his proximity. And then I feel guilty for feeling something good so soon. "You don't know what it's meant to me, though. You really don't. I don't know how I'd have dealt with this, if I'd been alone today."

"You don't have to be alone."

"I would be, though. My grandparents...I love them, but being around them right now would be impossible. We'd all be crying and crying, and I just...I just can't handle that. I can't let myself start crying. I mean, sometimes I just can't help it, but..." I lean forward, elbows on my knees, head hanging. "And at school, my friends wouldn't know what to say. It'd be awkward, and I'd just want to be alone, but the thing is, I *don't* want to be alone. I don't know how else to explain it."

"You don't have to explain it. I get it." He lets out a breath. "And you know, if you need to—talk about it. Or just...let go, you know? You can. If you need to cry, I mean. I don't know what I'm saying, just...I'm here, if you need to—talk, I guess."

"I just...I don't get it." I stare at the crescent moon rising over the roof of the building. "The officer who called me, he said she'd...the accident happened in the middle of the night. And, I mean, I don't know what she was doing then, you know? Like, she had a very orderly life. She had clients throughout the day, but her last one was always at seven in the evening. She'd have dinner, she'd either pick it up or she'd make something easy. And then she'd watch some TV, and she'd go to bed. I don't think she was ever out past midnight in all the years I lived at home. At least, not once she quit working the ER, I mean. So what the hell was she doing out at three in the morning?"

Ben is strangely silent. He doesn't answer, doesn't look at me. He just digs the end of his cane in the grass and spins it back and forth. Tension bleeds off him, and I'm not sure where it's coming from. I want to ask, but I don't.

This time, the silence is thick and tense. After a moment, Ben drains his beer and stands up. "Want another?"

I shrug. "Sure."

His abrupt silence and tension is odd and thick and unexpected.

So we go into his apartment through the sliding glass door off his back porch. He hands me a beer, and moves toward the back door, but I decide to sit on the couch and flip on the TV. He watches me click through channels until I find AMC and a rerun of last season's *The Walking Dead,* airing in preparation for the new season starting in a couple months. He watches me for a few moments, and then sits beside me, leaving a space between us.

It's clear, after half an hour or so, that something is eating at him. I know it was something I said, but I don't know how to address it, how to ask, what to say. I slide a glance at him, eyeing him sideways, as if I can decipher what's bothering him just by looking at him. His brows are drawn, and I get the sense he's not really watching the show. He's staring at the TV, but he's obviously a million miles away.

It's awkward, now. I'm here, he's here, but there's nothing between us. It's like he just shut down, like walls went up and any connection we might have made throughout the day has been erased. And I don't even know why. Worse yet, I can't figure out why that bothers me so much. Why I so badly want him to open up again, why I want so much for him to inch closer. I shouldn't want his heat near me, shouldn't want his proximity. But I do.

And why shouldn't I, though? Am I not allowed to feel anything but the grief? He's here and, in this moment, I can't remember a single reason why I shouldn't let myself explore whatever there might be between Ben and me. It won't lessen my pain over losing Mom. It won't soothe the hurt. But it might make me less lonely. It might ease the ache a little. And, right now, anything is better than the pulsing pressure of pain inside, grief buried deep and pushed down and not dealt with. It's down there, and it wants out, but I can't let it out. If I do it'll never stop. At some point I'll have to let myself truly feel it, but not now. It's too fresh, right now. And, in some way, I still don't even really believe Mom's gone. It's almost as if I'll get a text from her tomorrow morning, asking how classes are going. Like I could swing by her apartment and pretend I just came down to Texas to visit her. The reality of her death hasn't sunk in yet. Not totally.

And, in the meantime, I've got a hot, mysterious guy sitting beside me, one with honor enough to not only take care of my drunk ass, but tactfully and respectfully handle me throwing myself at him all but naked.

I don't know any other guy that would have done that. Maybe I just know assholes, but I can't think of one guy that would have been able to resist me literally throwing my naked ass at him.

Especially when I've seen and felt Ben's eyes on me, seen the flash of desire.

I glance at him again, and this time his eyes catch mine. His expression darkens, and I see that glimmer of attraction, see his eyes go to my lips, and then back to my eyes.

Fuck it.

I twist on the couch and lean in before I can second-guess myself. His lips are soft and strong and eager. I curl my hand around the back of his neck and slide my other palm against his ribs and lean closer, press tighter against him, and I taste the beer on his breath and feel his tongue slide against my teeth. His hands cross the space between us, one running slowly up from my knee to my thigh, the other going to my cheek, a roughened palm scraping across my cheekbone, fingers threading in the fine hair just above my ear. His hand is big, his pinky finger beneath my earlobe, his thumb tracing across my eyebrow.

His mouth moves against mine slowly and surely, and with each slide of lips against lips, our bodies glide closer and closer. I pull him against my mouth, deepen the kiss, breathe his breath and caress the hair at the back of his neck and slide my palm over the hard ridges of his ribs and the furrows of his abdominal muscles.

I gather the soft material of his T-shirt in my hand, bunch it and lift it and then I'm skittering my fingers over his flesh, rubbing my palm against his skin, roaming around to his back and up his spine, back down to his stomach and up the broad expanse of his chest. He mirrors my action, slipping his hand under my shirt and exploring up my back to just beneath my bra strap, and his hand is strong and gentle.

It's a kiss I don't want to break away from. Usually, a kiss is nothing more than a gateway to sex, a way to ease into nudity and penetration. But this is different. He's in no rush, kissing me slowly, thoroughly. His mouth explores mine, learns my kiss and my response. His tongue teases mine, flicking out against my teeth and tongue and then retreating until I'm hungry for his tongue inside my mouth, eager for it, demanding it, tasting the inside of his mouth and exploring his hard body and thick muscles and taut flesh.

His hands skim over my belly and roam the centimeters beneath my bra, sliding closer but not daring to touch. I don't want this to stop. I need this. I'm sober and doing this with my eyes wide open. I know this won't solve anything, and I'm not trying to use him as a salve or a rebound. I'm doing this because I want his body, because in the few short hours I've known him, I've grown to enjoy his presence and his personality. I don't know where this will go, after tonight, and I don't care. I just want *now*. I want his hands and his mouth and all of him, for as long as I can have him.

I push his shirt up and rip it off, toss it aside, and let my hands explore his body. God, he's ripped. He's not heavily muscled in a beefcake sort of way, he's more cut and toned and defined. He's *big*, though. Over six feet tall, easily, and probably weighs a good two hundred pounds of solid muscle.

I try to slow myself down, to delve back down into the kiss, to let my hands learn his torso, explore the mountain-ridge of his shoulders and the valleys of his abs and the thick iron of his arms. My hand slides from his shoulder to his bicep, clutches the bulging muscle, and then down his forearm, and then our hands are palm-to-palm, and then his fingers are curling between mine.

And the rightness of my hand tangled in his changes everything. It's simple, natural, and scary. It takes my breath away, and I have to break the kiss, touch my forehead to his and gasp for oxygen, and I realize we're both staring at our joined hands.

I pull away to look into his eyes, and I see the familiar weltering turmoil in his liquid brown gaze.

My free hand, resting on his shoulder, lifts seemingly of its own accord to touch the stubble on his cheek, and my thumb traces the shell of his ear. His gaze is intense and unwavering and indecipherable.

And then I'm attacking him, mouth hungry against his and we're twisting and he's falling backward onto the couch cushions, bringing me with him as we go horizontal. He's a hard presence beneath me, and I can feel his erection thick at my stomach. His hands curl over my shoulders, hesitate, and then slide down my back, over my spine until they pause again at the swell of my ass, and I can only wonder why he's hesitating, why he doesn't take what I'm so obviously offering.

He breaks the kiss, his fingers digging into my skin. "Echo…wait." There's pain in his voice alongside the heaviness of need. He doesn't want to wait any more than I do, but something is holding him back.

I move off him, and since he's taking up the entire couch all I can do is slide to the floor beside him. But I can't bring myself to break contact entirely, so I leave my hand on his chest and examine his face, hunting for clues.

"What, Ben? Did I misread the situation or something?"

He shakes his head. "No…yes." He sits up abruptly, one foot going to the floor near me, the other, his hurt leg, extended out in front of him. He runs his hands over his scalp, through his hair. "I just…I can't."

"Why?" I ask.

He only shakes his head, as if he can't or won't explain.

I grab his hand. "Ben. Talk to me. What's wrong?"

"Don't ask, Echo. Just...don't. Please. I need...I need a minute." He scoots forward and swings his other foot to the floor, struggles forward and to his feet, hopping to keep his weight off his injured knee.

I watch him leave through the back door, one hand on his cane, the other rubbing the back of his neck and scrubbing through his hair over and over. He's out in the long deep shadows cast by the moon and the lights from apartments and the lone orange lamp suspended from a power line over the courtyard.

What do I do? Let him go? Respect his privacy?

Fuck that.

I go after him.

Six: How It Happened
Ben

EVERYTHING INSIDE ME IS AT WAR. MY BODY WANTS ONE thing, my mind something else, my heart a different thing yet. And that's all aside from the guilt.

God, the guilt.

I can still feel Echo's lips on mine, feel her hands on my skin lifting my shirt up and off, feel her soft lush sexy body on mine, on top of me, kissing me and demanding more, attacking me and exploring me.

And holy *fuck* do I want her. I want her more than I've ever wanted anything or anyone. Or...almost anyone.

My heart aches, telling me I'm not over Kylie, telling me Echo is a rebound, telling me I'm still a fucking mess and I'm reaching out for anything to calm the furious emptiness inside of me. And my mind is telling me Echo is using me as a way to avoid dealing with her grief, and it's telling me that if she knew what Cheyenne had been doing out at two-thirty in the morning...if she knew what had happened moments before the crash...

I have to get away from her. I can't think when she's right here beside me, when I can smell the shampoo on her blond hair and the soap on her skin and the beer on her breath, when I can feel the heat radiating off her tanned silky flesh. I can't think when she kisses me, can't manage anything but to kiss her back and kiss her hard and beg silently for more.

I find myself out in the parking lot, leaning over the hood of my truck. I'm gasping for breath because I walked too fast and the pain in my knee is excruciating.

I don't hear Echo approach. She's just there, behind me. I feel her hands on my back, and then she's leaning her backside against the bumper, one hand on my shoulder, comforting me even though she had no clue why I bolted.

"Ben?" Her voice is soft and low with a musical lilt to it.

I don't even know how to respond or where to start, because I don't want to tell her anything. I don't want her to know. I don't know how to go about baring all my secrets. So I don't respond at all, which is just shitty as hell on my part.

She waits, and then twists and leans sideways against the hood, ducking down to try and catch my eye. "Benji?"

Oh hell no. That name...it hurts so bad, but coming from her it's new and strange and sweet and I can't help but shift my gaze to hers. "I'm sorry, Echo."

"What's wrong, Ben?"

I shake my head. "It's—just me."

"Look, you've got to give me something here, dude. You can't kiss me like that, and then just...shut down." She sidles closer, bumps me with her hip. Her hand is warm and small on my bare back, sliding in soothing circles. "I mean, I know I didn't imagine that. I know we don't know each other very well, but a kiss like that...we've got serious chemistry, if nothing else."

"Don't ask, Echo. Just don't. You don't want to know."

"Yeah, okay," she says, her voice dripping thickly with sarcasm. "Let me just pretend nothing happened real quick...oh, wait, no. I can't. So yeah, I am asking, because I do want to know."

"What if I don't want to tell?" I ask, my voice harsh now, unfairly so.

I pivot and walk away again, because I'm a coward, apparently. Back to my apartment, snatch my shirt and put it on, snag another beer and go out my front door and sit on the low step. A few seconds later, Echo is sitting beside me, a beer in her hand.

"Well, now I'm *really* curious," she says. "So you're gonna have to tell me something."

I guess I might as well get it over with, let it out.

I sigh. "It happened right over there." I point with my cane at the intersection, the left turn lane.

"What did?"

I swallow hard, set down my beer before I drop it. "The accident. Your mom's accident."

"Wh—*what?*" She's up and backing away, off the step and into the grass. She looks at me, and then twists and looks at the intersection. "What do you mean, Ben? How—? I don't even know what to ask. What was she doing here?"

I look up at her, because she deserves to see my eyes and see the truth. "She'd...she gave me a ride home after my session. I usually took the bus, but I'd tripped during therapy and my knee was hurting too bad to even walk to the bus. So she drove me home."

Echo is as still as a statue, staring at me, her brows pinched together, a million emotions warring on her face. "But...they said she died at—in the middle of the night. At like two-something, or three."

"Two-thirty-six. She died at two-thirty-six." It comes out as a whisper.

"How do you know? Why was she here, Ben?" Suspicion, now. The beginnings of anger.

"It's not what you think—"

She crosses the space between us in a few short angry steps, crouches in front of me, hands on my knees. "Then what was it, Ben? If it's not what I think, then what the *fuck* is it?"

I swallow hard, clench my fists. "She was my friend. She...I'm alone here, you know? And I'd just gotten injured, my knee..." I rub at my knee. "Football is all I know. And I'd just found it was over, that I'd never play again. She'd told me about how she'd been a dancer, how she screwed up her ankle and had to stop dancing competitively. I guess it was something we had in common."

She shakes her head. "No. Ben...come on, no. No." Her hand covers her mouth, her eyes shining with tears.

"She dropped me off, and I—I asked her if she wanted to come in. We watched a movie. That's it. That's it. I swear."

"Jesus, Ben. That's my *mother*."

"I know. God, I know." I try to look at her, meet her eyes, but she shakes her head again and backs up, falls to her ass. "But I told you, we watched a movie and that's it. We both fell asleep on the couch, and then she left."

Echo's eyes pierce me, pin me in place. "You're lying. You're fucking *lying* to me. Don't lie to me!"

I push myself to my feet; walk past her, toward the street and the intersection. I stop at the curb and stare out at the left turn lane, the light shining red. "I'm not lying."

She's there beside me because I can't seem to get away from her. "There's something else. I fucking feel it, Ben." She grabs my arms and turns me, stands chest-to-chest with me, looking up at me, her hands on my biceps. Her brown-gray-green eyes plead with me for the truth. "What happened, Ben? Just...just tell me exactly what happened. Please."

I don't know how to tell it. I don't. I swallow hard and sigh hard and think hard. "I...we...we almost kissed."

Echo doesn't move away, doesn't let go of my arms. She just blinks up at me. "What? What do you mean, 'almost kissed'?"

I duck my head and stare at the green grass beneath my bare feet. "We fell asleep, I told you

that. When we woke up, there was this...moment...
Cheyenne and I—we...almost kissed. We didn't,
though. She...she backed off and said she couldn't.
Because I was her client, and because she had a daughter my age." I try to breathe, try to force words past
my lips. "She got up to leave, and I could tell she was
tired. I didn't want her to go, because I could tell how
sleepy she was. I was worried for her. She tripped,
walking out the door, and I tried to get her to stay, and
I swear it was just to keep her safe, to keep anything
bad from happening. In the doorway, she stopped and
turned around, and that moment almost happened
again, but she repeated what she'd already said, that
she couldn't, that it just wasn't right. She couldn't.
And I got it. I really did. And it was more than that...
because I was so lonely and had been for so long, and
with everything else I've—she was my only friend,
and she was...your mother was a beautiful woman,
Echo. A beautiful person. And...I tried to keep her
from leaving, but she said she was fine, she'd be fine."
My voice breaks, there.

"Fuck. Ben...you almost kissed my mother? My
mom? And then you kiss *me?*"

"Now you get why I stopped." I choke out the
words. "I watched her drive away. I stood right here
on this step and watched her pull up in that left turn

lane. The light was red, and I watched her car sit there until it turned green. The whole intersection was empty. I mean, it was two-thirty in the morning, and she was so tired...so she didn't check for oncoming traffic. She just went. And this car...this red Mustang. It ran the light. It just...it didn't even slow down, even though the light had been red for so long, you know? And...and fuck, I watched it happen. I watched that Mustang smash into her door. It came from her left. I don't know how she didn't see it. I saw it happen. I saw her door just...crumple. Saw her truck roll, and I ran over to where she was, and she was already— already dead."

Echo just stares at me. "Ben..." she whispers, her voice cracking.

I shake my head. "I tried to stop her from leaving. I tried, Echo. I fucking...I couldn't do anything—" I can't take her silence, can't take the agony in her eyes, can't take the weight of my own guilt. "I'm sorry, Echo. I know that doesn't mean shit, but...I'm sorry. I'm so sorry."

Echo blinks, then scoots on her backside away from me, and I know how truly I deserve the anger in her eyes. She stands up, stumbles, rights herself. "I need...I need to think. I've got to—I've got to go." She starts walking, just walks away.

I force myself to my feet. "Echo. Wait." She stops but doesn't turn to look at me. I go inside and get my keys, bring them back out to where Echo is waiting. "Here. Take my truck."

"I don't know where I'm going—" She has the keys clutched in her hand, though. "I don't know where I'm going, or when I'll—I just need to think—I can't be around you right now. I'm too upset."

"I know. I get it. Just...take the truck."

She does. I watch her climb up into my truck, hear the engine turn over with a throaty rumble, and then she's gone.

I go inside, after a while.

It's all too easy to give in to the exhaustion. I don't know what time it is, and I don't even care. For the first time in my life, I give in to lethargy. I collapse on the couch, and even though I can't fall asleep, I just lie there, consumed by guilt and regret and the ache of Echo leaving.

All my life, I've been active, restless, energetic. Up early before school to hit the gym, and then practice after school. Even off-season I was in the gym early in the morning and I'd usually run a few miles in the evening. I was never idle. Sitting around and doing nothing made me crazy, and crazy made me feel useless and lazy and made my body buzz with unused energy.

But now, there's no more running, no more football. I could find a new therapist, but I don't see the point. I can walk. The knee will heal.

So I just lie there and pass the hours doing…I don't know what. I flip through channels, watch reruns and syndicated programming and sports clips. At one point, I even watch old grainy football games from the seventies and eighties on ESPN Classic.

Beyond the drawn blinds of the sliding back door, darkness fades to light, and eventually my eyes close.

When I wake up, sunlight shines bright and blinding. The TV is off. I sit up slowly, swing my feet to the floor, and scan the living room. I spot my keys on the round table that fills the space between kitchen and living room. I spot her sandals on the floor by the front door, her purse on the kitchen counter.

She's in my bed. Her jeans, T-shirt, and bra are in a neat pile on top of the dresser, and she's curled up on the very edge of the bed. The blanket is rumpled low over her hips, and she's got one hand tucked under her cheek, the other under the pillow. She's on her left side, facing the doorway, and I'm afforded a mouth-watering view of the fact that she didn't bother putting on one of my T-shirts.

My hands curl at my sides, and I have to force myself to stay in the doorway rather than going over to the bed. I want to stare at her, want to touch her, want to kiss her. In this moment, that's the only thing in my mind. Touch her, kiss her, slide into the bed beside her and hold her.

But I see her face, too, not just her breasts, and even in the relaxation of sleep, it's clear she's in pain.

I rip my gaze away, move to the bedside and draw the blanket up over her shoulders, more to cover her from my greedy gaze than anything else. But when the blanket touches her shoulder, she makes a cute little noise in the back of her throat, twists on the bed to face the other way, tucking the blanket more tightly around her, her feet shifting under the covers as she seeks a new position.

Her eyelids flutter, and I catch a slivered glimpse of her eyes. "Ben."

I tug the blanket higher around her. "Sssshhhh."

"I'm in your bed."

"It's fine. Go to sleep."

"'Kay." Her eyes flicker and flutter, and then her thick black lashes sweep against her cheek and she's asleep again, her breathing immediately going deep and even.

I leave her sleeping and hop in the shower, let the scorching hot water ease the knots in my shoulders.

When I leave the bathroom, a towel cinched around my hips, I find her fully awake, lying on her back with the blanket tucked under her arms, scrolling through her newsfeed on Facebook. As I emerge, dripping and hair mussed, she clicks her phone off and sets it aside, her eyes going to me.

"Hi," I say, moving past the foot of the bed toward my dresser, trying to act casual. Being essentially naked in a room with an essentially naked girl is anything but familiar to me.

She just stares at me, and I can tell she's hunting for words. "Ben...I drove around for a long, long time, thinking. And...I realized something."

I glance at her, a pair of underwear gripped in my hand. "What's that?"

"You think it's your fault."

"It is."

"No, it isn't, Ben. It's not. She was an adult. She made her decision. You expressed your concern, you offered to let her stay."

"I should have insisted. I should have...I don't know. Made her stay. She had no business driving."

She sits up higher, bringing the blanket with her. "Ben, she knew the risks. She was an ER nurse for ten years. She handled her share of patients injured in accidents just like hers. It's not your fault. She made the choice to drive, not you. What else could you have done, physically prevented her from leaving?"

"But if it weren't for me, she wouldn't have even been here."

Her gaze finally wavers, flits away from mine. "That's the part I'm still having trouble with." She touches the bed at her side. "Come sit."

"I'm not dressed," I protest.

"Me neither."

So I perch on the edge of the bed and swing my legs up, crossing my legs at the ankles and keeping the towel pinched between my knees.

Echo smirks and then slides over closer to me. "Modest, huh?"

I shrug, blushing. "I guess."

"It's cute. It's not like you haven't seen me in all my nearly-naked glory already."

I just shrug again and she sighs. "I just don't know what to think, Ben. I really don't. It's so hard for me to reconcile the idea of you kissing my mom with the fact that she was my *mom*. I mean, I get that she's…that she *was* a beautiful woman. Intellectually, I get that. But she was my mother. But I also know she was…lonely. I guess I'm only realizing that now, thinking about how something like that could hap-pen. I mean, I know Mom, and I know she's not…I know she wasn't a cougar. She had class and standards, you know?"

"Wow. Okay." I can't help the sarcastic tone.

Echo groans. "God, that came out really judgmental, didn't it? I'm sorry, I didn't mean it like that. It's just that she was twenty years older than you. *Twenty* years, Ben. That's a significant age difference. It's an entire generation, literally. But like I said, I'm trying to figure out, just for my own understanding, how she would even let herself get into a situation like that. And I realized, like I said, that she was lonely. I never knew my father, and I have no memory of my mom ever going on a date. Not one. Not in my entire life. She was dedicated to me and to work. I mean, maybe she went on dates or whatever while I was at school? I don't know. Somehow I don't think so. And I guess that makes me sad, I mean...everybody wants love, and...and sex, right?" She winces. "It's even harder for me to think about my mom in that context, but she was a woman, and she had to have those needs, right? So for whatever reason she let her guard down with you. I don't know. I mean, god, I get it. You're a great guy. You're easy to talk to, easy to be around, and shit, I'll be honest...you're hot as hell. But there just...there *had* to have been someone more age-appropriate at some point, right?"

I don't answer right away. "Well...I don't know what to say to all that. We didn't talk about anything like that. It never went there. We talked a lot, but it was always...surface stuff, you know? Or it was about my motivation, my injury, my interests and what I'm going to do with myself now that football is off the table. We didn't talk about you, or my past or hers, or anything except that initial conversation about her dance career." It's supremely awkward and difficult talking about this, for both of us. I bite the bullet and resign myself to being totally clear. "Look, it was... not something either of us were looking for. Certainly not me. I was here in San Antonio to play football, and that's it. I wasn't looking for anything. But then I got hurt and the only friends I had were guys from the football team. It became too hard to be around them, so I didn't really have any friends.

"And Cheyenne understood that. So, yeah, there was a level of attraction on my part. I never said or did anything, and I never really knew what she thought about me in that sense. I mean, I knew she was older than me by a good bit, but I didn't know how much until...until that day. And I mean...I was lonely, and I guess like you said, she was too. It makes sense, I guess, why a woman like her would even give the time of day to a guy like me. Because, like you said, she was twenty years older than me. But we were both lonely, and I invited her in, partly just to be polite and partly because, yeah, I wanted the company. I wasn't…thinking about…trying anything. Like I said, it just…sort of happened. But it didn't actually happen. You want the uncomfortable details? We were sitting on the couch, and in the process of watching the movie and then falling asleep, we'd gradually gotten closer and closer. And then we woke up, and there was just this strange moment of…*what if*…I guess. It was late, and we were both tired and just waking up, and…our lips touched for a fraction of second. Not even. And then she backed off and I guess she just realized all the different, very valid reasons why that couldn't and shouldn't happen. And it didn't. It was just this one weird moment, and I guess it was probably mostly just me."

Echo doesn't answer right away, and when she does, it's not what I expected her to say. "Why are you here, Ben? In San Antonio, I mean. You got hurt playing football. I know that. But…you're obviously not from here, so…why stay?"

I sigh. "I don't know. I honestly don't. I just…I'm not ready to go home, yet. That means admitting defeat, I guess. I left home for…several reasons. And if I go back—I don't know, I'll have to face reality. I'll have to actually start over. Figure out what the hell to do with my life. It's like…I have to figure out who I am, now. Because, honestly, football was it for me. Sounds pathetic, now that I say that out loud. My whole life was just about being a fucking jock. And now what?"

"So you're here avoiding reality?"

"Yeah, basically." I shrug. "Also, I haven't told my parents I got hurt. They'd be here in ten seconds flat, dragging me home and babying me and I just…I need to deal with this on my own for a bit first, I guess."

"You're lucky, then." She says this quietly. "You have both parents, and obviously they'd drop everything to come get you, if they knew you were in trouble."

I sigh. "They would. And I am lucky. I do know that. And I'll go back eventually. I mean, I have to. But I can't, yet. And not just because of the football injury thing. There are other reasons."

She glances sideways at me. "Care to share?"

I blink and breathe and hesitate. "Just…running away from heartbreak, that's all. I needed time and space, and it still feels too soon to go back and have to face everything I ran from."

I feel her gaze on me, so I finally turn my head to meet her eyes with mine. The air feels thick between us, rife with a million unspoken things. The kiss. What it meant, and how deep it went. I don't know what to say, suddenly, and clearly she doesn't either. We're close, physically, now. And we're both dangerously close to being naked. All that separates us is my towel and the blanket over Echo, and suddenly that doesn't feel like all that much. And despite the heaviness of what we've been talking about, all I can think about is how it felt to kiss Echo, and how badly I want to do it again.

"I want to kiss you again," Echo says, somehow reading my mind. "But...it makes me feel like a skank for wanting you in the midst of all that's going on. My mom hasn't been in the ground a week and I'm tangled up with a guy? And then there's everything that happened between you and her? It's confusing, and I don't know how to figure it out. I just know what I want. But I don't know if it's right or wrong. And I'm...not used to caring if it's right or wrong."

"I want to kiss you, too. I keep thinking about it. And the fact that it's all I can think about right now makes me feel like an asshole. So I guess...I get what you're saying."

"So what do we do?" she asks.

I shrug. "I don't know. Go with it, or don't. Seems like these are the only two choices we have, right?"

She fidgets with the fabric of the blanket, breathing deeply, brows drawn down in thought. "Right."

Her hair is loose and messy around her shoulders, tangled and knotted in places, her skin tan and delicate. I'm staring at her, because I can't help it. I see her pulse thudding in her throat. The blanket has slipped, baring some of her cleavage. A single gentle tug and she'd be exposed. My heart is in my throat, my mind in turmoil. Fear, doubt, nerves…these war with the raging wildfire of need and desire.

She's attracted to me, and me to her. We're the same age, in similar places in life. We've been brought together by a tragedy, and we can't seem to stay away from each other. She came back, and she didn't have to. She could have gone anywhere, she could have dropped off my keys and left. But instead she's here, in my bed, and now she's glancing sideways at me, breathing deeply and pinching the blanket between her fingers, and it almost feels like she's waiting for me.

Our gazes meet, and it's impossible to break away from her stunning, vivid eyes.

It's too easy, far, far too easy to let my doubts and fear and everything fall away. It's far, far too easy to lean into her, feel her shoulder pinned against the wall by mine as I tilt toward her, barely breathing. And god, she makes it that much easier when her soft warm hand slides across my shoulder and pulls me toward her. So I twist toward her, feeling the towel around my hips loosen but not caring, because her lips are damp and silken and strong on mine, and her tongue is insistent. My eyes are closed, and all I know in this moment is her kiss, because it's taking my breath and forming the entirety of my universe, and I don't want it to end, and I know somehow that she doesn't either. She kisses me desperately, hungrily, our lips scouring over each other's. We gasp for oxygen and I taste her breath intimate on my mouth, feel her hand sliding from my shoulder to my back and down to my waist.

And then we're sliding down, and the towel is coming undone, bunching around my hips, and I feel air cool on my hip as it eases open, and then I'm bared and naked on the bed, and the blanket and sheet is somehow not in the way either. I have to pause to breathe, and my eyes open, meet hers, green-gray-brown wide and liquid and heated with need as fiery as my own. She's naked, too, from the waist up. All she wears is a pair of underwear, a tiny triangle of black over her core with a thin string around her hips. She's kicked the covers away, and her hand is running up and down my back, her eyes not wavering from mine, and then her palm slides down and down and down and she's cupping my ass in her hand, squeezing, caressing, and then she's lifting up and kissing me, pulling me down.

I'm hard, achingly hard. Bursting with need from every seam and pore. And yet all I want to do is kiss her, so I let myself press her to the bed with my weight, one hand in the mattress at her side, the other tracing over her forehead, sliding honey-blond hair away, and I kiss her.

Her breasts are soft, crushed between us, and one of her knees rises and bends, sliding at my hip. Her hand remains on my ass, holding and squeezing as if she refuses to let go, as if she's found what she likes and won't let it go, can't get enough. That's how I feel, at least, as I delve into her mouth with my tongue, explore her lips and teeth and gums and tongue and breathe her breath and absorb the wonder of her skin against mine.

But then my knee makes itself known, and I have to break away and gasp in pain as the aching throb tells me I can't hold this position for long, levered over her like this.

And Echo, god, she seems to know this immediately. She pushes at my chest, and I fall to my side, then to my back, and she's moving over me, and Jesus, her tits are incredible, round and heavy and swaying, small dark pink areolae and hard button nipples, and my hands find them with a will of their own. I cup and lift them and Echo is sliding a knee across my hips, leaning over me, preparing to bend and kiss me, but her tits are too tempting, and I bring one to my lips, feather my tongue over her nipple and taste its hardness and the salt of her skin.

Echo moans, sinks down to sit on me, back arched and throat bared, breast pressed to my mouth, a hand on my chest. She writhes on me, and I feel her core sliding against my erection, and I'm close to losing it.

"Ben…" she breathes. Her voice is soft with bliss and with need.

All I want, all I need, is to hear her voice, to feel her skin, to explore her body.

And then she grabs my hand, the one not keeping her swaying breast at my lips, and brings my fingers to the scrap of black fabric.

I know what she's asking of me. Do I dare?

But she's insistent: "Ben…please. Touch me."

Seven: Chemistry
Echo

I'M A GIRL WHO KNOWS WHAT SHE WANTS. AND WHEN I know, I do something about it. I want Ben, so I do something about it. I know it's weird and there are reasons why this is a bad idea, but I don't care. He kisses like a god, with an urgency and a passion that takes my breath away. His hands are gentle and yet strong, and he has this way of letting me decide what I want, and then giving it to me.

I'm aching, hot all over with need. I'm frustrated and grieving and he's here, big and hard and muscular and sexy and naked. He's not just a distraction, although I could use one. I know he could make me feel good, and I need that. Shit, I know myself well enough to know if Ben and I bang, it won't be just once. We'll need it several times to really get it out of our systems. But then something else speaks, deep inside me, and says that there's more. I want Ben, that's easy enough to decide. But do I want to just bang him and go my way, the way it's been with every other guy? Or do I want more?

Hell, I don't know. That's too much to think about when his mouth is on mine and his skin is hot under mine and his hands are on me. One hand is gentle at my face, a thumb brushing at my flyaway hair, palm at my cheek, and now that thumb is at the corner of my lips, where our mouths join, and no one's ever kissed me this way, touched my face so tenderly and intimately and gently. It's a heady feeling, dizzying and arousing. Yet he's not pushing it. Surely it's evident how much I want this. Surely he knows by now that he can have me, that I'll not just let him, but I'll give back as good as I get. But he doesn't hurry things. He just kisses and caresses, a huge pleasant presence.

Normally, I'd be clawing at my panties and sliding him in, impatient to get started. I'm not afraid to take charge, especially when it comes to sex. Most, if not all, of my partners have been fairly clueless and clumsy if ardent, so if I want things to be at least somewhat satisfying for me, I have to sort of guide them. And that's fine. I get what I want, and so does the guy. Of course, what a guy wants from sex and what a girl needs are usually very different.

But with Ben, it's different. I don't know how, or why. I don't want to push him; I don't want to take charge. I want him to be what I need without having to be shown. Because…I think I sense that he can be.

Yet…he's holding back. And I'm going insane with need. I ache inside. My thighs quiver with need. My core is damp, and I know he can smell my desire. But yet even after I've rolled him to ease his weight off his injured knee, and he's discovered my tits and his mouth latches on and sucks and licks, sending zinging thrills of heated bliss though me, he doesn't push it past that. Maybe he's playing a game, pushing me to the edge of sanity. Making me wait.

That'd be hot.

And yet as I gasp and breathe and arch my back, frantic with how good his mouth feels on my nipple, he still keeps his hands away from my core, cupping my boobs and letting me grind on him. God, yes, I feel his erection, and even before I've seen it I can tell he's endowed like a god. And I *want* it. I want his cock. I need it. I'm crazy for it. But I'm even more desperate to come. He's kissed me senseless and now he's driving me wild with his mouth on my tits, and I need more. *More.*

I find myself clutching the back of his head, my fingers buried in his thick soft black hair, keeping his mouth against my breast, sitting astride him with my back arched to press him closer, my head hanging back on my neck, and I *need* him to touch me.

So I do something unusual for me: I ask him. "Ben...please. Touch me."

I'm not an ask-for-it type of girl. I'm a take what I want and if you don't satisfy me, there won't be seconds. And honestly, there aren't usually seconds. I never ask. I know what I want. I know how to get it. I know what I look like and I know guys like it. But somehow, with Ben, everything is just...different. *He's* different, and I'm different with him.

I take his wrist in my hand and show him what I want, bringing his fingers to my core. The air is cold against my saliva-wet nipples when his mouth leaves my skin, and I look down to see his nearly black eyes wide and dark and intense on mine. I lift up on my knees. One of his hands rests on my hip, the other at the apex of my thighs, reaching nearer and nearer. He slides his hand around my hip and takes my ass cheek in his palm. I bite my lip at the strength in his grip and the delicacy of his touch, the way he caresses me as if unsure if he's allowed to, as if he's marveling that I'm letting him touch me, rather than desperate for him to quit playing around and just fucking take me.

I say nothing, just kneel over him and release his wrist now that it's clear what I want. When his wrist is freed, he slips his hand in the narrow gap between my thighs, and I watch him as he caresses my inner thigh, and then his middle finger traces up my opening over the material of my thong, and I know there's a wet spot there from my leaking juices. I'm literally wet for him, and I know he sees, feels, smells it. His eyes are heavy-lidded, his chest rising and falling with deep breaths. For my part, I'm breathless in anticipation.

And then he traces back down, and now his finger hooks under the elastic of the thong and pulls the triangle of black aside, baring my pussy for him. He makes a sound in his throat, a murmur of appreciation, I think. I just watch, unable to move or think or breathe or speak. His middle finger skates over my naked opening, and I tremble all over.

A gasped moan leaves me when his fingertip eases in, and now there's just the very tip of his finger inside me, but it's enough to have me wanting to writhe and beg for more. But I don't. I keep still and try to keep silent, because he's slowly drawing his finger down and then back up, and my eyes cross and my eyelids slide closed on their own, fluttering.

He drags his fingertip upward, and he finds my clit. I gasp again, unable to prevent myself. And then he brings his finger in a slow, maddening circle, and I can't help but move my hips in a circle to match, needing more and more. And Ben gives me more. His finger slides into me, piercing me fully, and I whimper as he draws it back out, slicking my essence through me and over my clitoris.

My tits ache. I cup them and squeeze, lift, and writhe as he starts to touch me in a rhythm now, sliding in, circle twice, and slide in, circle twice. I let out a groan when he adds a second finger.

I feel him lift up and strain toward me, so I plant a palm on his chest, pinning him to the bed, lift my core off his body, and offer my breast to him, bring it to his mouth. He sighs and groans in his chest, and then laves his tongue over my nipple and I'm lost to the lighting bolt striking me at the touch of his mouth. His index and middle fingers move in me, circle and circle, and I feel my hair hanging over one shoulder, probably tickling his chest, feel something huge and hot expanding inside me. I'm gasping nonstop, and then a hot wire tugs inside me, a bolt of surging need connecting my tits to my clit and to the orgasm building inside me.

I ride his fingers, now, shamelessly grinding on his touch for more, and he gives me more, more, until

I'm wild with the need to fall over the edge. There is not one single thought inside me except the need for him to get me there, and I'm on the edge. His teeth worry over my nipple gently, and I gasp, and then he sucks the nipple into his mouth and his tongue flickers over it, and his fingers circle me with a speed that matches the urgency of my grinding hips.

"Ben...shit...oh god...I'm coming, Benji..." I feel the momentary tense of his body beneath me when I use that nickname, but I'm lost to the climax washing over me, surging through me, gripping me and wringing me.

I'm helpless, now, caught by the climax.

And Ben does something totally unexpected. He rolls me to my back, and before I can protest, his face is between my thighs and his finger is keeping my thong pulled aside, and his tongue is lapping at me, and the orgasm shatters, or I shatter, a throaty moan ripping out of me. I clutch his face to me, let my knees draw up and fall open, because his tongue is driving and circling my clit and I'm riding his face, writhing and moaning and helpless to contain myself with the potency of my orgasm.

Finally I'm shivering and gasping and shuddering with the aftershocks, and I expect Ben to rise up over me, but he doesn't. I have to push him away from me, because I can't take the stimulation for a moment.

He rises to lie beside me, watching me, a small satisfied grin on his face as he stares at me.

I gasp for breath, waiting for him. But he doesn't do anything, just looks at me. "What?" I ask, unnerved by his silence and by the fact that he's not taking his pleasure yet.

"You're incredible," he says. "So gorgeous."

I give a little shrug and smile. "Thanks."

"No, for real. You are stunningly beautiful, and sexy as hell."

I roll toward him, still shaking and breathless. "Thank you, Benji," I say with a happy, flattered, giddy grin. His eyes close as if in pain. I frown. "Should I not call you that?"

His eyes flick open and go to me. I see determination cross his features. "No. It's fine."

I rest a knee on his thigh, a hand on his belly, and can't help but glance at his cock, straining hard and huge, bigger even than I'd initially guessed. It's thick, with a wide, bulbous head leaking clear fluid, veins that stand out, long and ever so slightly curved back towards his body, laying flat against his belly. His balls are heavy and dark, prickly with trimmed black hair.

God, he's gorgeous, and I'm going to seriously enjoy what he's packing.

But something in his voice stops me from touching him just yet. "You don't sound convinced about that."

He shrugs. "I am. Seriously. It's fine."

"Let me guess. Benji was a nickname the girl who broke your heart gave you."

He nods. "Got it in one."

"Well, I'm appropriating it." I lean over him and press a kiss to his chest. "But for real, if you don't like it, just tell me."

He shakes his head. "It's just a reminder, and I need to get over it. And I like the way you say it, anyway."

"Okay then...Benji." I rest my chin on his pectoral muscle and look up at him. My hands skate over his chest, toying with his tiny nipple and then down to the muscle sheathing his ribs, and to his hard abs. "So...now what?" I lace my words heavily with suggestion.

His eyes go to mine. "I don't know." A grin curves his lips. "Now what?"

I'm aching for him, but I don't want to rush this. I want to enjoy him, I want to drag out every moment, want to tease out this delicious foreplay as long as possible. So I keep exploring his torso with my hand, the other tucked between us, my knee on his thigh, my foot against his calf. I run my palm up his side and over his belly, teasing lower and lower with each random circuit around his body. And I watch him the whole time. At first, his eyes remain on mine, dark and brooding and impenetrable. But as my hand slips lower and lower, his eyes gradually close.

I flatten my palm against his belly and slide it under his erection, a teasing not-quite touch. He sucks in a sharp breath and pulls in his stomach. I grin a little at that. And then I can't wait any longer. I slowly curl my fingers around his girth, and he stops breathing entirely. His face is a mask of rapture and wonder, and I can't help wondering how long it's been for him. Judging by his reactions to everything, quite a long time.

Which is fine. I'm finding myself not just willing to take it slow, but looking forward to the tantalizing journey. We'll take it step by step, and enjoy every moment. He has this way of making me want to savor each second, each touch, each kiss and caress. I don't know what it is, if it's just some subtlety in his personality. I don't know. But I'm going slow and loving it.

I don't even pump my hand, at first. I just hold his cock in my fist and enjoy the view, the way so much of him juts up and out over my hand as I grip him at the root. My hand seems pale against his dark flesh, and I like even that subtle contrast. Slowly, I slide my hand upward, relishing the stutter of his skin against mine, and the way his belly sucks in and his breath exhales suddenly, involuntarily. I roll my palm over his head and squeeze, and then glide my fist back down enough to rub my thumb over the tip, smearing the pre-come over him.

I glance up and see that he's watching through slitted lids, his face a mask of bliss and focus. He's breathing deeply, now.

I caress his length slowly downward, and then I cup his sac, feel its heaviness in my palm. My cheek is on his chest, and I'm watching myself touch him, and even though this is by no means new for me, this somehow feels different. As if I'm doing and feeling and experiencing this through new eyes.

With each slow slide of my fist up his length, I curl and twist my palm over his head, rub his tip with my thumb and then pump my fist to his root. As my hand presses against his belly on the downward slide, Ben lifts up, presses into my hand. His breathing is ragged. He's getting close and holding back. His hands are knotted in the flat sheet at his sides, as if he's not sure where to put them. So I let go of his cock and take his hand in mine, press it to my head, into my hair. I resume the slow caress of his length and he weaves his fingers into my hair, smoothing it back off my face, and his other hand caresses my shoulder and down my back as far as he can reach.

When his hips begin to move with the stroke of my fingers around his considerable thickness, I press my lips to the flesh of his chest, and then to his ribs, moving over him gradually now, until I can kiss from hip to hip, chest to navel. He tastes clean and smells of soap and man.

"Oh…ssshhhhhiiiiit…." He gasps. "That feels so good."

"Yeah?" I kiss his belly, mere centimeters from the head of his cock. "Which part?"

"Everything. Your hand, the way you're…touching me. You kissing me like that."

"Are you close?" I ask.

"Yeah…"

"You're holding back, aren't you, Benji?" My cheek is resting on his belly now, my eyes locked on his cock, watching it squeeze out of my fist, the head dark and straining toward my mouth.

"Yeah, I am," he admits, with a groan.

"Don't hold back," I say, sliding my face over his skin, closer and closer.

"Echo...you don't have to—" he starts, but then I've got him in my mouth, and I have to keep my jaw spread wide to take his thick cock.

I wrap my lips around him and slide my mouth around him until I feel him at the back of my throat, and he groans, gasps.

Letting him fall out of my mouth, I look up at him with a grin. "I don't have to what, Benji?"

"Do that," he groans. "You don't have to do that."

"I know." I punctuate this by licking the pre-come off his tip, and then curl my fist around his root and put my lips to his cock and suck at the head. "But I'm going to anyway."

"Oh god. I'm close, Echo."

I hum as I slide him into my mouth. I cup his balls and press my fingers under them, and he lifts his hips off the mattress, his fingers tightening in my hair. Oh yeah, I like that, the way he's got a grip in my hair and isn't quite pulling, but almost. I bob, now, taking him as deep as my gag reflex will let me and then backing away. I swirl my tongue around the head of his cock, tasting his essence, feeling him throb between my lips. He strains, almost thrusting at me. I hum again, a moan of encouragement. His hips move, and I can tell he's trying to not fuck my mouth. So I back my mouth away and take him in my fist, pump him hard and suck, swirling my tongue against the tiny slit at the top of his cock, tasting the moisture pooling there. He is thrusting now, involuntarily moving into my fist. I bob with him until I hear him groan, and then I let go of him and move my head in synch with his thrusting, sinking down as he pushes in, pulling away as he draws back. And now he's moaning loudly and both his fists are tangled in my hair, holding my hair and gently encouraging me to keep going.

"Oh my—fuck, oh fuck—" he grunts, and I feel him tense all over. "I'm—I'm coming, Echo… Jesus—ohhhhhh…"

His warning comes just in time for me to prepare. His hips thrust up, and his cock nudges the back of my throat, and I feel the come burst out of him, a gush of liquid down my throat. I pull my lips up and then back down, fucking him with my mouth, hard and fast, and he comes again, and this time I taste it, a thick hot wash of come in my mouth, and he comes a third time, and I've got to swallow before the next wave surges out of him, and I'm bobbing and stroking him with my tongue, feeling spurt after spurt of seed explode out of him, until I'm sucking it from him and he's groaning and stroking my head and feathering my hair away from my face.

When he's softening in my mouth, I release him and slide up to rest my cheek on his shoulder. He wraps an arm around me, cradling me close.

"Holy shit, Echo."

"You came *a lot*," I say, wiping at my lips.

He looks down at me. "I came *hard*."

"Yeah you did." I brush at a stray lock of black hair on his forehead. "But then, so did I. *Really* hard."

He's still breathing hard as we lie together. Eventually, he glances at me. "I don't even know what time it is, I just know I'm hungry."

"Not me," I say, giggling. "I just had breakfast."

He laughs with me. "You're sure you don't need anything else?"

"Nope. Lots of protein in come, I hear." I grin up at him, and my smile widens as I see that he's blushing again. Seriously, this guy and his blushing is so damned cute. "For real, though, I could go for breakfast."

He lifts up to peer over me at the clock. "Holy shit. It's twelve-thirty."

I shrug. "Makes sense. I didn't get back until after four."

"I wasn't sure you'd be back, honestly."

I lift up on an elbow and look down at him. He twines a lock of my hair around his finger. "I just needed to think, Ben. It was a lot to take in." I rub my hand over his chest. "I thought about leaving your truck here and just...taking off, but...it didn't seem right. And I didn't *want* to. That kiss...it was—I couldn't stop thinking about it. I wanted to talk to you once more, at least. Tell you I...I don't blame you. It wasn't your fault. And even what happened with you and Mom, as weird as it is for me to think about it, I get it."

"And now?"

I shrug. "And now...we've got chemistry, Benji." I slide closer to him, press my lips to his and taste my own essence on him. "And I like it."

"There's a lot you don't know about me," he says, looking at me and sliding a finger across my temple.

"And there's a lot you don't know about me. I mean, do we know anything about each other, really? Information-wise, I mean. No, we don't. But that doesn't change the fact that I feel a physical pull to you. Attraction, yes, but...something else, too. I don't know." I slide out of bed, and face him as I get dressed, enjoying the fact that he can't take his eyes off me as I hook my bra on and shimmy into my jeans. "So get your fine ass out of bed and put on some clothes."

He grins. "Yes ma'am."

Now it's my turn to stare at his magnificent body as he tugs on underwear, sadly covering his big, dangling dick, followed by a pair of jeans and a t-shirt.

We head out and I drive us to a nearby burger place Mom and I used to go to a lot, but all the way there my thoughts keep returning to what he said: *There's a lot you don't know about me.*

And god, it's true, isn't it? I don't know shit about him, or him about me.

He's moody during lunch. Conversation flows easily, but I occasionally get a sense of something deeper going on in his head. I want to ask, but I also don't. Being with him feels insular, like the world and life beyond this thing between us doesn't exist, or doesn't matter. I mean, I know I have a lot to do. Mom's house needs to be cleaned out. I have to go through her stuff, and I don't even know where to begin or what to do with it all. And I have to figure out if she had a will or anything like that. And eventually I have to get back to school. I got a leave of absence granted, but it won't hold forever. And once this bubble around Ben and me pops, all of that will come crashing back down around me and I'll have to deal with it all. And this place, San Antonio, will become a place of memories, a place that once was home, but isn't any longer.

So I don't pry into whatever is percolating behind Ben's eyes.

We eat lunch, have a beer each even though it's barely one in the afternoon, and we avoid talking about anything deep. And through it all, the only thing I really want is to go back to his apartment, get him naked, and fuck him until neither of us can move.

He pays again, and then we're in his truck and I'm heading to his apartment.

He glances at me. "Um, do you want to swing by your grandparents' house? Get your stuff? I mean... if you wanted to stay with me while you're in San Antonio, I'd think you might want your bag, at least, right?" He clears his throat. "Assuming you want to stay, I mean."

"Hell yeah, I do. But we can't just 'swing by' their house. It's kind of far. A good two-hour round trip, depending on traffic. And...are you sure you'd want to come with me? They'd...ask questions."

"It's up to you, Echo. You can do whatever you want. I wouldn't mind questions. I mean, we're friends, right?"

I shrug. "Sure. But I'm pretty sure it'd be obvious there's more, especially to Grandma. She don't miss a trick."

He laughs. "You sounded very Texas just then."

I grin and can't help laughing. "Well, I did grow up here, so it comes back every once in a while." I cut a glance at him. "I don't know, though. Do I want to go there? Not really. It'd just be…hard. And my bag only has a couple changes of clothes and my makeup. Nothing super important, you know? I mean, I wasn't planning on being here very long."

We both sober at that.

"No," he says, quietly. "I suppose not."

I try to turn the conversation back to something light. "So, I guess my point is there's nothing I really need. I can buy more clothes, and I don't plan on putting on any makeup any time soon." I glance at him and wink.

His smile is bright and hopeful and amused. "You weren't, huh?"

I shrug. "Nope. I don't usually wear much anyway. Some eyeliner and lip gloss to class, maybe a bit more if I'm going out with my friends."

Clearly not the response he was expecting, judging by the look on his face. "Oh. Right. Well you don't need it at all. You're gorgeous."

I can't help but glow a little at his compliment. "Thanks." I lean toward him. "Also, I don't wear makeup to bed."

A smile spreads across his face, and he glances at me. "Neither do I."

I laugh and smack his shoulder. "I'd hope not, doofus."

He grabs my wrist, and then slides his fingers through mine. This does odd things to me. It makes my heart thud a little harder, even as part of me melts and part of me heats up and my belly flutters and I press my thighs together to stem the pressure building there. All from the small, simple gesture of him taking my hand.

I drive us back to his apartment as fast as I legally can.

Eight: Bare Truth and Bare Skin

So…yeah, I should know by now that nothing ever goes as planned.

We get back to his apartment in record time, and I've got my tongue down his throat before he can get his key out of his door. He stumbles inside, slams the door closed with his cane, which he tosses aside along with his keys. Ben's hands find my ass, knead and grip, and mine go to his stomach, lift his shirt off him and I toss it away, then start on his jeans. All this while our mouths clash and collide, tongues slash and stutter. My heart hammers in my chest, even though I've done this more times than I care to count. I'm not exactly a chaste girl, you might say.

But this is different.

God, I keep going back to that thought, and never make any more sense of it. He's just different, and I don't know why, or how. Or what it means, if anything.

He's got my jeans unbuttoned and his hands are digging under the denim and finding skin, rolling down the string of my thong and squeezing and cupping the flesh of my admittedly generous bottom. For my part, I'm greedily unzipping his jeans and helping him get them off, pushing them down, and then forcing myself to slow down, to pull slowly and teasingly at his tight black boxer-briefs until his huge hard dick is thick and tall between us, and I'm caressing it hungrily, sliding my palm up and down his length. And oh no, he's not idle. His hands push away my shirt, fumble at my bra and bare my tits, and then he's sliding his rough palms down my sides and under the string of my thong, working it free from my ass-crack and I'm stepping out of it.

And just like that we're naked, and we haven't even left the front door.

I take his hands in mine and walk backward, pulling him into his room. But then he turns the tables, spinning and sitting on the edge of the bed and tugging me to him, kissing my chest and my stomach, clutching and caressing my ass, licking my tits and between them, and then his fingers find my opening and I gasp as he slides two fingers into me, his palm cupping my bare flesh. And in that moment I'm glad I used one of his disposable razors to shave the other day.

I ride his fingers until I'm gasping, and then I push him down and lie on him, rise astride him, kiss him, reach between us to grasp his erection…but he grabs my hips and lifts me, pulls me forward and settles me on him. I kneel over his face and he hooks his arms over my thighs, finds my opening and parts me, laps at me with his tongue, and before I know it I'm gasping and groaning and coming, but he's relentless and moves his fingers into me, two thick fingers inside me and fucks me with them and licks and licks and sucks at my clit and I come again.

When I'm not sure I can withstand another orgasm, I lift up and off him. "Ben, enough. I want you."

I shimmy down his body until I feel the thick round head of his cock at my entrance, but then he tenses and grips my hips to free me in place.

"Echo, wait," he growls, his voice low and rough.

I look down at his face, see the tension and the fear and the doubt and even pain, and I can't figure any of it out. "Why? I thought you wanted this?"

"I do, Jesus I do. So fucking bad it literally hurts."

"Then why are you stopping me?" I grip his cock in my hand and stroke him. "I want you, Ben. I want this, with you, right *now*. I'm clean, and I've got an IUD. We're covered, if that's what you're worried about."

He shakes his head. "No. I mean, yeah, that crossed my mind. But...that's not—that's not why I stopped you."

I groan in frustration. "Then what the hell is the problem? Is it the thing with Mom, again? Ben, I told you. I don't blame you, and you shouldn't blame yourself. As for the other part, like you said, nothing actually happened, so it's—"

He shifts under my caress, and then lifts me off him. I move to sit cross-legged on the bed, not bothering to hide my irritation. Ben flexes his knee, and then moves to sit on the bed facing me, his erection straining. "There's something you should know."

"Well, I know you're not gay, because I've felt the evidence to the contrary, several times now. So what could you possibly have to tell me that would change me wanting to have sex with you?" I shift closer to him, and move so I'm sitting on his lap. He winces, adjusts the angle of his knee so my weight isn't bothering it, and then I wrap my legs around his hip and drape my arms over his shoulders. I press my lips to his neck and then his ear. "Because Ben…I *really* want to have sex with you. A lot of hot and possibly kinky sex. So…what?"

He swallows hard and blinks and looks at me, swallows again, and then rests his forehead against mine. "I—this is going to sound stupid, but it's true. I'm a virgin."

I laugh immediately because god, he's *got* to be joking. "Um yeah, *sure*. Okay."

He frowns, and swallows again, as if fear and embarrassment are overwhelming him, and I start to feel the beginnings of something boiling inside me. "It's not a joke, Echo. I swear."

"But…" I shake my head. "Earlier, we—you went down on me. You have, more than once now. And there's no fucking way in hell that was your first time. You're too damned good at it. The way you touch me, the way you kiss me…what the fuck are you *talking* about, Benji?"

He sighs. "I've done that stuff before, yeah. But actual sex, like intercourse? No, I've never done that."

I can only blink at him. "I…Jesus, Ben. How—I mean, how does that happen?"

"That's a long story."

"A two-beer story, or three?"

"Three, I'd say." He won't look at me.

I slide back off his lap, my curiosity and emotions in turmoil. He looks distraught as I hop to the floor, and I know I've got to hear this, but I also know I still want him. So I move behind him, wrap my arms around his waist and kiss his shoulder, the back of his neck.

"Hey Benji-Boy?" I whisper in his ear.

"Yeah?" He twists to look at me, hesitation and need on his face.

I let my hands drift down between his legs and clasp both palms around him. "You owe me a hell of story. But nothing's changed."

I don't wait for his response. I bring six bottles and an opener and set it all on the side table, pop two bottles open, and then settle myself on the bed.

Ben takes his beer and leans back against the wall beside me. "So...the heartbreak I told you about? It all goes back to that. Her name is Kylie. My parents and hers are best friends, and Kylie and I grew up across the street from each other. I was there when her parents brought her home from the hospital. We grew up together. We spent literally every single day together from the time she was born. We were inseparable. And even when we got to the age where we were noticing the opposite sex, neither of us were ever interested in anyone else, even though nothing happened between us."

He swallows a huge gulp of beer and then stares down into the suds in the bottle. "The problem was...I was in love with her. I remember the day I first realized she wasn't just my best friend, but that she was a *girl,* you know? I was fourteen, she was... not quite twelve? Around there. And she developed early, you know what I mean? By twelve she looked fourteen easily. And were at the beach together, at my parents' lake house. We were swimming, playing some game. I don't remember what. Chasing each other, splashing, whatever. And suddenly I couldn't stop staring at her. Like, all of a sudden I realized she had these parts that I really liked looking at, right? And she was my best friend, but all the hormonal puberty stuff? It was all focused on her. And it wasn't just hormones, though, you know? I knew her better than anyone. I knew how talented she was and how cool and just awesome she was. I just...fell head over heels for her."

"Sounds like that was inevitable, though," I remark.

He shrugs and nods. "Yeah, maybe. But I realized that she was only eleven or twelve, and I couldn't... say or do anything. Obviously."

I grin at him. "But you jerked off thinking about her, didn't you?"

He blushes furiously and starts peeling the label off his beer. "Yeah, I did."

I can't help laughing. "I'm just teasing you, Ben. You're fucking adorable when you blush."

He pins me with a glower. "Yeah, well, I can't help it. So, yeah, I jerked off thinking about her. I was a fourteen-year-old kid, so pretty much anything got me going. But Kylie was it, man. She was all I thought about. All my buddies started trying to get girls to go out with them and tried to cop a feel and whatever, and they bragged about getting to second base or whatever, but I didn't get into anything like that. I was waiting for Kylie."

I start to sense the shape of the story. "Oh. Shit."

He nods. "Yeah. I waited, and I waited. She turned fourteen, and then fifteen, and I'd never even had a girlfriend, and she'd never shown any interest in other guys, thank god, but I just couldn't figure out how to...how to broach the issue. How to tell her, out of the blue, that I'd been in love with her since she was fucking eleven.

"I mean, how do you start *that* conversation? I tried so many times. We'd be sitting on her porch talking and doing homework, or watching TV, or driving around in my car, and I'd be thinking about what I'd say, and I'd even open my mouth, but I couldn't get the words out."

He sighs and drains his beer, takes another. "I never could. I turned eighteen, nineteen, went to college near home and lived with my parents, and she was always right there. Never dated anyone, just never seemed interested. I thought that was a sign that we were meant to be together. So I made a plan. She'd graduate and we'd go on a road trip together. Just the two of us, the whole summer. Just go somewhere. Anywhere. And we'd...I wouldn't have to tell her. She'd just realize. And we'd get together, and I'd eventually tell her how long I'd loved her. I never said a thing. I never let on how I felt. I didn't know how, you know? We'd go to the lake and I'd have to hide how the sight of her in a bikini turned me on—especially as she got older and really filled out. I'd hide in the water and keep my distance. I kept assholes away from her. I protected her. I took care of her. Drove her to school, dropped her off, and we were always just... best friends. That was always the same."

I finish my beer and start another. "And then..."

He nods. "And then she met *Oz*." He says the name with venom, spits it. "Shit, it's hard to talk about this. I've never said any of this to anyone. Not ever, not to anyone."

I reach out and tangle our fingers together, rest our hands on my thigh. "So what happened with Oz? And why does it sound like you hate him?"

He sighs, closes his eyes and visibly summons the words. "I don't hate him. I just…well, part of me does, I guess. He was a new guy, showed up her senior year. He was older than her. About my age, I think. Obviously older. And he was…from the other side of the tracks, you know? Tattoos and piercings and metal shirts, big attitude, badass motorcycle. A real bad boy. I didn't like him from the first time I saw him, and… and she did. She got on his motorcycle the first time she met him, and rode off with him. And that was it. I knew it then, I knew…that was it. She had her arms around his waist and she was holding on to him like… like she wouldn't ever let go. And she had this look on her face…like…like she was *happy*. But in a way I'd never made her. Excited. Exhilarated." He sounds so bitter, so angry. "I got pissed. I was stupid. But I didn't trust him. He just reeked of bad boy, you know? Like I knew he did drugs, and drank and all that. Kylie was too good, too innocent and pure for a fucking hardass like him. I tried to protect her from him."

"Uh-oh," I say. "I bet that didn't go over well."

He laughs mirthlessly. "Yeah, no. It drove her to him all the more. It was jealousy, like *mad* jealousy. She was supposed to be mine. Half a year more and she would have been. But he came along, and...fucked it all up. So I was pissed off and jealous and then kind of turned into a huge dick. But it was also honest worry. He had these scars on his forearms that made me just sick with worry, like what darkness is he pulling her into? And there wasn't a goddamn thing I could do. I tried. I warned her. I tried to tell her how I felt about him, but she just...shut me down cold. Pinned me on it, you know? Pegged me as jealous. Just...she didn't realize how deep the jealousy went."

"Because you'd never told her how you really felt," I fill in.

"Right." He takes a couple sips and keeps going. "So I tried to move on. I could see she was happy with him. And there was nothing I could do. She was just... gone. It was too hard to be around her because they were always together, so I pulled away. Started dating chicks at the university. And...we'd fool around. I was able to bullshit my way past the fact that I'd never had a girlfriend until my sophomore year of college, which was fucking pathetic enough as it was. But...I couldn't ever get past messing around. Not because the chicks weren't willing, though. It was me. We'd mess around and whatever, but when it came time to actually sleep together, I just…couldn't. That was something that was supposed to happen with Kylie, and I couldn't get that thought out of my head. I fucking tried. I was in bed with a girl, like…right there, as close as we were to it just now. And I panicked. I jetted out of there and never saw her again. She was cool about it, though. I claimed I was sick or something stupid, and she just went with it, didn't make me feel bad, didn't tell anyone.

"I'd also been hoping dating other girls would maybe make Kylie jealous or something, but it didn't. She didn't care. She had Oz. And fuck, I could tell Oz was good to her. They were good together, and I couldn't deny it. So it turns out that she and Oz got into an accident on his motorcycle. I got pissed and defensive, and went after him. Like, I knew this would happen, I knew he'd hurt her. We got in a fight, and… he got hit by a car. Almost died. Went into a coma and almost didn't wake up."

"Oh my god."

He nods. "Yeah. That's not the crazy part, though. So…I find out his name isn't actually Oz. It's Benjamin."

"What? You guys have the same name?"

There's an odd look in his eye as he barks a laugh. "Actually, our first and middle names are the exact same. Benjamin Aziz. My mom is half-Lebanese, and…his dad was my mom's brother. We're both named after him."

I stare at him. "You're kidding me. He's your cousin?"

I nod. "Yeah. None of us realized it until his mom and my mom met for the first time. It was a fucked-up story. His dad committed suicide before he was born, and his mom moved around a lot, just messed up from the whole thing. He never knew anything about him, and he and his mom just…bizarrely, coincidentally ended up in our lives. So I can't hate him, because he's a good guy, and he loves Kylie like fucking crazy. But he not only stole the girl I loved, but my best friend, too.

"Because I just…it hurt too bad to be around them. Around her. I ended up telling her how I felt. I told her I'd loved her our whole lives, and that she was supposed to be mine. And she was…this is the part that fucking hurts the worst. She told me she'd had a crush on me, too, when she was younger. She'd waited for me to make a move, wished I'd kiss her, and I almost had so, *so* many times, but always chickened out. But Kylie got sick of waiting, and didn't want to risk our friendship by making a move herself. Neither did I, you know? I was afraid. What if she didn't love me back? What if I told her I loved her or kissed her or whatever…and she rejected me? I was scared, and I lost my chance. I left home not long after that, and haven't been back since. That was over a year and a half ago."

"Damn, Ben," I breathe. "That's fucked up."

He laughs. "Yeah. No kidding."

"And there's been no one else since then?" I can't help asking.

He shrugs. "Same deal as before I left. I drove around the country for a long time. I'd find work somewhere and hang for a while, and I'd mess around with a girl I worked with or something. But I couldn't ever bring myself to go all the way, but at that point it was more about how fucking embarrassing it is to be a twenty-two-year-old male virgin. It's pathetic, and I couldn't tell them. They were just random girls. But with you…it's different. I don't know—" He halts, glances at me, emotions boiling just under the surface. "I don't know why, why it's different with you. But it is. And now…now you know." He sets his now-empty second beer down, leaning across me to do so.

I'm at a loss. He's a virgin. I don't even know how to process that, how I'm supposed to feel about it. In one sense, it makes me feel exactly the way he's afraid it would: a little embarrassed for him, and a little worried about having to teach him things, wait for him to figure things out. But then...so far he's always made sure I come first, and hard. He pays attention to how I'm feeling, and seems to intuitively know what I want, what I need. He's not pathetic. Anything but, really. He's hot and sexy and except for this particular thing, he's confident, a man who knows who he is.

I glance at him, and see that he's still and silent, staring out the window, obviously in thought or maybe just waiting for me. He looks dejected, as if assuming that, because I now know his deep dark secret, I won't want him anymore.

Understandable, but not true.

I toss back the last of my beer and set it down beside me, slide down and roll to my side, facing him. I reach out with my hand and rest it on his thigh, keeping my eyes on his.

He looks down at me, a flash of surprise crossing his face, quickly replaced by hope and nascent desire. "You're still here."

I smile up at him, waiting. "Sure am."

His eyes heat up, but he doesn't move to touch me yet. "You don't care that I'm a virgin?"

I shrug. "It's a surprise, that's for sure, but I don't think less of you for it."

He joins me in the horizontal, angles his body toward me. His palm touches my cheek, and he leans toward me, a smile playing across his lips. "So, you're still here, in my bed, and you're still naked."

I wrap my fingers around the back of his neck and draw him down to me. "Naked in your bed," I murmur, lifting up to kiss him softly, "and ready to deflower you."

He grunts a laugh. "I don't think the term 'deflower' applies to guys."

"Ruin your innocence?" I reach between us and find him hardening again. I stroke him with a slow and gentle caress.

He smirks and bends to kiss my clavicle, and then the slope of my right boob. "I'm not exactly innocent, as you may have noticed."

I gasp as he covers my aching nipple with his mouth. I press his head against me with one hand and stroke his now-erect cock with the other. "True…"

He's over me now, and I feel him between my legs. But I also feel the tension in his belly, the way he continually flexes his knee as if fighting to contain the pain of kneeling. I let him kiss me, and I guide him to my entrance with one hand, cup his ass and pull him to me, lift my hips and drive him deep, watching his face as he enters me with a slow deep drive.

I can't help a whimper from escaping me as he pierces me, because he's huge and hard and fills me like I've never been filled, he stretches me to a pleasant aching burn, and I wrap my legs around his waist and grind on him, bring my lips to his ear and nip at his earlobe.

"How's it feel, Benji?" I whisper.

"Fucking incredible," he rumbles. "You feel...I didn't know it would feel this way."

I hold onto both hard globes of his taut ass and encourage him to move. "Fuck me, Benji," I whisper, and then bite his earlobe again and stretch it out, let it go, and nip at the skin of his neck. "Let me feel you move."

He groans and trembles. "Not sure how—how long I'll be able to—"

"You're close, huh?"

He buries his face between my breasts, and his hips glide against mine, and his thick cock slides deeper until we're crushed hips-to-hips and he's shaking, tensed, growling in his throat. "Yeah. Sorry, I'm...I'm trying to—"

I push at his shoulder. "Lie down."

He pulls out, gasping, and moves to his back. Slowly, I move to straddle him. His dick glistens with wetness, lying hard and thick against his belly. He's breathing hard, sweating, every muscle tensed and taut as he struggles to hold back. It's impressive, actually, how much control he has, considering. I slide my ass over his belly, my palms on his chest, leaning over him. My breasts sway and drag against his flesh. He cups them, and then his hands go to my hips and he caresses my ass, the backs of my thighs.

Reaching between us, I grip his cock and press the head to my slit, nestle him between the lips, and then slowly feed him into my channel. He groans and trembles, his fingers tightening on my hips.

"Hold it for me, Benji," I groan, hanging my head as he pierces me. "Not yet, okay? Just…hold on."

"Trying." His grip on my hips is almost painful. "You just feel so fucking good it's getting impossible to last much longer."

When he's in me, I push up so I'm kneeling upright, balanced on him with one hand on his belly, the other holding my hair out of my face. I stare down at him, and our eyes lock, his dark brown gaze hot and desperate and hard with determination. I hold it there, just the tip of him inside me. I'm pretty sure I know how this is going to go, and I want to make sure we both get the most out of every second.

But then Ben surprises me. He slides his palms up from my hips to my ribs, and then cups my breasts. "Don't move, Echo. Just…stay right there, just like that."

One of his big hands covers my breast, rough palm scratching my nipple, and then he pinches the sensitive button and rolls it, flicks it with his thumb until I'm biting my lip and stifling a gasp. He moves his hand to the other side, and gives that nipple the same attention.

With his other hand, he drags his fingers down my belly to my clit, feathers a soft touch over it. "Touch yourself, Echo," he tells me, his voice low and fierce. "Make yourself come."

"I don't need to come. I already did."

"But I want to watch you come. I need to."

My eyes locked on his, I bring my middle and ring fingers to my clit, replacing his touch with my own. He cups my tits and toys with them. Struggling to hold still, knowing if I move too much he'll come, I start a rhythmic circling, finding the rhythm I know works best. It's a slow touch at first, but it doesn't take long before I'm gasping at the heat building inside me, and I'm fighting to keep my hips still, and then my eyes slide closed because I'm groaning.

I feel Ben watching me, feel him tensed and frozen solid beneath me, hear his ragged breath. And then I hear and feel nothing but the detonation building inside me. "I'm—I'm there, Ben. I'm coming."

"I feel it," he growls. "I feel you tightening. Come hard for me, Echo."

It's a wave crashing through me, sudden and hot and powerful, making my insides clamp, lightning zapping through me, and I feel my pussy clamping down, hear a wild shriek rip out of me.

Ben's hands clutch my hips, and I throw my head back on my neck, arch my spine, palms flat on his belly, and I sink down on him. He pulls me down as I impale myself on him, hard, and I scream as he thrusts up. My climax shatters through me harder yet and he's growling and cursing— "Oh fuck, Echo, fuck, you feel so good..." —and I feel him throbbing inside me as he prepares to unleash his own orgasm.

I fall forward as my climax wrings through me, unable to stay balanced upright any longer, and now I clash my mouth over his and taste blood as my teeth bash into his lips, but he doesn't protest, only kisses me harder and his hands clutch my ass in a kneading vise-grip and pulls me onto him, and now I'm writhing, lifting up and forward and crashing down, fucking him desperately.

And then he's gone, two thrusts and done, and I feel his come spurt hot and wet inside me and I stroke onto him even faster and harder, milking it out of him. Another thick gush fills me and he's groaning wordlessly, thrusting with a stuttering rhythm, and I'm still coming too, whispering breathlessly "Fuck, fuck, oh my fucking god, Ben!"

His hips glide and flutter and pulse, and his cock throbs inside me, and I'm shaking with the after-shocks, unable to stop moving on him as each thrust makes me shudder and curse.

Finally, eventually, I can't move anymore, can only collapse onto him, bury my face in his neck, tasting sweat on his skin. His palms skate over my shoulders and back and spine and ass and thighs, my ribs and into my hair and back down, smearing my own sweat.

"There," I mutter. "Now you're not a virgin."

"Holy shit."

I smile against his neck. "Was it what you thought it'd be?"

"Nope." He shakes his head. "It was a whole fucking lot more."

I'm still shuddering, still gasping for breath. It was a whole lot more for me too, but I don't know how to say that, because it kind of scares me, so I don't say anything. I just leave his softened dick inside me and cling to his neck and push away the thoughts and emotions roiling inside me.

I need to say something, though. There's going to be the *so how was it for you* question, at some point, and that's always just awkward. So I forestall it. "That, Benji-boy, was some good fucking."

"Was it?"

I nod. "It was." I lift up and press my palms to the pillow on either side of his head. "Really good."

And I'm telling the truth, too. I'm not the type of girl to fake an orgasm or claim it was good when it wasn't. I may not be blunt with the truth if it was bad, but I won't lie about it. And what just happened with Ben, it was...*really* good. Top ten, ever. And I'm immediately hungry for more.

"Got a towel?" I ask.

He gets up and grabs a clean towel from the bathroom, but instead of handing it to me, stands beside me and hesitates. "Let me."

So I show him how to clean me—top to bottom—and then he sets the towel aside and climbs into the bed beside me. His eyes roam my body. And then his hands follow suit, fingertips grazing my skin in random patterns, hip to hip across my belly, up between my breasts, tracing my shoulder and arm, around the mounded flesh of one breast and then the other. I just watch him touch me, content to let him do as he wishes and wait in this easy, companionable silence until he's ready for more.

Nine: In the Bubble
Ben

I can't seem to stop touching her. And, lucky me, she doesn't seem inclined to make me. She just lies there on top of the sheet, naked and beautiful, her hair a tangled mess again, her skin flushed. Her eyes are closed, but I know she's not asleep. I don't know what she's thinking, and I don't ask. I just let my hands skate over her flesh, touching her everywhere, cupping her full high breasts and the bell-curve of her hips, her taut belly and her muscular thighs and her face and her hair.

Her eyes flick open and she glances at me. "You really like touching me, don't you?"

"How could I not? You're this incredibly sexy woman, and you're naked in my bed, and you're letting me touch you. Guy's gotta make the most of the opportunity."

She smiles at me, white teeth and red lips. "I'm not going anywhere just yet, Benji."

"Yeah, well, maybe I'm just greedy," I say.

She lets out a breath, then rolls to her side, and my hand comes to rest on her hip. "I guess I can handle that." Her eyes move from mine to my shoulders and chest and arms, and then her hand follows the path of her eyes. "I might be slightly greedy myself."

I watch her hand as it skates in a sinuous slide down my chest, through the path of hair on my belly leading downward, and then she's cupping my balls and rolling them in her palm and fingers. We both watch her as she takes my softened dick in her hand and massages it, toys with the head of it between her fingers. Within moments, my cock begins to unfurl, straightening and hardening. A smile curves Echo's lips upward as she works me into hardness, palming my erection as it begins to ache and strain.

"Well. Look at that. Ready again already." Her eyes flick up to mine. "How greedy are you really, Benji-boy?"

"Get on and find out."

Her pupils dilate, and her breath catches. "It's like that, is it?"

"It's like that."

I feel powerful. I feel ravenous. I feel like every moment not inside her is a moment wasted. My heart begins to pound as she rolls toward me, slides her thigh over mine and presses her small hands to my chest. I take her by the hips and lift her off the bed, settle her lithe, lush curves onto my body. Her hair hangs in a blonde cascade on either side of her face, her lips part and she sucks in a sharp breath as I cup the generous swell of her ass. Her shins press into the mattress on either side of my legs, her palms support her weight on my chest, her tits sway.

She nestles my cock at her opening. Her eyes are more hazel in this moment than any other shade, and they're locked on mine, and I couldn't even begin to fathom what she's thinking right now. I need to be inside her. I lift up and thrust, but she moves away.

"Ah-ah-ah," she says, a sultry smile on her lips. "Not yet."

She flutters her hips so her pussy slides around my cock, smearing her juices on me and making me growl. It's a tease, though, because I don't get any deeper, not the way I need. I grip her hips in my hands and try to pull her down, but she grins and just shakes her head.

"I don't think so, Benji. I like it like this." She rolls her hips and the head of my cock moves shallowly in and out of her opening, a maddening tease of what I need.

"Jesus, Echo," I growl.

"What?" she asks, her face and voice the essence of innocence.

I thrust, and yet again she moves with me so I fail to get any deeper. Frustrated, I wrap my arms around her shoulders and roll so she's beneath me. I take her wrists and pinion them in one hand above her head, and with my other hand I clutch one of her thighs and press her knee upward, leaning into it to alleviate some of the pressure on my game knee. Her eyes are wide and her chest heaves as she sucks in deep breaths.

I fix my eyes on hers, holding still for a moment with just the tip of my dick nestled between the plump lips of her pussy. And then, grunting with relief, I thrust deep, hard and fast.

"Fuck!" Echo shrieks, and her entire body writhes in shock and—judging by her wide-eyed gasping—pleasure.

"Exactly," I tell her, my voice low, pulling out slowly and then driving deep again. "Fuck."

Her mouth falls open and her eyes go wild, her head tipping back. She fights against my grip on her wrists, but her hips rise and her pussy slides to envelop my aching cock, and she whimpers. Her thigh is a thick soft weight in my hand, and I tighten my grip on the expanse of muscle and flesh as I drive in yet again. My knee hurts, but in this moment I couldn't care less.

I still don't feel like I'm deep enough, like I'm where I need to be. So I shift forward, closer to her, and Echo seems to read my thoughts or to know what I need. She lifts her other leg and nudges me upright. My knee protests, but I ignore it, because now the silky backs of her thighs are flush against my chest, her feet are hanging over my shoulders and I'm so deep inside her hot wet pussy that I feel swallowed by her.

I thrust slowly, and her brows draw down and her eyes go wide. "Yeah, Ben, that feels *so* good," she groans. "Harder."

So I fuck harder, curling my hands around her thighs and pumping into her so my hips meet her ass with a loud slap. "Like that?"

In the moment that I'm deepest, she lets out a throaty groan. "Oh yeah...just like that. Again, Benji. Fuck me again."

She scrapes her hands through her hair, clutching it at the scalp and arches her back off the mattress. She's gasping as I drive into her. Again and again I thrust hard and deep and slow until I'm lost in the rhythm, drowning in the way my cock pounds into her and the primal way she groans at each resounding *slap* of flesh on flesh.

"Holy shit..." I moan, feeling my balls tighten and my cock begin to ache and my muscle shake, "I'm close."

"Don't stop, Benji, don't you dare stop," she growls though gritted teeth. "Keep fucking me until you come."

"What about you?" I ask, knowing somehow that she's not anywhere close.

"Oh...I'll get mine," she says, her eyes dark and gleaming with promise. "Don't you worry about that. I'll get mine."

"Get it now, then," I tell her, not slowing my rhythm. "Touch your pussy, Echo. Come with me."

Her fingers dive down between her thighs and I feel her swiping at her clit, and now her growls grow louder and higher-pitched second by second, and her hips start to circle, meeting me thrust for thrust now, where before I think she was just taking it from me. I feel a distant throbbing in my knee, but it's nothing in comparison to the aching pressure in my balls. I start to lose my rhythm right as I feel her pussy clamp and pulse around my cock, and now her fingers are flying madly around her clit and she's groaning non-stop, eyes squeezed closed, spine arched off the bed, and her legs close around me, clenched in the throes of her building climax.

"I'm coming, Ben!" she shrieks, breathless, "oh fuck, oh fuck, right now Benji, I'm coming right now…"

The way she says that name, that nickname, I never thought I'd be able to hear without hurting, but the way she says it feels good, feels like it belongs to her now.

She screams loud and her feet come off my shoulders and plant in the mattress, pressing her upward, and then she's locking her heels around my back and I'm falling forward, all my weight on my one good knee, the other leg extended. I have to be crushing her with so much of my weight on her like this, but her hands clutch and scrabble at me, pull me closer, scratch at my ass to get me moving harder and faster and she's thrusting up into me wildly, and all can do is try to keep up with her. I'm grunting like an animal as I feel my sac tighten and explode, and then I'm pouring myself into her, emptying my balls into her tight pussy, and she's biting at my ear and my shoulder, her nails clawing down my back, and my cock is pounding into her crazily—*slapslapslapslap*—wet squishing sucking heat and clenching muscles and sweat and the smell of sex and her breath on me and I'm biting her nipple until she shrieks in equal parts pleasure and pain.

I have a realization right then, at the climax of my orgasm: she likes it kind of rough, and she likes it when I take control.

I file that away for later, and we move together, finding a synchronized rhythm as our mutual orgasm shudders and begins to fade.

Finally, she's still and gasping raggedly for breath, and I'm collapsed on her, limp and empty and sated and amazed. My knee fucking kills so bad it's hard to breathe, but I don't care. The pain is worth the pleasure.

"Jesus fucking Christ, Benji," she pants, her hands resting proprietarily on my ass in a way that does something shuddery to my heart.

"That was..." I start, but I don't even have the right words for what that was.

"Intense," she finishes for me.

"Yeah," I agree. I start to move off her. "I've got to be crushing the actual life out of you."

She tightens her grip on my ass. "Uh-uh. I kind of like it."

"Being crushed?"

She laughs. "Yeah. Call me crazy."

I grin, my mouth curving against the soft flesh of her breasts. "Crazy girl."

I don't know how much time passes with us lying like that, her buried beneath me, her hands roaming up my back and always returning to my ass.

Eventually she fakes a pained groan and pushes at me. "All right, you big lunk. Get off me so I can go pee."

I roll to my back, gasping a groan and flexing my knee, but keeping my eyes on Echo as she shimmies off the bed. I watch her fine round ass sway, and then I hear her pee and wash her hands, and she's coming back toward me, big tits trembling and rocking side to side as she strides toward me. God, even the way she walks is seductive and sexy and mesmerizing, like there's music I don't hear and she's dancing to it.

She lies down beside me, tucking a hand under her head, resting her other palm on her diaphragm. She stares at the ceiling, and I just watch her breathe— or more truthfully, watch the way her chest swells and her breasts shift with each breath. I just can't get enough of looking at her, and that does something to my heart, to my gut, to my instincts and my head, to my everything.

I grew up with Kylie, I was in love with her for six, almost seven years and there wasn't this intense attraction, even to her. It honestly scares me, because I don't know this girl *at all*. I don't know what she's thinking, what she's feeling, and she's hard to read. She doesn't wear her thoughts or emotions on her face, so all I have to go by are her words and actions, and we all know how misleading those can be in regards to a person's real feelings. I feel this starvation when it comes to Echo, like I've been hungry my whole life, living on an empty stomach, wasting away and living off my own insides, and Echo is a plate of food set in front of me. I want to gorge myself. I feel ravenous and wild. The intensity, the potency of my physical attraction alone is…frightening. And I want to *know* her, want to be able to read her emotions on her face and know her physical cues and know what she's scared of, and what she wants and needs, I want to know, I want to know. But I don't know how to ask, how to tell her what I'm feeling, because I'm feeling so many powerful things and they're all just too much.

"What are you thinking?" I finally ask.

She pivots her head to look at me. Her face is blank at first, as if she's only just now registering that

I even spoke, and then she smiles faintly. "Just that I like it here, in your room. In this bubble of you and me. I don't want to leave it."

"Me either."

She returns her gaze to the ceiling. "You don't have to. But I do."

"Why?"

She lets out a sigh. "Well, aside from the fact that I have a life outside not just this room, but this city…I have to sort out Mom's stuff." She swallows hard. "I have to figure out what to do with it all. I have to get her house sold, and…her car, and…" She's blinking hard, swallowing, and then she's pressing the heels of her palms into her eyes. "And I don't even know where to start. So I'm kind of using you, Ben. I don't want to go through her shit. I don't want to feel all that. Here, with you…I can pretend like none of it exists, like this is all there is. You and me, fucking and drinking and going out for food. But…I can't keep pretending. I'm running out of time."

I feel the bubble pop, pierced by her words. She feels it, and so do I. I move off the bed, tug on clean underwear and jeans and T-shirt, and then I find her clothes and hand them to her. She sits up, eyes wary, takes her underwear and swings her feet off the bed, slides the thong on without standing up. Next is the bra, and then she's doing that sexy jump-wiggle-shimmy to get her ass stuffed into her jeans.

As she shrugs into her shirt, she glances at me. "So that's it, huh?" There's a note of coldness in her voice.

I just smile at her softly, knowing what she's assuming. "Yep. That's it." I let her think it for a moment longer.

I pull on socks and my cross-trainers while she finds her own shoes, and then she's hiking her purse over her shoulder, and I find my keys. There's a strange familiarity to the rhythm of us getting ready like this. I watch as she pauses by the front door, pulling her hair back into a neat, low ponytail.

Her hand on the knob, she glances back at me in confusion as I stuff my wallet into my front pocket and join her at the door. "Where are you going?"

"*We* are going to your mom's house. I'm helping you sort her things."

Echo blinks several times, as if processing. And then she shakes her head. "No, Ben. No. I have to—"

I slide my arm around her waist and pull her back toward me. "What, did you think I was kicking you out, just like that? Like, wham-bam-thank-you-ma'am?"

She ducks her head and stares at her feet. "Yeah, kind of." Her voice goes to a barely audible whisper. "That's how it usually works."

I don't know how to process that. Usually works? She's used to being…what? Fucked and sent home? There's a *usually* to this, for her? It makes me sad and angry and bizarrely jealous and insecure and sick to my stomach.

"Echo…god, you think I'd just—get what I wanted and send you on your way?" I look down at her, try to nudge her chin up, but she resists. "Do I seem like that type of guy? Like that's all I wanted, was sex?"

She won't look at me. She pulls away from me and jerks the door open, fleeing. "I'm just gonna catch the bus. I'll see you later."

I follow her out the door, pause to lock it behind me, but by now she's far enough away that I'd have to run to catch her, and running is out of the question. My knee is stiff and locked and throbbing from overusing it already, so I can barely walk, and I forgot my cane inside. She's running, actually jogging away from me. I have to catch her. I know if I let her go like this, it's over.

And I don't want it to be over.

So I hobble to my truck and climb in, start it, and reverse out. My knee screams in protest at even the slight flexing of using the pedals, but there's no choice for me. Not in this, not with her. I peel out of the parking lot and down the street after Echo. She's almost to the bus stop; so I floor it and swerve around the bus, squeal to a halt at the curb.

I roll down the passenger window. "Get in, Echo."

She ignores me, stands at the bus stop sign, clinging to the pole like it's the only thing keeping her upright. I slam on my flashers and put it in park, hop out and limp around the hood. I jerk open the passenger door and grab Echo's hand.

"Let go. Leave me alone. I'm not doing this with you, Ben." Her voice is flat, cold.

"Yes. You are." I sweep my arms under her knees and around her shoulders, lift her clean off the ground. I deposit her in the passenger seat, teeth clenched at the pain of walking, of carrying her, and determined to not let her see. But she sees anyway.

"Goddamn it, Ben." She glares at me as I struggle into the driver's seat. "You're gonna fuck up your knee even worse."

"Yeah, probably," I agree.

"You can't just kidnap me like this."

"Yes, I can. And I just did." I ignore the middle fingers from the traffic skirling around my truck, the blaring horns, the questioning stares. I pull out into traffic and head in the direction of Cheyenne's studio, knowing she lived near it.

"Fuck, you're impossible." She leans her head back against the headrest, eyes closed.

"True enough."

"What do you want from me?"

"Why are you shutting down like this?" I turn off the radio and glance at her as I stop at a traffic light.

"You don't know me. I don't know you. We had some good sex, and now it's over. Drop me off and go home." She delivers this monotone, staccato.

"We can fix the not knowing each other. And yes, we had good sex, but there was more to it."

She shakes her head. "For you, maybe."

"Liar."

She ignores this, points to the right. "Turn at the next intersection."

"If you thought I was kicking you out," I tell her, trying a different tactic, "I'm sorry. I should have been clearer."

She shrugs. "That's how it works, Ben. We've known each other less than three days. You think this is love at first sight or something? You think we, what? Fell in insta-love? Get real, dude."

I flinch at the venom in her tone. "Jesus, Echo. Bitter, much?"

"Like I said, you don't know the first fucking thing about me." This is delivered quietly, with far less venom.

"But you know me, don't you? I told you—"

"And I didn't ask you to, did I?" She shouts this, and it's shocking, the sudden shift from whisper to shout. "You could have just fucked me and I wouldn't have known any different. But you saddled me with your stupid fucking sob story, and now I'm supposed to stick around and feel sorry for you and teach you all about sex, right? Hang out in your bachelor pad and show you how to fuck like a pro? I could, too. I've been around the block a few times. Well, guess what? I have no interest in playing that game with you. We had a moment, sure. But now it's over. Turn left here."

She stares out the window as I pull into a subdivision of small houses, one- and two-bedroom single-family homes worth maybe a hundred and fifty grand at most, most of them with faded, peeling paint and sagging gutters and ten-year-old cars in the driveways. She directs me deeper into the neighborhood, letting the thick, tense silence build between us. Finally, she points to a tiny blue house with gray shutters and a small patch of overgrown yellowing grass. There's a black mailbox attached to the wall by the front door, the kind with the flap on top, and it's overflowing with junk mail and catalogues and magazines and envelopes. Several newspapers in translucent pink bags sit on the front stoop in a pile. A green hose lies in a haphazard coil in the driveway at the side of the house, and a chain link fence separates her driveway from the side yard of the house next door. There's a detached garage, and another tiny patch of dying grass out back.

I pull into the driveway, and Echo is out of the truck before I have it in park. "Thanks for the ride, Ben. See ya." She closes the door.

I put it in park, shut it off, and get out. Echo watches me lumber awkwardly after her to the front door. She just stares at me, and when I'm on the stoop with her, she finally sighs and pinches the bridge of her nose. "Ben, how clear do I have to be?"

"I hear what you're saying, Echo, but it doesn't match the way you were even half an hour ago. I don't know what you're thinking, or what you're feeling, and I don't expect you to actually do something totally crazy like actually *tell me,* so I'm gonna stay and help, and you can just go ahead and deal with it." I meet her gaze steadily, keeping the hurt her words inflicted off my face and out of my eyes. "You can't do this alone, and you're not going to."

Her hazel-green eyes stare into mine, her brows drawn. Eventually she just sighs and unlocks the front door and pushes it open. "Fine. Whatever. Suit yourself. But don't expect—"

"I never expected anything, Echo." I move past her, assessing the interior of the house.

There's a tiled entranceway where the door opens to a coat closet, with a living room to the right. A picture window faces the street, with a couch on the wall kitty-corner, a TV mounted to the wall opposite the couch, and a cheap coffee table between them. Beyond the living room is the kitchen, separated by nothing but an abrupt transition from threadbare tan carpet to cracked and bubbling linoleum.

The house smells musty, with hints of mold and rotting food. There's a styrofoam container on the coffee table, the lid closed with the handle of a fork sticking out between the lips of the clamshell, two empty Coors cans beside it. A hallway off the kitchen leads, I assume, to the bathroom and bedrooms.

Echo just stands in the entrance, hands fisted at her sides, struggling to breathe. "This house. Jesus, this house." I wait for her to continue, and eventually she does. "I grew up in this house. She never moved after I left for school. She said she was going to, and I think she even looked at apartments, but she never moved."

I close the front door and lean against the wall to get my weight off my knee, content to wait for her.

"I don't want to be here. I don't know how to do this." She sniffles. "I'm a bitch, and you don't deserve it. I'm sorry. Just...go, okay? I'll be fine."

I notice she didn't take back anything she said, though. So I still don't know which version of Echo is the truth, the Echo that was in my bed, or the Echo standing before me now.

I take her by the shoulders and turn her to face me. "I'm not leaving, so just listen. Here's what's going to happen: we start in the kitchen, clean out the cabinets and the fridge and all that. I'll run out and get a bunch of boxes and some contractor bags. Okay?" She nods, silent, and keeps her eyes on the floor. "Okay. So you start there. Use whatever garbage bags there are here to clean up the trash first, and I'll be right back." She nods again, and looks so mixed up and full of agony that I want to kiss her and take it all way, but I don't.

I wrap my arms around her shoulders and pull her against me for a quick hug, and I kiss the top of her head. "I won't say it'll be all right. But I will say that you'll be okay. Someday. For now, just...keep breathing, okay?"

She lets out a shuddery breath and pushes away from me, sets her purse on the floor near the coat closet and kicks off her shoes, moves into the kitchen.

I watch as she digs a box of garbage bags out from under the sink, shakes one open. I leave her there and pick up a flat of moving boxes, a tape gun, and packing paper from a U-Haul store, and then stop by Home Depot for a box of contractor bags. When I get back to the house—only finding it again after several wrong turns—Echo is standing in the kitchen with three full garbage bags around her feet, flipping through a cookbook.

She glances at me, and then goes back to the cookbook, her expression distant, as if seeing memories rather than me.

I haul the bags outside and toss them to the curb. I empty the fridge and freezer item by item, leaving only the half-empty box of Coors. We'll need those, I think. When the fridge is empty, I start on the cabinets and drawers. Echo glances at me now and then, but seems absorbed in the cookbook, which I realize now has notes in the margins, recipes and adjustments scrawled in the whitespace. The handwriting, I realize, isn't feminine, but masculine.

I dump the silverware drawer into a bag, and start on the flatware.

Echo glances up as I'm about to toss a couple of plates into the bag. "Not those!" she cries. She stands up, sets the cookbook aside, and takes the plates and bowls from me. "The other stuff is fine. But this set... not these."

I realize the plates I was about to throw away are fragile and old looking, from an antique set of fine china. I set aside four more plates, six bowls, six tea plates and matching mugs, and six appetizer plates. "Family china or something?"

She nods. "Yeah. It belonged to Grandma. She gave it to Mom when she got married. It's...very old."

"And the cookbook?" I ask.

She's quiet for a long moment, turning a bowl over and over in her hands. "It was...my father's." She glances at me. "And no, I'm sorry, there's no way in hell I'm getting into *that* right now."

"I wasn't going to ask," I lie.

She softens a bit. I bring in a box and assemble it, tape the edges together. I wrap the china in several layers of packing paper and stack it all in the box, set the box aside, and resume emptying the kitchen. Three contractor bags later, the kitchen is empty. I take a couple bags into the bathroom. It's getting more personal now. There's a hair dryer on the sink, still plugged in, a curling iron beside it, two tackle boxes of makeup, and a box of tampons on the floor beside the toilet.

I hear a stereo turn on, static of the tuner as Echo finds a station. A guitar chord thrums, and "Country

Must Be Country Wide" by Brantley Gilbert starts. Cheyenne liked country music. I don't know what kind of music Echo likes. Shit, I don't know where she goes to school, what she studies. She might have a boyfriend back at school. I shake off that train of thought.

"Echo?" I call out. She peeks her head into the bathroom. "Anything in here I should set aside?"

Echo steps in, peeks into the cabinet under the sink, rifles through the makeup. "Leave the makeup. Everything else goes."

So I toss everything, the cleaning products and the bottles of shampoo and conditioner and hair oil and face oil and body lotion and whatever else the two dozen bottles might be. The pink and white Venus razor sitting on the corner of the tub. The pink goofy sponge thing. At one point, I toss something into the garbage bag and a whiff of something erupts, the scent of shampoo from the slightly opened top. The scent hits me hard, because I have a sudden and powerful olfactory memory of that shampoo scent on Cheyenne's hair.

I finish in the bathroom, drag the heavy bag out to the curb, and return to find Echo sitting on the couch, flipping through a photo album, tears streaming down her cheeks. There's a stack of photo albums on the coffee table, a jewelry box, the two tackle boxes of makeup, a couple stacks of dog-eared paperbacks, a wood-handled hairbrush with fine blond hairs still tangled in the bristles.

"I'm trying to find all the...personal stuff. The sentimental things," Echo says without looking at me. "Just so you don't think I'm not doing anything."

"I didn't think that."

She flips a page, touches a photograph with an index finger, and sniffles. "Why are you helping me?"

"It's too much for one person to do alone." I sit down on the couch beside her, stretching out my throbbing, aching knee. "And whatever else we may or may not be, I'm your friend. And friends help each other."

She sniffles again. "You suck." But she says it gently, so it means the exact opposite.

"I know."

Echo flips the page, and I glance down at the pictures. There's Echo as a little girl, platinum blond hair in pigtails, wearing Mickey ears, flashing double thumbs-up and a gap-toothed grin in front of the Magic Kingdom castle.

"There are pictures of me, and pictures of Mom, but none of us together." She touches a picture of herself on a carousel horse, from the same trip, taken from the horse beside hers, I imagine. "It was just her and me for most of my life. No one to take pictures of us together."

She turns the page, and then another, and then I stop her, pointing at a photograph. "There's one of the two of you."

It's a shitty photograph, blurry, the frame tilted sideways. It looks like it was taken in the backyard of this very house. Echo laughs. "Yeah. Great-Grandpa Gene took that. He was a hundred, literally. Everyone else was inside. It was my birthday. Mom was taking a picture of me, and Grandpa Gene just took the camera and snapped this."

"Well, it's not a bad photo for a centenarian."

"I think he had a heart attack a couple days later." She glances at me. "So, what's left?"

"Just the bedrooms."

"The hardest part, then."

I nod. "Yep."

She stands up, sets the album on the coffee table, and precedes me into the smaller bedroom. Echo's, it looks like. I wasn't sure what I expected from Echo's childhood bedroom, but it's not what I find. There are posters on the wall, but not of boy bands or horses or rock bands, but rather posters of Broadway stars. I recognize Idina Menzel and Kristin Chenoweth,

Phantom of the Opera, Cats, Wicked, Rock of Ages, and there are other posters of other singers I don't know. There's one of Yo-Yo Ma, and there's an artistic piece depicting the blinding lights and crowd as seen from on-stage, the back of a woman's head and her hands cupping an old-school type of microphone, the rectangular kind.

There's a rack of CDs between a desk and the double bed, and it's jammed to bursting with CDs, overflowing, double-stacked and more piled on top of others. The music spans genre: I see Kenny Chesney and Garth Brooks and George Strait and the Dixie Chicks and Sara Evans and Miranda Lambert, Sarah Bareilles and Sarah Brightman and a bunch of other presumably classical singers, as well as pop artists like One Republic and Maroon Five and Muse and Train and bands crossing more into rock from the eighties, nineties, and into the new millennium. Basically, any and every kind of music possible. I even see a few hard rock albums from Korn and Linkin Park and Three Doors Down.

There's surprisingly little else. The desk with a jar of pens and a pair of scissors, a chest of drawers, a closet, the bed with a patchwork quilt neatly tucked under the edges of the mattress.

"Impressive music collection," I say.

Echo snorts. "That's not even a fraction of my collection, just what fit on that little shelf." She crosses into the room and crouches to examine the plastic jewel cases. "It is fairly representative of my taste, though."

"You like a little of everything, then."

She nods. "More like a lot of everything. Music is what I do, after all."

"Really?" I try to sound casual when I'm anything but.

She shrugs. "Yeah. It's my major: vocal performance."

I'm not sure why just yet, but something inside me sinks. "Oh. Wow, that's...awesome. Where—" My voice cuts out, oddly, and have to start over. "Where do you go?"

"Belmont." She's looking at me, now, hearing the off note in my voice. "What's wrong?"

"Belmont. In Nashville." There's only one Belmont University, so the clarification is pointless.

"Doing It Our Way" by Gloriana comes on, both fitting and painfully out of place.

"Yeah," she says, standing up and turning to look at me. "What?"

I shrug and shake my head, not willing to face what the realization has done to me, what I'm feeling and thinking. I refuse to acknowledge it. "Nothing." I lift the bag in my hand. "So what stays and what goes in here?"

She doesn't take her eyes off me. "Everything goes. I cleaned this room out when I moved to Nashville. Those jewel cases are empty. I have the discs at school." She moves in front of me as I take a step deeper into the room, stopping me with a hand on my chest. "Ben, what's the deal?"

"Nothing."

She sighs. "Now who's shutting down?"

I groan and drop the bag, sit on the bed. "I'm from Nashville."

She stares at me. "What?"

I nod. "Yeah. Lived there my whole life, from the time I was three. I was born in Ann Arbor, Michigan, but we moved to Nashville when I was three. I'm about thirty credits shy of a bachelor's from Vanderbilt. I was the starting quarterback there for three years straight."

Echo blinks. "Shut the fuck up. You're kidding, right?"

I shake my head. "Nope."

"I have friends who go to Vandy. I mean…Jesus. I dated a guy who was on the football team—two years ago?"

"What was his name?" I ask, feeling shaky.

"Marcus Shaker."

I fall backward onto the bed. "You dated that asshole? Jesus. He's a hell of a tight end, but he's a total dickbag."

"You know him?"

I stare at her. "Like I said, I was the starting quarterback."

"Wait." She waves her hands in a 'hold on' gesture. "Ben…like Benjamin Dorsey?"

I nod. "That's me."

She tilts her head back. "Holy shit. Marcus hates your ass."

I laugh. "I know, and the feeling is mutual." I glance at her. "Wanna know what our beef is?"

"Sure."

"We were at a frat party one weekend. Our sophomore year. I caught him roughing up this chick in the bathroom. Pawing at her, calling her names. Had his hand up her skirt, and she was fighting him off, but…she wasn't winning." I shake my head, remembering. "I pounded his ass into the ground. He missed three games because of that fight. I reported it, but the girl refused to press charges, and the school never did shit about it. But he got a lesson from me, that's for damn sure."

"That—that sounds like Marcus," Echo whispers. "I didn't date him long."

Something is off in her voice, in her posture. "Echo?"

She shakes her head, turns away, head ducked, fingers plucking at frayed white threads of a hole in the thigh of her jeans. "Don't worry about it."

"Because saying that makes me worry less."

She shrugs. "You stopped him that time. But that wasn't the only time he did something like that."

"Meaning he tried it with you?"

Echo blows out a short, sharp breath, head tilted back on her neck. "It doesn't matter. Not anymore. I dealt with it a long time ago. Just…drop it, okay?"

"Echo, come on, you can't just—"

"I said *drop it!*" She turns, shouting. "It's old news, and none of your business."

I slide up behind her, my hands curling around her arms. "Echo, Jesus—"

She shakes me off. "I'm not talking about it, Ben. I don't need your help." She turns, takes the bag from me, pushes me out of the bedroom, through the living room to the front door; I let her push me, though I'm not sure why. "You've done enough. Thank you, and goodbye."

"So it's like that, huh?"

She holds the front door open, gestures out. "It's like that."

I stop in the doorway, turn to look at her. We're close. She's holding the front door, standing in the tiny foyer, eyes hard, posture ramrod-stiff, but her lower lip trembles and her fist on the doorknob is white-knuckled.

"More Than Miles" by Brantley Gilbert plays on the radio.

I'm at a total loss for words. "Echo, I—"

She just shakes her head and cuts me off. "Nothing to say, Ben. It's not about Mom, it's not about Marcus. It's just…I can't do this with you."

"Why not?" I close in, stand so close she has to peer up at me. "Why are you pushing me away?"

"Because you're getting too close, Ben. And that's the last thing on earth I have the time or emotional energy for."

I glance down and see the outline of her phone in the hip pocket of her tight jeans. I pry it out, hand it to her. "Unlock it real quick."

"Why?"

"Just do it." So she does it, hands it back. I dial my cell number, and after my phone has rung twice, I hang up the call and save her number into my phone. And then I call her phone from mine and save my number under "Benji." I hand it back to her. "Can I at least see you before you leave?"

She shrugs. "I don't know. I don't know anything right now. I just know I'm overwhelmed and you're making it worse. You're confusing me, and I don't need that right now."

"Fair enough." I start to turn away, but then change my mind.

I grab her face in both hands and kiss her hard and deep, wrestling her lips with mine, slashing her tongue with mine. I cup her cheek in one hand and slide my other hand to her waist and crush her against my body.

She lets me kiss her, stunned, for several seconds, and then I break away. She gazes up at me, two fingers to her lips, like she can't believe I just did that. "You suck," she whispers.

And then she pulls me back in, closes the front door, and then we spin and her spine is pinned against the door and Echo is lifting up on her toes to kiss me. She tries to go gently, but I'm having none of that. I don't know what's driving me. It's not mere lust, though there's that in spades. I want to prove something to her, but again, I'm not sure what.

When her lips touch mine, shivering and trembling, her breath soughing slowly over my tongue,

I breathe in her scent and then dive in to steal her oxygen, demand her kiss, demand heat, demand fire. And she gives it. She lifts up on her toes and clutches my shirtfront and gasps and relinquishes gentility in favor of aggression.

My hands seek skin, her shirt rises and I find it, palm her spine and the soft curves of her sides, just above the waist of her jeans, and then my fingers are toying with the string of her thong peeking up over the low-rise jeans and hers are busy at my chest, pushing at my shirt.

But I'm not content to merely kiss. Not after what we had together this afternoon. I break the kiss and grab her by the shoulders, spin her in place so her front is pressed up against the door, and I slide my palms around her waist to her belly, press in flat and dig my fingers under the waistband of her jeans, against her skin. She gasps and sucks in her stomach, rests her forehead against the door and lets out the breath in a whimper when my fingertips graze her opening. She's limp against the door, yet also taut and tense at the same time. I pop the button of her jeans and lower the zipper and shove them down, and she's pushing back against me, grabbing my hand and pressing it to her now-bare core, dipping at the knees as I touch her, find her wet and willing. She's gasping out loud within moments, and then she's reaching blindly behind her for my zipper, and before I know it, my own pants are around my ankles and I'm pressing up against her.

We both hesitate at the same moment, freezing, not breathing. I lower my face to her neck, pull my body away, breathing shakily. "Not here, Echo. Not like this."

"No." She doesn't move, though, as if she's feeling the fight of need versus knowledge; I know I am.

I owe it to her to be stronger. So I bend, find the scrap of material that she calls underwear and lift it for her, tug it into place, and then do the same for her jeans. I tug, tug, and she lets me, not moving, breathing deeply and slowly as I get her jeans into place. She spins and pushes me away.

"Stop, stop. I can't handle it when you do that. I'm barely handling myself right now as it is. You being sweet and dressing me like that…I can't handle it." I don't apologize. I just bend and lift up my own clothing, but she grabs my wrists and stops me. "Let me help you out with your problem," she says, glancing down at my straining erection.

I shake my head and back out of reach. "No. That'd be even worse than if we'd done what we just started." I pull my boxers into place and zip my jeans, button them. Now that we're both clothed, I let myself get within touching distance again, but I don't actually touch her, because that would be catalytic and dangerous. "Has anything changed?"

"Between us?" she asks, and I nod. She closes her eyes, wipes at her face with both hands, and then falls back against the door. "No. I don't know how to change it. Us fucking wouldn't change it. Here, your place, anywhere. It'd feel incredible, but it wouldn't change anything."

"Then we're right back where we started before I kissed you."

She shrugs and nods. "Yeah. If we fucked, it would put us right back in the bubble, and—as much as I like it in the bubble, I have to face reality at some point."

"So you still want me to go?" I hate how my heart thumps and aches.

She won't look at me as she nods and reaches for the doorknob, moving out of the way so I can step fully outside. "Yeah. *Want you to go* may be too strong a way to put it, but yeah, it's best if you go."

"Okay then." I step carefully down the two wobbly stairs to the sidewalk and cross the grass to my truck. "You have my number."

"I know." She waves, like it's any old goodbye. "Drive safe."

"Yeah."

And then I'm gone, back out to the main road, to my apartment, where I contemplate the fact that Echo and I were just a few miles apart, that we even know some of the same people but never crossed paths until now, until this. And I think about how this makes the thought of going back home to Nashville all the harder. Before, it was like skulking home with my tail between my legs. And then I got injured and I just couldn't face even the idea of going back and hearing all the talk, the whispers, the curiosity about why I'd vanished so suddenly.

And now, if I go back, I'll know not only is Kylie there with Oz—married now—but Echo as well.

What the fuck am I supposed to do?

And of course, just to rub it in, the radio plays "The One That Got Away" by Jake Owen.

Ten: Ben-Shaped Hole
Echo

IT'S ELEVEN O'CLOCK AT NIGHT, AND MOM'S HOUSE IS done. I tossed almost all of her clothes, because she was taller and skinnier than me, which irked me pretty much my whole life, from the time I was old enough to be jealous of her figure. I kept a pair of her shoes, killer red heels I'd always envied and that she'd never let me borrow. I also kept a leather bomber jacket that was old and worn and likely belonged to my father, as well as her favorite cream knit sweater. I have two boxes of sentimental stuff, picture frames and photo albums and her jewelry, and her favorite books. The curb is piled high with bags that I labeled as either "trash" or "free stuff", as this neighborhood always gets trash-picker traffic the night before the garbage is collected. Someone will take the bags of goods and the rest will get thrown away. I leave the furniture, the TV. I clean the place top to bottom, scrubbing and vacuuming and mopping and wiping until the house looks like it had never been lived in. Grandpa and Grandma will sell the house and take care of whatever else has to be done.

And I do it all without sobbing.

When I'm done, I book a flight back to Nashville for early the next day.

Then I call Grandpa. "Hey there, sweet-pea. We was gettin' worried about you," he says by way of hello, his voice low and thickly Texas-accented.

"I needed time to deal, Grandpa. Sorry, didn't mean to worry you."

"Where ya at?"

"Mom's—Mom's house. I just finished…going through everything."

He's silent for a moment. "You shouldn't have done that on your own, sweet-pea. Your grandma and I woulda helped you. We're old, but we ain't helpless."

"It was mine to do." I swallow hard. "I had help, too."

"That boy you left with?" His voice brooks no argument, meaning, I'd better damn well explain, because even if I am twenty-two, I still have to answer to my elders.

"Yeah. Ben."

"Echo." It's a none-too-subtle warning.

"Just let it be, Gramps. Please?" My voice shakes. "I just…I need a ride to the airport in the morning."

He lets out a breath. "You're stayin' with us tonight, then?" It's a concession, which means a lot to me, since Grandpa isn't one for conceding anything, ever.

"Yes, sir."

"Be there in forty-five. Just hang tight."

"Thanks, Grandpa."

"No sweat, sweet-pea."

I sit on the stoop with the boxes at my feet, killing time on The Berry, and then Instagram. That last one is a mistake. I end up in my own photograph history, swiping through the pictures of Mom and me the last time we were together. It was the Fourth of July, and we spent it with Grandma and Grandpa at a lake near their house, grilling and drinking beer and setting off firecrackers. Mom and I got along great, since we'd decided on an unspoken rule to totally ignore my choice of schools and career.

I hold back the sobs, even still.

I keep holding them back when Grandpa shows up, his Wranglers as tight as ever, his shirt plaid and pearl-buttoned, his boots worn and scuffed. I hold them back as we drive in silence back to their house in his rattling, chugging, diesel Ram pickup that's older than me. I hold the tears back when Grandpa hugs me stiffly outside the truck in the gravel drive out front with the crickets singing and the moon high. And I hold them back when Grandma hugs me tearfully and makes me sit down to eat reheated roast beef and mashed potatoes and pecan pie.

I nearly lose it, though, when the ancient radio mounted under the cabinet next to the kitchen sink plays "Even If It Breaks Your Heart" by the Eli Young Band. I force myself to keep it together, even when "Leave the Pieces" by The Wreckers plays, but that one is hard, because I want to be as strong as the lyrics in that song, but don't feel like I am.

So now I'm lying in the narrow bedroom off the kitchen that's always been mine when I visit my grandparents, staring at the fifty-year-old painting of a cabin on a snowy hillside with tall pine trees in the background. That painting has always been how I get to sleep in this room. The moon shines through the window over the bed, streaming silver light onto the painting on the wall, and I imagine myself in that scene, a little log cabin with a fire cheerfully blazing, snow falling peacefully outside in thick fat flakes.

It's not working tonight, though.

I miss Mom.

I miss Ben.

I miss Nashville and my life and my friends and how things were before I got that call.

Most of all, I wish I could take back the things I said to Mom the last time we called.

I grab my phone off the little bedside table and stare at Ben's entry in my phone book. I want to call him, want to hear his voice. But even wanting that scares me, because I don't do that. I don't do emotional connections to guys.

I learned not to do that a long time ago, the hard way. I learned it when Dad left Mom when I was eight. I learned it at fourteen when the high school junior I just *knew* was in love with me took my virginity, then told everyone at school. I learned it again with the next "boyfriend", who ditched me the very second I finally let him have sex with me; literally, he finished, zipped up, left, and I never saw him again.

And I kept learning it with every guy I thought I liked, every boyfriend I stubbornly hoped would actually fall in love with me. But none of them ever did. They all acted like they liked me, like I meant something, and once I'd put out a few times and they got what they wanted, they took off and left me wondering what I'd done wrong. It wasn't until Marcus that I realized how stupid I'd been.

I put thoughts of Marcus out of my head. And I certainly don't call Ben.

I text him instead: *Thanks for your help today.*

His response comes quickly: **no prob.**

I don't know what else to say. I have to think for a long time. I type several things, then erase them. Finally, I send the simple truth. *I'm sorry. Under different circumstances maybe we could have taken it somewhere. But it is what it is.*

Under different circumstances. You know how many times I've heard that?

I already said I was sorry.

Don't be sorry. You headed back to school soon?

Tomorrow AM.

Well…I don't know what else to say but have a safe flight, then.

That sounds so distant, so unlike Ben, that it actually hurts. My fingers type without consulting my brain: *You're making me second guess myself, Benji.*

I'll come get you right now, wherever you are.

I choke when I read that. I nearly tell him yes, I nearly give him Grandma and Grandpa's address, but

I don't. Because if I was confused before, him coming to get me in the middle of the night would only confuse me more. And as nice as he's being right now, I know it won't last.

No. Sorry. Just no.

You know, I've always known women were confusing, but Echo, I really don't understand you.

Me either. That's part of the problem.

Goodbye, Echo.

That sounds so permanent.

I don't know if I can ever go back to Nashville.

And I can't stay here. There's nothing left for me in San Antonio. Nothing but memories. It was Mom's home, it's not mine. And now she's gone, and I just can't stay.

I get that. But that's not why you're pushing me away.

No, it's not.

But you won't tell me why.

I did.

No, you gave me excuses.

Damn it, Ben. I don't know what else you want me to tell you.

Exactly my point. There was a pause of several seconds, and then he sent a follow up text: *Go to sleep, Echo. Go back to Nashville tomorrow and just keep breathing. You'll be okay, someday. One day at a time.*

I can't figure out what else to say after that, so I don't text anything back. In the morning, Grandpa drives me to the airport and sees me off at security. He promises to ship me the boxes of Mom's things. I manage to keep it together all the way to Nashville, all the way to the apartment I share with three other girls.

Thank god for those girls, because they live for three things: partying, boys, and music.

I'll need huge doses of all three to move on.

Addendum: I'll need huge doses of partying and music to move on. I'm done with boys for a long, long time.

Which has nothing to do with the strange, empty hole I feel inside me...a hole that is frighteningly Ben-shaped.

Even admitting to myself that I feel Ben's absence like a chasm within me has me trying to fill that hole with whiskey.

Lots and lots of whiskey.

Eleven: Going Home
Ben

I MANAGED TO WASTE A WEEK. I DON'T EVEN KNOW WHAT I did for that week, to be honest. A whole bunch of not much. A whole bunch of feeling sorry for myself, hating life, hating women, hating football, hating my life. Just…hating in general. Drinking. Avoiding my phone, refusing steadfastly to look at the last texts I'd exchanged with Echo. Also steadfastly refusing to call Mom and Dad.

It was inevitable, though. I had nothing left here. Nothing left anywhere.

It's almost funny how big a bitch hindsight is; once Echo was gone, I realized with lightning-bolt suddenness and vivid clarity that I'd fallen in love with her. I mean, sure, I knew nothing about her. But it wasn't just a physical attraction. It wasn't just the sex. It was just...*her*. I want to know everything about her, I want to know what happened to her father, I want to know why her mother was alone for so long. I want to know why Echo is so shut down, so unable to talk about herself. She didn't make a big deal of it until right at the end but, looking back, I realize that she always deftly avoided talking about herself. I want to talk to her from dawn till dusk and find out everything about her, and I want to hold her and shelter her secrets and...I want her to be happy.

I know that feeling, loving someone enough to want their happiness to be my priority. It's why I left Nashville, after all. Kylie deserved happiness, and she'd found it with Oz. I couldn't give her anything, couldn't stomach seeing her happy with him, couldn't stomach seeing her at all, so I left. It was as much for her as for myself, I now know. I needed the space and time, as well. I needed experiences that didn't include Mom and Dad and Kylie and football.

I grew up while I was gone.

Not all the way, though, because I still need Mom and Dad. Now I don't know what to do. I'd thought I'd found myself on this journey around the country, but it turns out once football was taken away I still don't know who I am.

So I'm sitting on my couch just past dawn, my cell in hand, ESPN on the TV, muted, trying to make myself call home.

And then my phone rings. It's Mom.

"Benny!" Her voice is so soothing, so familiar, that lilt from growing up fluent in three languages. "You haven't called in so long, I was getting worried. I just…felt like I had to call."

My throat is thick, choked off with heat. "Mom."

She hears it, of course. "Benny? What's wrong, sweetie?"

Twenty-two, a grown man, and she still calls me Benny. "I don't even know—ahem—" I have to pause and clear my throat and start over. "I don't even know where to start, Mom."

She's quiet for a long, long moment. "I think it's time to come home, Benjamin."

"I can't."

"It's been almost two years, honey. If you're not over her by now, no amount of running away will change that."

Ouch. "It's not that, Mom."

She sighs. "Let me get your father. Hold on."

Shit. Shitshitshit. I can talk around Mom, because she won't push an issue. She doesn't have that directness in her. Dad, however, will dive straight into the heart of the matter and won't give up until I've spilled it all out for him.

"Son." His voice comes on the line after a moment.

"Hey, Dad."

He must have been working out, as I can hear his breath huffing quickly. "So. Out with it."

"I got hurt," I say.

"Explain."

"Took a hit to the knee. A bad one."

"How long are you out for? You need surgery?"

I swallow hard. "I already had surgery, and a month of PT. And…I'm out permanently."

He doesn't answer right away. "Shit."

"Yeah."

"And this happened when?"

"Month, almost a month and a half ago." My damned voice is small, like I'm a little boy again.

"And you're just now telling us?" He sounds pissed, but with Dad pissed usually comes from worry. "What the hell, Ben?"

"I—I don't know. I didn't want to tell you. I didn't want it to be…real, I guess. I don't know, Dad." I have to swallow and blink. "I had to handle it on my own."

"I'll be there this afternoon." His voice is gentle but allows for no arguments. "Get your shit together."

"Dad, I don't know what I'm—"

"Which is why you're coming home."

"You don't understand—"

"And you can explain on the drive home. This ain't up for discussion, son."

I don't have the energy or the will to fight it. "See you soon."

"Damn straight. Be ready."

He shows up at the door of my apartment at one that afternoon. He doesn't knock, just walks in as I'm stuffing the last of my clothes in a duffel bag. He stands in the door of my bedroom, massive arms crossed over his chest, brows drawn, staring at the cane leaning against the bed.

I ignore him until I have the bag zipped, set it on the floor beside the other suitcase and duffel bag that contain all my clothes and other belongings, of which there aren't many. I take the cane in hand, turn slowly to face my father. Take a hesitant step toward him. My knee is really messed up again. Once Cheyenne died and I met Echo, I'd stopped exercising it and started overusing it, so now it's stiff all the time and sore and always throbs with pain. To the point that any progress I'd made with Cheyenne has probably been totally undone. I can barely walk on it, even with the cane. Not that I'd admit that to Dad.

"Jesus, Ben. You need a *cane?*"

"Not forever. Just…for a while." I take another step.

His eyes waver, and then he rushes across the space between us, wraps me in a bear hug. "Ben. God, Ben. You went through this alone?"

"I'll never play again, Dad." My voice cracks, and I have to breathe hard and deep to keep it all at bay. "I may never even be able to run again."

"What happened?"

"Just a bad tackle. I had two on me, taking me down. Then this other guy comes at me, and just… drilled my knee. Hit me from the side, all his weight in a flying tackle and my knee just crumpled. Done. Just…done."

"And you went through the surgery, the therapy, the loss of your career, and you didn't even fucking tell me? Ben, I don't get it. I just don't get it." He pushes back and paces away.

I balance on my cane. "I didn't know how to deal with it. My career was over. I didn't know what to say, I didn't know…anything. Like I said on the phone, I just needed to deal with it on my own first."

Dad scrubs at his face with both hands. "I guess I can respect that. I don't like it, though. I wish you'd called. I'd have been here with you. Mom and I both would have."

"I know. I just couldn't." I shake my head. "I'm ready to go. Just got those three bags."

Dad grabs all three, hikes one over his shoulder and carries one in each hand, and then leads the way out to my truck. I follow him, hating that he has to carry my shit for me. He tosses the bags in the bed of the truck, bungees them in place and covers them with the rolled-up tarp I keep in the bed for that purpose, and then slides into the driver's seat. It took me that long just to get into the passenger seat.

After swinging by the manager's office to settle up, we're out of San Antonio within half an hour, and I don't look back. There's less than nothing there for me.

The first two hours pass in silence, the radio on, tuned to country. I want to change it, because country does nothing but remind me of Cheyenne and Echo. But Dad has a rule: the driver controls the radio. And he likes country. So I'm stuck with the memories.

Finally, as the third hour begins, Dad glances at me, and his eyes are knowing. "There's a girl, ain't there?"

"What?"

He shrugs. "That look on your face, it's the expression of a man with woman troubles. Only one person on earth can put that look on my face, and that's your momma. So, what's up?"

I shake my head. "I don't even know where to start, Dad. I really don't."

"It's not still Kylie, is it?"

"No. It's not about Kylie." I roll down the window to block out "Oh Juliet" by Joel Crouse.

How do you explain what happened? With Cheyenne, first, and then, even more difficult, with Echo. It seems impossible. How do you explain the significance of what happened with Echo?

I can almost taste your kiss…

Jesus, that song is fucking killing me. It's the reverse of what happened, in some ways, because I feel like it's my heart that was broken, not hers, but the emotion behind it is just slaughtering me.

I punch viciously at the radio until something else, anything else, comes on. I leave it at a pop station, something electronic and recycled and auto-tuned and polished with a packaged, factory-processed shine. The kind of empty bullshit that I loathe, but it holds no emotion and no sting of pain.

Dad glances at me with something awfully close to amusement in his eyes. "Well, that explains a lot."

I growl. "I don't think I can talk about it, Dad."

"Is it worse than everything with Kylie?"

I shrug. "Different. Everything with Kylie was a long time building, and it was mostly my own fault for waiting so long. This is different."

"Well, I'll let you be for now. We got us a long drive ahead of us, though, so if you feel like talking about it…"

"I can't, Dad. I just can't. It's too much, too soon, and I don't even know where to start or what I'm gonna do."

"If there's a question of what you're gonna do, then it ain't over, is it?"

I sigh. "Not really. Here's the short version: I met her in San Antonio. Under…unusual circumstances, and just leave it at that. Turns out, though, that she goes to Belmont. And I *really* don't want to go back to Nashville, for a lot of reasons. I'm as over Kylie as I can get, but it's still going to be hell having to see her. Plus, my football career is over, and all my friends at school are football buddies. I don't know what I'm going to do. I don't—I don't know who I am, Dad. And being in Nashville is just going to confuse me even further. Kylie, football…and now Echo is there too…it's the last place on Earth I want to be. But I couldn't stay in San Antonio any longer, and with my knee fucked up I can't drive for long, and I don't know where else to go."

"Got yourself a pile of troubles, it sounds like." Dad switches the radio station, but tunes it to a more traditional country station, the older stuff, George Strait, Clint Black, Alan Jackson, Garth Brooks. "What's the deal with…Echo, you said her name is?"

"Yeah. Echo. It's hard to explain. Partly because I don't even know what the problem really is. She wouldn't say. She just…shut me down, but I could tell the reasons she gave weren't the real ones."

Dad mulls on it. "Well, in my experience, when a woman shuts down like that, it's out of fear or the need to protect herself, usually a bit of both. She may be afraid of what she's feeling, you know? I mean, obviously I don't know her or the situation, but that's my experience." He glances at me. "You want my advice?"

"Sure."

"When we get home, take some time to settle in, first, okay? Let me get you in to see Doc Petersen, get another opinion on your knee. And then I think you need to face the mess you left behind in regard to Kylie." He glances at me, eyes sharp. "She and Oz got married, you know that, right? They're living in Nashville. They're happy. But I can tell she's upset about you, how things ended. You left real sudden, you know? And before you left, things were—"

"I was an asshole. Please don't remind me."

"I think she just wants her friend back—"

"I really don't know how I'll handle that," I interrupt. "I don't know how I'll feel seeing her again. I feel like I've had enough time and space to know that I'm past the craziness I felt back then, you know? Especially because I've got all this with Echo on my plate. But it'll be hard, regardless."

"I guess all I want to say is just don't *not* handle it. You two were best friends for far too long to let it sit."

I nod. "Yeah. You're right. I'll handle it, I promise."

"Good."

We drive in companionable silence for many hours after that, sometimes talking, mostly not; Dad and I are alike in that we don't need to talk for long periods of time. Somewhere past midnight, I convince Dad to let me drive for a bit so he can take a break. He falls asleep quickly, head against the window, and I let the road hypnotize me, let my thoughts spiral loose and free. I let myself think about Echo, about how much I miss her, how much I want to not even go home first, how I want to find her at Belmont and demand a resolution, demand truth. I let myself think about Kylie, too, for the first time in a long time.

I can't say I would have done anything differently, given the chance, because I'm just not sure how else

I could have felt, under the circumstances. But I do wish I'd been a better friend, thought about Kylie more and myself less. I was worried, though, you know? Given initial impressions and first reactions—judging totally by appearances and rumors—Oz should have been trouble, could have been really bad for Kylie. Could have taken her down the wrong path. But fortunately for her, he turned out to be a decent guy who really does love her. But it could have turned out much differently.

It didn't, though, and like Dad said, I owe it to the friendship we had to fix things.

I've been home for two weeks, resting, staying home, lying low and keeping to myself, trying to figure out what the hell I'm going to do. Moping, basically. Finally Dad all but drags me to Doc Petersen's office in step one of the fix-Ben's-life program.

"I'm afraid I'm going to have to concur with the doctor in San Antonio," Dr. Petersen says, a sympathetic expression on his aged face. "Given a lot of hard work, you'll see normal everyday mobility. Walking, even jogging, won't be a problem. But competitive ball? Especially on the professional level? Impossible, I'm afraid. If you're tough enough, you might get a season or two out of it, but one injury, push it too hard, and you'll be worse off than ever. And even if you were careful, the strain would eventually just be too much."

I nod, and flinch at Dad's hand landing heavily but comfortingly on my shoulder. "I see. Thanks, Doc."

He smiles at me. "It's the end of a dream, son, and I know it's hard to hear. I've been treating athletes my entire life, and this is by no means the first time I've delivered news like this. It's hard. It just sucks, in modern parlance. But even if you can't play professionally anymore, you can still be involved in the game, right? For some, it's too hard to be around what they can no longer do. But for others, coaching is a way to be part of the game they love. Think about it. I know your father can help you in that direction, if you were to so choose." He stands up and claps me on the bicep. "Like I said, it's the end of one dream, son, but that doesn't mean it's the end of everything."

I nod, and the doctor leaves Dad and me. "I know, Dad. Finish my degree first, and then think about what's next."

He laughs and slaps my shoulder. "You got it, son. A college degree, even if you don't end up in that field, will never be wasted."

"My credits are all toward political science, Dad."
I laugh with sarcastic self-deprecation. "What the hell
was I thinking?"

He shakes his head and laughs. "You know, I
always wondered that myself, but there ain't much
you can tell a kid your age."

"At this point, I think I might be willing to
listen."

Dad shrugs. "You've got time, kiddo. You're
what, thirty credit hours short of a degree? That's a
couple semesters, Ben. Just finish it. Then you've got a
degree to show for yourself, and you can rethink your
career in the meantime. With so little left to complete
your degree, it'd be kind of stupid to try to totally
change your major, if you ask me. If you decide on
something else, you'll have your basic requirements
out of the way, so you could get a second bachelor's
or a master's or something and only have to take
catch-up pre-reqs.

"And, like Doc Petersen said, there's always
coaching. Volunteer to coach Little League, or apply
to coach at a high school or junior high. Get some
coaching experience under your belt, and I can talk
to Mike about getting you on the Titan sidelines.
There's a whole world of possibility out there for you,
Ben. You just gotta figure out what you want. This

is one closed door. There's countless other doors still standing open."

"But that was the *one* door I'd been working toward my whole life. I remember sitting in the box with Mom at six years old, watching you play, and just *knowing* I'd do that, too." I have to swallow hard past the lump. "I don't know what I was thinking when I chose poli-sci. I was thinking it didn't matter because I'd be playing pro ball."

Dad nods. "I know." He claps me on the shoulder yet again and leads the way out of the exam room. "Come on. I'll buy you a beer."

I look at him skeptically. "Dad. It's barely noon."

"So it'll be a lunchtime beer."

I grin. "Sounds good."

So we sit at a burger joint and drink beer and talk about the next season for Dad. It would be his last, he's decided. Not surprising news to anyone. He's played hard for a long, long time, and put up some receiving records that will probably not be broken anytime soon.

When we're done, Dad slips me a scrap of paper with familiar feminine writing on it.

Ben, meet me for coffee at 1:30. She'd written the name and address of a coffee shop near Belmont beneath that and signed her name with a swirling scrawl: *Kylie.*

"It's quarter after one, kiddo. Best get moving," Dad says. "And Ben? I know it's gonna be hard, but just...think before you speak, okay?"

I just nod. Once upon a time I probably would have taken umbrage at that, so I take it as a sign of having matured that I am able to see it for the wise and likely difficult-to-heed advice it is.

He hands me the keys to his Rover. "I can walk to the stadium from here. Just be careful, okay?"

"Thanks," I say, waving as he heads out.

By the time I find a parking spot within a couple blocks of the coffee shop, it's already a few minutes past 1:30. I take it slowly, allowing myself to lean on my cane and not use my knee too much.

She's sitting in a thick leather armchair, sipping coffee from a ceramic mug, flipping idly through a house copy of *TIME* magazine, positioned so she can keep an eye on the door. She sees me the moment I enter, and her face lights up as she leaps out of her chair, sloshing coffee on the floor as she hurries to set the mug down.

"BEN!" she shrieks, rushing toward me. Her arms go around my neck as she slams into me; it's like none of it ever happened, in that fraction of a moment. "Benji...oh my god...Benji, it's really you!"

My heart flops, squeezes, and aches, and I don't know how to decipher the rush of a thousand different emotions. "Ky. God, I've missed you." And…I had. I really, really had. I just hadn't let myself realize it until now.

Benji. How do I handle the ache those two syllables engender? It was her nickname for me, and then it was Echo's, and now? Does it belong to both? Neither? God, I don't know. I don't know. I just know it's good to see her, but that initial joy is quickly tempered by the other emotions connected to Kylie.

She lets me go and backs away, and I plant my cane and lean on it. Her eyes go to it. "Ben? What's… what's with the cane?"

I shake my head. "Let me get a cup of coffee and we can catch up."

She gestures at the table between her chair and another, which she'd claimed with her purse. A mug of black coffee sits on the table, and I'm sure she's sugared it to within an inch of its life, just the way I like it. "Got you covered."

So we sit, and I'm acutely aware of Kylie's gaze following my limping progress across the coffee shop, and the careful, ginger way I sit, extending my leg. I grab my mug and sip at the coffee, and take in the reality of Kylie. She's more gorgeous than ever. Her curly red-blond hair is longer than it's ever been, bound in a loose, low ponytail, flyaway strands drifting across her forehead and brushing her chin and shoulders. She's wearing a below-the-knee khaki skirt and a white V-neck T-shirt, and while her clothes aren't revealing, they accentuate her curves with classy, sexy, sophistication. She's got calf-length black leather boots on with a heel that makes her even taller and makes her long legs longer. She's wearing minimal makeup, as usual, and the purse she slides between a hip and the chair is a black leather Dior.

Life has been good to her, it seems.

And then she casually drapes a hand over her knee so the track lights overhead glint and gleam off the diamond ring. It's a brutal reminder: she's not my Kylie anymore. Her electric blue eyes fix on me, and then follow my gaze to her ring. "Oz and I—"

"Got married. I know, I heard. Congratulations." I struggle to sound genuine, and I'm surprised by how bitter I feel, suddenly. Which is stupid. I'm not in love with Kylie anymore. I'm not. Right? So why do I feel this way?

"Ben—" she starts, her glow of contented happiness fading.

I hold up a hand, silencing her, and take a deep breath. "Kylie, let me get a few things out, okay? The first and most important is that I'm sorry. I treated you—and Oz—like shit. I was an asshole. I did and said things I had no place doing or saying, and I'm sorry. I hope you can forgive me. I wasn't the friend you deserved. I should've—I should've seen how happy you were with him and let you—. I should not have gotten all up in your shit about it. I didn't give Oz a chance."

Kylie's eyes water. "Ben, of course...of course! I was hurt, yeah. I mean, you were so angry and I didn't get it, not until you told me—" She breaks off, glances down. "Until you explained how you feel."

"Felt," I clarify. "Past tense, at this point. But look, I'll be honest. I was an asshole, yeah, I own that, but I had pretty good reasons, I think. I'd been in love with you for so long, you know? And I'd...harbored it, kept it in, waited...at first I was waiting for you to be old enough to date, and then by the time you were I'd kept quiet about how I felt about you for so long that I didn't know how to tell you, and...I was just plain scared. I was scared of you telling me you didn't feel the same way, I was scared that if I just kissed you, you'd—laugh, or push me off, or just...I don't know. Act like you couldn't understand why I'd do that, you know?

"Most of all, you were my best friend and I was scared to risk that. I thought I had time on my side.

You'd never been into guys, never dated anyone, and neither had I. Me, because I was waiting for you, and then holding out hope that I'd figure out a way to tell you. And then I thought I'd wait till you graduated and we'd go on this road trip, and it would just...*happen* between us, and I wouldn't have to actually tell you I'd had this secret love for seven years."

"Ben, Jesus—"

"Hold on. Just...wait. Just listen." I fortify myself with more coffee, and collect my thoughts. "I waited too long. Oz showed up, and you fell in love with him. And I realized I'd lost my chance. I felt like my shot had been...*stolen,* you know? Unfair, I guess, since it was my own fault for being a fucking pussy about it, but that's how I felt. And I was honestly worried about you, okay? You have to admit, based on what any of us—what *I* could see about Oz, it was scary. None of us knew him, none of us got to see what you did...what you do see."

She nods. "I totally get that, Ben, I do. And to be honest about it, that's part of the appeal. That's part of what drew me to him. He was—he *is*—so different from what I'd ever known. He was a little scary and dangerous, and I'd always been the good girl, always been safe and careful and played by the rules and done the responsible thing. And Oz was a chance to have something different, to see a part of life unlike anything else."

"I can see that," I admit.

She wraps both hands around her mug and glances at me across the rim. Her blue eyes are shielded, guarded. "Ben, you said...you said it was past tense. The way you—being in love with me."

I nod. "Yeah. I'm sorry I had to take off the way I did, but I—I couldn't figure out how to be happy for you. And that's what you deserved. I cared about you, but your dad told me that if I really did *love* you, I'd do what was best for *you,* and figure out how to live with that for myself. And the only way I could do that was to get away. So I left."

"Where'd you go?"

I shrug. "Everywhere. I spent a good year just... drifting. I would stop in a little town somewhere and find work and stay there for a few weeks or a month. Spent time in...oh, man...Iowa, South Dakota, Montana, Idaho, down the Pacific coast. I learned to surf in California, that was fun. I just drifted and worked and...honestly, tried not to think about you." I can't look at her as I explain this. "It was months and months of not thinking about you at all. Because that was easier than...missing you, and hurting over it."

She lets out a little noise that's part sigh, part sob. "God, Ben. That sounds like it was…"

"Exactly what I needed. It was lonely, yeah. But it was better than hanging around here and seeing you and being bitter. I never would have gotten over you if I hadn't left. I couldn't be sitting here talking to you if I hadn't left." I hesitate, drink some coffee, and watch the black liquid swirl in the mug. "It would have destroyed me, staying here."

"And now?"

I shrug again. "And now…hopefully we can be friends. You look great." I rush to cover that. "Happy, I mean. You look…happy."

She smiles. "I am. I really am. Oz and I…it's incredible. I'm studying music management at Belmont, and we're gigging here in the city during the semesters and going on tour with Mom and Dad during breaks and the summer. Oz and Dad finally opened their classic car restoration business, and… yeah. Things are great." She leans toward me. "The only thing missing has been you, Benji."

I wince at that. "Kylie, I—please don't call me that."

"Benji? Why not?"

I shrug miserably. "I'm over the pain and the bitterness, but that…still hurts, I guess."

But Kylie is far too perceptive to fall for that. "There's someone else, isn't there?"

"Sort of," I admit.

She doesn't respond right away. "You know, the thing I was the most upset with you about was the hypocrisy of being mad at me for being with Oz when you were with all those other girls."

"I never slept with any of them." I'm not sure why that comes out, why I tell her that.

"You—but you—what?"

"I let you think I had on purpose. The whole… the only reason I ever went out with any of them was to make you jealous." I duck my head. "But I could never…go all the way with them."

"God, Ben, that's—"

"Fucked up, I know." I sigh and tilt my head to look up at the ceiling rather than at her. "That's not true, though. Making you jealous was the primary reason. It was also a half-assed attempt to try to move on. To force myself to get over you."

"Get over me by getting under someone else, huh?"

I shrug. "That was the idea, but I couldn't do it. I'd get close and end up thinking about you, and—I'd have to stop."

"But you let me think the worst anyway."

"At that point, when I told you that…I don't think I cared, honestly. Nothing mattered but how I felt like you'd been stolen from me."

"That's kind of a dick move," Kylie says. "Letting me think you'd fucked all these other girls and then getting pissed at me for falling in love with someone and wanting to be with him."

"I know," I admit. "I know. And I'm sorry for that, too."

She just blinks at me, and I still know her well enough to see the anger in her expression. "That pisses me off all over again. Like, that's so many layers of deception, Ben."

"I know."

"Any other lies you need to clean up?"

"I was a virgin. When I left Nashville, I mean. You want the whole truth, there it is."

She looks stunned. "No shit. Really?"

"Really."

Her eyes narrow. "But you're not anymore."

"No." I carefully keep my gaze away from hers.

"So, who is she?"

I'm really, really not sure that's something I can talk about with her. "I…don't know if we're there yet, Ky."

She nods. "Fair enough." But she can't let it go, though. "Is it serious? Did you just come back to talk to me, or…"

"No, I'm back for good."

"You didn't answer my—"

"Kylie," I cut in, my voice firm. "I can't talk about it with you. I want to fix things with you. I want us to be friends. I loved you as a best friend for seventeen years, above and beyond anything else. I'm here talking to you because I want that back. I know I fucked up in a lot of ways, and I've apologized for it. But…I just…I *cannot* talk about Echo right now."

Immediately, Kylie's expression goes far too carefully neutral. "Echo. Echo Leveaux?"

I lean back in the chair and cover my face with both hands. "Of course you know her."

"She's…*incredible*." Her voice takes on a note of awe. "I've heard her sing at school and with her band, and…Ben, she's—legit, she's the most amazing vocalist I've ever heard."

I rear back in shock. *"What?"* I knew she had to be good to study at Belmont, but coming from Kylie, this kind of raving is like the Pope calling you holy. Kylie knows music and she knows talent, so I respect her opinion on this topic more than just about anyone else's.

"How could you not know?"

"I didn't meet her in Nashville. I met her in San Antonio. I've never heard her sing."

Kylie considers her response carefully. "Let's go back a bit. The cane, the limp. What happened? The last thing your parents told me was that you were playing semi-pro football in Texas."

"Not semi-pro, actually. It was an experimental minor league. A way to keep an eye on upcoming talent other than the NCAA. A lot of the experts are saying college ball is increasingly broken as a path to the pros." I wave my hand. "Whatever. Not important. Yeah, that's what I was doing. I was on the verge of getting drafted. Another season or two in San Antonio and I'd have been picked up, no contest. But I got hurt. Took a nasty hit to my knee and it just…shattered."

"Will you be okay?"

I tilt my head from side to side. "Okay? Yeah. I'll lose the cane in few months, hopefully. But I'll never play ball again."

"Oh…Ben." She knows exactly how much football meant to me. "I'm so sorry."

"Me, too. But…it is what it is, and I just have to deal with it."

"It is what it is," Kylie repeats. "I hate that phrase. It's a cop-out excuse to explain away what you can't accept."

"What am I supposed to do, Kylie? It's a medical fact that I will never play competitive football ever again. The surgeon in San Antonio told me that, and Doc Petersen told me that not even two hours ago. I'm done. My football career is over. It's a fact."

"You're more than a football player, Ben," Kylie says.

I lean my head back and sigh. "God, I fucking know that. I've been told that a hundred times already. Cheyenne told me that. Echo told me that. Dad told me that. Dr. Petersen told me that. I fucking know there's more to life than fucking football!"

"Cheyenne?" she says, by way of avoiding my outburst.

"My physical therapist in San Antonio. And Echo's mom, incidentally."

"Ah. I see."

I laugh bitterly. "No, you know what? You really couldn't even begin to see."

"So, tell me, Ben." She leans forward and touches my knee. "We're friends, right? Best friends? Best friends tell each other things. And I sense you need to talk about this."

I shake my head. "It's too long a story, too fucked up, too difficult. And yeah, we're friends, but I'm not sure we're there yet. I'm not sure *I'm* there yet, at least."

"All right, then."

"It's not that I don't trust you, or—that I don't want to talk about it." I groan and sit forward. "But I don't. I do, but I don't. I don't know. I'm just so mixed up about everything right now. You, this, us? It's still not easy. Part of me sees you and everything comes back all over again. But then there's all the shit with Echo, and losing football, and—everything. So it's not you, it's just…everything is too much."

"Sounds like you have a lot of thinking to do."

I laugh. "Yeah, but where do I start?"

She doesn't answer right away. She just sits and stares into the dregs of her coffee for a long time, thinking. "Start here, with you and me. I'm glad you're back. And…for what it's worth to you, I forgive you. I'm sorry things worked out the way they did…or, at least, I'm sorry you got hurt. I can't be sorry for finding Oz, but I'm sorry you got hurt in the process. I never wanted to hurt you, I just didn't know. If you'd said something years before, maybe—but there's no sense rehashing the past. You're my oldest friend. I've known you literally my entire life, and the past…what, almost two years? It's been hard without you. I've missed you. We all have. So…you don't have to confide your secrets in me, but just know that I'm here. I'll listen. I'm your friend, and I love you. Like a—not like a sister, but—like a friend, I guess. Like family, I love you. I want you to be happy. I want us to put the past behind us, okay?"

I nod. "Thank you." I meet her eyes, and she's not the only one with emotion rife in her eyes. "And Kylie? I'm glad you're happy. I really am. Maybe someday I can meet with Oz and he and I can sort out our shit."

Her eyes shine. "I know he'd like that a lot. He doesn't have a lot of family, and he doesn't make friends easily, so if you and he could—patch things, I guess, it'd be wonderful to see him have his cousin in his life."

"I'll do my best."

Kylie digs her phone out of her purse and glances at the time. "I've got studio time in a few minutes, so I've got to go. But let's do this again, okay? Soon?"

I stand up and we hover awkwardly, and then we both laugh and give in to hugging. And it's good to hug her. "Yeah, soon."

She doesn't let go right away, though. "And Ben? All I'll say is this: if I don't get to call you Benji any-more, you'd damn well better make sure she deserves to use the nickname *I* gave you."

I rub her arms and then I have to let go. "Yeah, well…I guess I'll just have to see how shit shakes loose, right?"

"Right." She moves past me, waving. But then she stops once more and turns back. "And Ben, do yourself a favor: go on YouTube and look up a band called Echo the Stars. A girl's music...it says a lot about her." And then she's gone in a flutter of khaki skirts and clicking boot heels.

I go home, up to my old bedroom, and I flip open my laptop. I type "Echo the Stars" into the YouTube search bar, click on the first video that pops up, a song called "Only the Moon." It's clearly a handheld video camera on a tripod set up in the back of a bar somewhere on Lower Broadway.

Echo, her blond hair down and curled into loose spirals, stands at a microphone center stage. A guy stands to her right with a mandolin, lank brown hair in his blue eyes. Another guy stands to her left with a banjo in his hands and an acoustic guitar on a stand behind him. There's another guy with a fiddle behind them standing beside the drummer, an electric guitar on a stand next to him, and a female upright bassist with her own microphone on the other side of the drummer. Then there's the drummer himself, who has an elaborate setup, a huge multi-tiered drum kit in front of him with an array of hand drums to his left, and a didgeridoo leaning against the wall on his right.

Judging by the variety of instruments, I have no clue what kind of music they're going to play, but I'm already fascinated.

I hit play, and there's the sound of applause dying out as Echo thanks the crowd. The mandolin player picks at the strings, adjusts a tuner, and then he and Echo glance at each other and exchange nods.

"Okay, this is 'Only the Moon.' It's one of our originals," she says.

The drummer swivels away from the drums and takes the didgeridoo, inhales deeply, purses his lips, and blows into the instrument. A deep, buzzing sound rises, the kind of sound you can feel in your chest even through the computer speakers, and it continues for a long moment, unbroken. And then the guy playing the didg takes a breath, pauses, and starts again, this time somehow making the instrument produce a high-pitched, buzzier sound, and the mandolin joins in, picking a high, circular counterpoint. The banjo player has traded that instrument for his guitar, and he starts in with a drum-like chord: *thummmm—thummmm—thummmm*. Next is the electric guitar and the upright bass, finishing the melody.

Echo is last, sucking in a deep breath, and then she lets out a long, high, wordless wail that carries and carries until she lets the note trail off. And then she sings, in a voice of starlight and angelfire and aching purity:

> *"It's a long, long road to walk alone,*
> *A dark and winding path that I must roam,*
> *And I've only the moon to keep me company,*
> *Only the moon to watch me on my way.*
> *A broken heart chose this path,*
> *A heart cracked by grief sent me this way.*
> *And I've only the moon to sing me down the road,*
> *Only the moon to warm me in this cold.*
> *My feet falter, my tears drip,*
> *Fall like rain, so much salt on my lip.*
> *And I've only the moon to watch me weep,*
> *Only the moon my secrets to keep.*
> *I left you there,*
> *I knew your heart,*
> *And I left you there,*
> *With only the moon to light your way,*
> *With only the moon to hear you say,*
> *Come back, come back, come back.*
> *Oh, oh, oh, oh,*
> *I've only the moon to sing me down the road,*
> *Only the moon to warm me in the cold,*
> *Only the moon to watch me weep,*
> *Only the moon my secrets to keep,*
> *Only the moon to hear me say,*
> *Come back, come back, come back..."*

And then she repeats the refrain, "only the moon" in the same grief-wrought wail, the instruments all playing in a crashing clash of colliding sounds, the didgeridoo puffing and buzzing like the breath of a predator, the mandolin circling and circling high rolling circuitous notes, the acoustic guitar providing a fast chugging base-rhythm, the electric guitar mirroring Echo's sung melody, the bass thrumming beneath it all louder and louder like the rumble of distant thunder, until all the instruments fade away and all that remains is Echo's haunting wail and the reverberating bass.

Echo's hands lift to hover by her face as she holds the final note for an impossible length of time, fluttering as she runs out of breath, and then she lets the note go and the bass is silenced. Echo slumps forward, clinging to the mic stand as if about to collapse, head hanging, hair falling in a blond curtain around her face, and just before the video cuts to the sound of deafening applause, I could swear I see her shoulders shake with sobs.

I look for the upload date, my heart thudding, goosebumps shivering on my skin. I find it, and discover that Echo uploaded this song less than a week ago.

"Holy shit. Holy shit." I stare at the screen, scroll down through several pages of videos by Echo the Stars. "She's fucking incredible."

That song, though…is it about me? Or her mom? Or…both, maybe?

All I know is, I have to find her.

Twelve: Alone With My Whiskey and My Regret
Echo

"ECHO? ECHO! COME ON, HON. GET UP." THE VOICE IS male, distant, and pissed. The world shakes horribly. "You need to get up, Echo. Our set starts in twenty minutes and you're not dressed."

Set?

Shit. The gig. But I'm so tired, and everything hurts, and I'm drunk. Really drunk. My eyes won't open. The world shakes again, harder.

"Stop…" I mumble. "Stop the…th' shaking. N'more. No…no more shaking."

"Then get your ass up, Echo. We can't do the show without you." It's Brayden MacKellan, my band's mandolin player, my best friend and, right now, my own personal conscience/torturer. "You're fucking wasted...*again*." He manages to pack a hell of a lot of disapproval and disappointment into that one word.

"Hurts." I blink my eyes, and three of Brayden weave into my field of vision. I try to focus.

"I know, hon." He kneels down, and even watching him move makes me dizzy. "But you need to get up and get moving. We're getting paid huge for this. We can't back out, and we can't do it without you, so I really need you to figure your shit out, okay? Now come on. I've got a shower going for you."

Ooh. A shower. Yay. I let him help me up, fall against him, smell the coffee on him, and the faint tang of beer and cologne. Mmm.

"You smell yummy, Bray-bay."

"I know. That's the smell of sober, Echo."

"Shu'up, asshole." I blink at him, both of him... no, all three of him.

He helps me into the bathroom, closes the door behind us, and starts peeling at my clothes. Which are sticky with what might be spilled booze, or possibly my own puke.

"You're lucky you've got me, Echo," Brayden says. "I don't think anyone else would do this for you."

Ben would have, but I can't think about Ben; I've got Brayden, and he'll have to do.

I nod my head sloppily. "I know. You love me."

"I sure as hell do. But you're also lucky I'm playing for the other team right now, because I'm really not sure you can handle the shower by yourself."

Brayden plays for both teams, so depending on his mood and the day of the week he might be hooking up with a guy, or a girl, or both. It's complicated, and I stay out of it. Of course, we did have that one night after our first gig together. He was the first friend I made at Belmont my first year, and he was in a straight phase. He's beautiful, Brayden is, with long and artfully messy brown hair and piercing, expressive indigo eyes. He's tall and thin, wiry and lean and sort of delicate-seeming, but he has an inner core of strength and an air of careless insouciance.

We realized our musical chemistry was off the charts and started writing songs together, and eventually we booked a gig, nailed the set, and then nailed each other. Which was when he decided to admit to being bisexual, and that he didn't think he and I would work out long term as a couple, and he didn't do long term anyway. Which was fine, because neither did I, and he wasn't what I wanted sexually anyway, being a little too effeminate for my tastes. The little tryst didn't affect our friendship or our music, and we added members to our band over the next couple years until we became Echo the Stars. The core is still Brayden and I, and we're hella tight.

I don't hesitate when he gets me naked and shoves me into the shower.

Which is ice cold.

"BRAYDEN!" I shriek and try to climb out, but he keeps me under the spray until I stop struggling. "YOU ASSHOLE!"

"Chill out, Echo!"

"Don't tell me to chill out, you dick! This water is like fucking ice!"

Brayden has the gall to laugh, until I stop fighting him and yank him so he nearly falls into the tub with me. "You're gonna get me wet, and we don't have time for me to change!" he squeals, thrashing. "Okay, okay!"

"Make it hot, you asshole. And get me some clothes."

He turns the knob so the water goes hot, and I sigh in relief. The cold water did wake me up a little, though. I'm far from sober, but I'm awake enough to function, at least. And god knows I've got plenty of experience functioning while wasted.

I just don't know how to deal, otherwise, especially now.

I get clean, holding on to the wall most of the time. When I'm out, Brayden has my favorite pair of holey jeans and my favorite T-shirt, and my favorite boots. He knows me. Kind of like a sister, in a lot of ways. Only, he's a he, and we fucked once. So not like a sister. But still.

Drunk thoughts don't make any sense.

Bray hustles me out the door and into his Jeep, and he hauls ass across Nashville to the bar where we're supposed to be playing...ten minutes ago, by the time we arrive. The bar manager is pissed, the rest of the band is pissed, and the crowd is pissed. At least I'm not the only drunk one, now, though.

I weave carefully onto stage, grab the mic and lean into it. Stare out at the crowd, which goes quiet when I appear. Being on stage centers me, calms me. The alcohol buzzes and burns in my blood, boils in my stomach.

"So, I'm kind of wasted," I admit into the microphone. "Like really hammered. But don't worry, I can still sing my ass off."

The crowded bar shakes with the howls of the audience. We've built a cult following in the last year or so, which has a lot to do with YouTube and social media—all Brayden's work—and our kick-ass live shows.

But this, the moment before the lyrics pour out of me, this is where I live.

And it's something Mom never understood. It's the cause of our fight. She didn't want me to start a band, especially because my studies at school do suffer a bit. I'm dedicated to this band, to this life. She wanted me to focus on classical music. Go a more "elegant" route than gigging in dingy bars and honky-tonks in Nashville. She wanted me to...I don't even know. Sing opera? Go to Broadway? I don't know. She liked the "classical" thing, and I don't think she really understood what that meant, or what she really wanted for me. When I started gigging with Echo the Stars, she was livid. She didn't even want me to go to Belmont. She wanted me to try out for Juilliard or a conservatory. Or go to a university closer to home. Anything but Nashville, anything but a band. I think she knew if I started a band, I'd be less likely to finish school. And damn it if she wasn't right. The more gigs we book, the more we get paid, the more attention we garner, the less relevant class seems. I just want to sing. I love being on stage with Brayden and Mim and the guys. Nothing matters when I've got the mic.

Like now.

The only thing that can numb the pain and the guilt more than booze is performing. So I cup the mic and hold the stand for balance, and I let Bray's masterful mandolin playing wash over me, tap my toe when

Will comes in with the banjo, and weave a swaying dance when Atticus taps the bongos with the heels of his palms and fingertips, creating a quick, driving rhythm. Vance and Mim are quiet for this number, sitting off to the side until we're ready for them. For now, it's just Bray, Atticus, Will, and me.

I dive into the music, letting it take me away.

"I don't need to love, you know,
Don't need the heartache,
Don't need the high or the low,
Don't need anyone but me,
I don't need to cling to you
Late at night, through the stars as they sing,
Don't need love, old or new.
I just need me.
Because I'm all there is,
I'm all right,
I'm all right,
And I don't need love.
I've ached and I've hurt and I've cried,
I've loved and lost and love has died,
I've learned the lessons, and now I know,
I don't need to love,
Don't need the high or the low,
Don't need anyone but me
Because I'm all there is,

And I'm all right,
I'm all right."

There's an instrumental break, and then I repeat the last few lines, Mim harmonizing.

And then we play "Only the Moon" which nearly makes me cry, so we do a cover of "Broussard's Lament" by Sarah Jarosz, and then "Henry Lee" by Crooked Still, with Mim playing the cello rather than the bass and Vance on the fiddle. I'm lucky as hell to have these talented multi-instrumentalists in Will, Mim, Vance and Atticus; Bray and I both only do one thing, but we do that one thing *really* well. I mean, when you come across insane talent like those four, musicians who can seamlessly switch from instrument to instrument like they do, you go with it. You hang on to 'em and you make beautiful music with them. You do *not* waste it sitting in class learning shit you'll never use. I learned composition by composing; I learned harmony by harmonizing.

I find my pace, find the groove where the music pulls me away.

We do "Undone in Sorrow" by Crooked Still, which really showcases Vance's show-stopping fiddle skills, and then we take a break. I take a bottle of Sam Adams and sit out back behind the bar, drinking and thinking.

And of course, Bray joins me. "From an artistic perspective, I should appreciate this funk you're in. Even piss-drunk, you sing your guts out up there. Better, even, maybe. And the songs you've written? Amazing. But...as your friend, I'm worried for you, hon." He shakes his head to toss a hank of brown hair out of his eyes. "You're drinking all the time, and you won't talk about what happened."

"My fucking mother died, Bray. That's what fucking happened." I take a long swig.

"I know, but...I know you. I've sweat and bled on stage with you. I've held your hair while you puked your guts out, and I held you through that pregnancy scare you had our freshman year, and I stood by you through that whole shit with fucking Marcus. And now, suddenly, whatever this is you have going on, you've shut me out of it." He leans toward me, rests his head on my shoulder as he digs a cigarette out of his hip pocket. "And that scares me."

"I'm just fucked up, Bray. That's all."

He blows a stream of smoke. "Bullshit. That's total bullshit, and you know it. I mean, yeah, you're mega fucked up, I get *that*. So am I. But it's not just about your mom dying. I mean, I know you two weren't on the best terms lately, and—"

"Bray-bay, I love you, buddy, but shut up. Just… shut up." I hate the way I sound, and the way he pulls away from me and smokes in silence. "I'm sorry, Bray. I really am. I just…it all hurts too much, and you can't help. The last time I talked to her, we screamed at each other. I called her a meddling bitch, and she called me an ungrateful spawn, and—that was the last time I talked to her."

"Shit, honey. I had no idea."

"And it's not just that. It's also that…that all I ever wanted was for her to see how much I love doing this—" I wave toward the bar, the stage, the rest of the band, "and she couldn't just be happy to see me using my talent. She was jealous that I get to follow my dreams when hers was—was taken from her."

Bray stares at me with compassion in his eyes. "Echo, I—"

"She's *gone*, Bray!" I shout. "She's dead, and I'll never get to fix any of it. I'll never get to tell her how much she—she meant to me, that I loved her so…so much. She was all I had. Well, except for Grandma and Grandpa, and thank god for them, but…she was my *mom*…and she's—she's dead."

"God, Echo. Just…god. I'm so sorry." He wraps his arm around me, and he accepts the truth I gave him.

It's the truth, sure, but it doesn't touch on the rest of what has me fucked up. It doesn't touch Ben, or my regret, or my heartbreak, or my guilt. But he accepts it, and we go back on stage.

We play more covers, another few original songs, and then the rest of the band leaves the stage and only Brayden and I remain.

"Okay, we're gonna take ya'll back to when it was just Brayden and me. This is a song I wrote during a...a very painful time in my life. And to be totally honest, I'm in a very similar place right now, so this song is really appropriate, I guess. Just don't get too mad if I have a hard time near the end, okay?"

The crowd goes quiet. Bray stands at my side, mandolin cradled in his delicate hands, his expressive dark blue eyes on me, waiting, encouraging. Finally, he nods at me, and starts the melody. It's slow, mournful.

> *"Oh god, it's like a hole,*
> *Ripped into my chest,*
> *And I can see my bones,*
> *Each and every one.*
> *My bones, they prick and stab,*
> *Poke and slash,*
> *And I wish sometimes*
> *That I was dead,*

Laying on a slab.
If I was dead, I wouldn't have to feel this,
I wouldn't have to know this pain,
Wouldn't have to bear it,
Because this kind of pain,
You can't help but wear it,
When it cuts you deep,
Slashes at your heart, and tears it.
Oh god, it's like a hole,
Tearing me in two,
And from that wound
Bleeds my life,
Bleeds my heart,
Bleeds the last of my innocence.
From that hole bleeds my soul,
Bleeds my soul,
Thus bleeds my soul.
You see it, all this blood?
Of course you don't,
Because it only bleeds within,
It's not the blood that's red,
The blood that's hot and wet.
It's the blood of will,
Blood of peace,
Blood of innocence.
You can't see this blood,

Can you?
Because it's only on my soul.
I wish, I wish, I wish,
Oh god I wish I could show it to you,
So you could see the hole you left,
When you forced me to the floor.
So you could see what perfect pain you wrought,
Such perfect pain,
Created by your drunken hands,
By your brutal breath,
Hot on me in that dark,
You caused such agony,
Such perfect pain,
That perfect pain,
That awful, perfect pain."

I'm fighting sobs by the time the last note of the mandolin fades, and Brayden is holding me up with one arm, mandolin slung around his back, and the crowd isn't cheering or clapping, only silent, so still and quiet and watching me. I can't collapse now. I can't.

"That was called 'Perfect Pain'. But don't— *ahem*—" I have to pause and collect myself, swallow past the knot in my throat, try a deep breath and start over. "Don't worry. I won't leave you hanging with something that dark. How about one more?"

This time it's Atticus who starts us off with a single huge hand-drum between his thighs, sitting on a stool to my left, Bray to my right picking a quick lilting tune, Atticus thumping steadily like a dancing heartbeat, Mim on his left with a mic and a stand, ready to sing harmony.

"I don't know you,
But that's okay.
I don't know you,
But I will, soon enough.
There's just the beat of the music,
And the beat of my heart,
And the touch of your hands,
And the spark on our tongues.
That's all we need,
If only for tonight,
If only till the hot sun rises,
If only till you see my flaws,
And you see my makeup
Streaked and smeared,
Only till you see me fix my skirt
And forget to write your number down.
It's enough for tonight,
If only till the buzz wears off,
Till the whiskey all runs out.
I don't need tomorrow,

I don't need to know you,

I don't need your name,

Or even one of your secrets,

I only need you for tonight.

I only need the beat of my heart,

And the touch of your hands,

I only need the spark on our tongues.

I only need the whiskey of your kiss

And the silence as we fumble our way to sunrise.

It's enough, it's enough,

It's got to be enough,

Because honey, it's all we'll ever get,

It's all I have to give,

If only for tonight.

You get me till the hot sun rises,

Till the whiskey runs dry,

Till I fix my skirt,

And forget to write your number down,

Till I wash the makeup off,

Till I change my skirt,

If only until I go out tomorrow night,

And sing this song again.

Because honey, I only need tonight,

And I don't need your name,

I just need the spark on our tongues

And the beat of the music,

And the whiskey of your kiss,
Only for tonight."

That's the song that has the most views on
YouTube, the song that everyone knows the words to.
Like tonight, it erases the ache of the song that came
before, leaving the crowd cheering and carrying on,
identifying with me somehow.

Only now, it feels cheap. It feels like all my jus-
tifications for how I've lived my life up till now have
been empty and vain. Like I should have known better. Because all this time Ben was a few miles away.

I let the applause wash over me and keep a smile
on my face and wait until Bray gives the cue for us to
leave the stage. We pack up quickly and stuff our gear
into Bray's Jeep, Atticus's pickup, and Vance's full-size
van. We split our pay, and everyone goes their own
way. Usually we'd party afterward, but the rest of the
band is pissed at me for being late and showing up
drunk, even though we fucking killed it…like always.
They don't get it, I decide. Fuck 'em. At least for now.
I love them, normally. But they don't get it.

Brayden drives me home, and thank god my
roommates are gone again, at some sorority function,
I think. I don't know, and I don't care. My roommates
are nice enough girls, but they're vapid at best.

I kick off my boots and peel my shirt off before I'm even in my bedroom, and then I grab the half-empty bottle of Jim Beam from under my bed and take a long chugging swig straight from the bottle as I unbutton my jeans.

"Jesus, Echo. Can't you give it a rest?"

"Fuck no, Bray-bay. I've got demons to chase."

"You're gonna hurt yourself."

"Too late for that, buddy."

He sighs in frustration and disgust. "You haven't been sober since you got home. Not for one second. You're gonna fucking pickle yourself. By which I mean you're gonna end up in the hospital."

I kick my pants off and collapse onto my bed in my bra and underwear. Bray is just straight enough to run a glance over me as I sprawl on my bed. The whiskey hits me and I let it run my mouth for me.

"Fancy another go?" I say in a fake accent, leaning forward, propping myself up with both hands on the bottle. "For ol' time's sake?"

He looks hurt, and pissed. "Fuck you, Echo. We're friends, and I'm worried about you."

"Don't be. I'll be fine."

"We have another gig on Friday. Try to be reasonably sober, will you?"

"Not a chance. But good try." Brayden leaves in a huff of anger and worry, and I'm alone with my whiskey and my regret. I lift the bottle to my lips and speak a benediction into the whiskey: "I'm sorry, Mom. I miss you." A long swig, and another whispered admission: "I'm sorry, Benji-boy. I'm so sorry. I was stupid, and I let you go."

Before long, the bottle is empty, and the world is spinning, and I feel sick, but at least the ache of everything is gone.

Thirteen: O.D.
Ben

I'VE HAD HER NUMBER THIS WHOLE TIME, AND SHE'S HAD mine.

But I haven't called her, nor has she called me.

Nor have we texted.

Nothing.

For over a month.

In between finishing the last few classes I need for my bachelor's, I've watched every Echo the Stars video there is, and I'm stunned breathless by Echo's talent. Kylie wasn't kidding: the girl can *sing*. But it's her lyrics that really push it over the edge, for me at least. I mean, the music is stunning. Complex, intricate, bursting with raw talent and passion and creativity. But Echo's lyrics…they're open and deep and aching with pain and meaning. She doesn't pull any punches. She writes from the heart, from the gut, from the soul, and some of the songs are almost embarrassingly personal in nature. She bares it all, leaves it all on stage. It's shocking, sometimes brutal and painful, and always mesmerizing.

Eventually, I decide to watch them play live. So I find their next date, a Saturday show in a packed bar. I show up early to drink, find a spot at the end of the bar where I'll be able to see the stage. They're supposed to go on at nine and I'm there at eight. I pace myself, drink slowly. 8:30 rolls around and band members show up to set up the equipment, plug in instruments and monitors and effects pedals, adjust mics and sound levels, but I don't see *her*. 8:59…and the band is milling around off-stage. I see the cellist/ bassist on her cell phone, gesturing frantically, angrily.

Finally, she gets up on the stage and takes the center mic. "So we're supposed to be playing right now, and obviously we're not. Our vocalist is running late, but she'll be here any minute. Sorry."

There's grumbling, but no one leaves. The house technician turns on some music from the in-house system, "Anji" by Simon & Garfunkel.

9:30, and finally there's noise from the back of the house, a door opening then closing, followed by heavy steps. The mandolin player shows up, basically carrying Echo. She's wasted. He snags a stool on the way to the stage, sets it up front and center and deposits Echo on it. She sits unsteadily, pawing at her hair, pulling a strand out of her mouth. Her eyes are bleary, wild. She doesn't see me, yet.

"Sorry, sorry. Bad day." She drags the mic closer, lowers it, screws it tight once more. "No sense wasting time with preamble, right? I'm Echo Leveaux, and this is Brayden MacKellan, Vance Lawson, Mim Lang, Atticus Vaughn, and Will Wolf, and we are Echo the Stars. But then you know that, don't you?" She sounds surprisingly lucid for how clearly hammered she is. She points at the drummer. "Hit it, Atticus."

The drummer, Atticus Vaughn, lays a fast, intricate beat, joined by Mim Lang on an upright bass, picking and thumping and slapping, and then everyone is playing. The first half of the song is all instrumental, and I can see Echo composing herself, breathing and closing her eyes and swaying with the music, and then finally she unlatches the mic from the stand and brings it to her lips.

"Don't you know, Mother,
How I love you?

How could you, Mother, when all we did was fight?
How could you, Mother, when you've gone into the light?
Don't you know, Mother,
How I miss you?
How could you, Mother, when you're gone?
How could you, when it's been so long?
I wasted so much time,
Wasted so much life.
Don't you know, Mother, don't you know?
Do you get messages in Heaven?
Or wherever you are...
Do you hear me, late at night,
When I cry until the sun shines bright?
Do you hear me, Mother?
I'm telling you now, I'm sorry.
I'm telling you now, I wish I'd said it then,
When I still had you here,
When I still had you near.
I'm sending this message to Heaven, Mom,
Do you hear me?
Do you hear me?
I'm sorry, Mom, I'm sorry,
I love you, Mom, I love you,
And I want to come home,
I want you to come home.
I'm sending this message to Heaven,

But I don't think it will make it there,
And neither will I."

She gasps and curls in on herself as she finishes the lyrics, and the band plays on a couple minutes longer, and then Brayden leans against her as he plays one last lilting circular melody on his mandolin. She's sobbing, and everyone, including her bandmates, is clearly wondering what to do, what to say. She pulls it together, after a moment.

"Sorry. I'm sorry, guys. My mom died recently, and I'm just—I'm trying to deal with it. Not well, clearly." She laughs bitterly. "I mean, how do you deal with that kind of regret, you know? You heard the song...I have so many regrets. So much I never got to say. I didn't feel any of this until recently...when she died I was just numb at first, you know? Just... numb. It didn't feel real. I still cried, but the reality of it, that she was really, permanently gone, it hadn't hit. I— I tried to call her. Right after I got back to Nashville, after the funeral. I wasn't even thinking, I just dialed her number, wanting to talk to her, to tell her something, to resolve the stupid shit we'd been arguing about, and—her number was disconnected. I didn't even have an old voicemail to hear her voice one more time. Just..." she waves a hand and makes her voice go high and robotic, "'We're sorry, the number you are trying to reach is no longer in service.'"

"Echo, honey, let's play another song, huh?" Brayden says, trying to ease her out of her rant.

"No, Bray, I need to say this. I need—they need to know why I'm like this." She waves him off, and now she doesn't seem quite so stable, emotionally or physically. "I didn't even get to say goodbye. I tried to call her, and she didn't answer, she wasn't there... and—I just miss her. But you know, it's not even that. It's—it's...there was this guy, right?" She sways on her seat, gripping the mic stand for balance. "There was this guy. We met, and we had this thing. You know... this *thing*. This big, important...*thing*. And I let it go. I let him go. But I didn't just let him go, did I? Oh no. Not Echo, I couldn't do anything that easy, could I? No, I had to push him away. Make him think I didn't— make him think I didn't feel what he... " She weaves unsteadily on the stool, shades her eyes, peering out at the crowd.

She sees me.

"I...am I drunker than I thought, or is that you out there, Ben?" She stands up slowly, with the careful precision of the very, very drunk, and stares at me. "It is you. Goddammit. You shouldn't be here. You said... you said you weren't coming back, and now you're here. And you're seeing me like this." She looks like she's about to pass out, swaying on her feet.

I'm standing up, moving toward the crowd toward her. "Echo?"

She looks at me. "I'm sorry, Ben."

I'm almost there, reaching for her. "It's okay, it's okay—"

"No, it's not, because I took some—" she curls forward, teetering, and vomits at her feet. "Oh god—"

She pitches forward and I catch her before she tumbles off the stage, and then I've got her in my arms. "Echo?"

She looks up at me, and her skin is pale and yellowing and the whites of her eyes are yellow too. "Not—not okay. I took a bunch of Vicodin, Ben—I'm sorry, I'm sorry, I just couldn't take it anymore—" and then she vomits again, on me, on the floor.

I glance at Brayden. "Call an ambulance."

Brayden just stares at Echo, who is limp now and barely breathing. "Echo? Jesus, what did you do?"

"CALL A FUCKING AMBULANCE!" I shout, and he jerks into motion, digging his cell phone out of his pocket and stabbing at it.

I tune out as he relays information to the operator, my sole focus on Echo. Her head lolls backward, and I roll her in my arms so she's facing down. Drool and blood-laced vomit streams from her lips, and she's gagging, gasping, groaning, crying, mumbling unintelligibly.

"Echo, stay with me baby, it's me, it's Benji, I'm here, okay? I'm here, you'll be okay, just stay with me, just hang on, okay?" My voice shakes, trembles, and it's hard to carry her without putting weight on my knee, but I don't dare put her down, so I balance against the stage.

I hear sirens, fucking sirens. My head spins, my heart clenches. I'm hallucinating, or remembering. I'm seeing the fight with Oz on Kylie's front porch, Oz stumbling backward, slamming into and rolling off the hood of a car, blood on the windshield and on the road as he hits the concrete, and then the sirens; I'm seeing Cheyenne's F-150 at the light, the red Mustang flying through the intersection and bashing into the driver's side door, toppling it over, and the blood and her head hanging, already dead, and the sirens approaching, uniformed EMS and the subtle shake of a head, because she's already dead.

And now…

Now there's sirens approaching yet again and Echo is unresponsive in my arms, and I'm unable to breathe, I need to breathe, need to breathe with her, need to breathe for her, but I can't because I'm sobbing, carrying her in a limping run toward the medics and the stretcher as they slam open the bar door and rush through the parting crowd. They take her from me and I'm answering questions automatically, but I don't know, I don't know, I don't know her blood type or what she drank or how many pills she took.

Brayden is beside me, his shoulder under my armpit keeping me upright, providing answers. "I saw an empty fifth of whiskey, but I don't know if she drank the entire thing at once. The Vicodin was mine, and there were only ten pills left." He chokes and we're supporting each other now as he falters. "She twisted her ankle a few months ago and I left the bottle for her, and I just forgot it—I didn't think she'd do this, she's never—never tried anything like this before…"

We're at the ambulance and they're lifting the stretcher into the back of the vehicle. One of the medics stops both of us with his hands outstretched. "Are either of you family?"

"She doesn't have any family here," Brayden answers. "I'm the closest thing she has."

"One of you can ride along." He gestures to the ambulance, and Brayden climbs in with a glance at me.

"Meet us at the hospital!" he shouts as the doors close.

The last I see of her is an oxygen mask going over her face, one of the medics saying something about "naloxone", and then the doors are closed and the ambulance is gone. I hobble as fast as I can toward my car. I don't know where my cane is. I can't find the Silverado, my mind drawing a blank. But then it's there in front of me and I'm twisting the key and tearing out of the parking space. I make it to the hospital in record time, find a parking spot in the ER lot and I've got another long walk to the doors, my knee screaming and on fire, but I ignore it, ignore it, grit my teeth and limp as fast as I can.

When I get into the waiting room, I see Brayden with his hands fisted in his hair, head tipped back, eyes closed, pacing back and forth in front of a stretch of empty chairs. He sees me, comes toward me.

"They're pumping her stomach right now. We won't know much until she wakes up, assuming—assuming she does."

"Is there a danger she won't?" I ask.

He nods. "Yeah. I'm not sure when she took the pills, or how many, or how much she drank on top of them. She could—she might have liver damage, maybe even brain damage...but at least she's still breathing, right? There could also be heart failure. We just don't know. There's nothing we can do but wait."

I turn away and take a step, two, and then my knee gives out on me and I collapse, catch myself on a chair and climb into it. "Shit. What the hell happened to her?"

"Her mom died," Brayden says. "It was sudden—"

"I know," I interrupt. "I was with her in San Antonio." I can't bring myself to tell him the truth.

"Ohhhh," Brayden says, realization in his voice. "You're the *other* reason she's so fucked up in the head, aren't you?"

"She wasn't like this the last time I saw her. She got drunk after the funeral, but after that she seemed… upset, obviously, because shit, who wouldn't be? But suicidal? I had no idea she'd…I didn't think she was capable of doing this to herself."

Brayden sits beside me. "I've known her since our freshman year at Belmont, and I didn't think she was either." He extends his hand. "I'm Brayden."

I shake his hand. "Ben."

"Our girl's been through some shit, and she's never been this bad." Brayden puts his head in his hands and palms his forehead. "Breakups, being cheated on, a pregnancy scare…she was always solid. She'd drink, go into her head for a while, and in time she'd be fine. Even when she was raped she didn't get this bad."

"Raped?" My voice goes thin as a razor and twice as sharp. "You mean what happened with Marcus Shaker?"

Brayden's head comes up. "You know about him?"

"Yeah, I know him," I growl. "I went to Vanderbilt with him. We played football together."

"Yeah, well, your football buddy raped Echo."

I shoot to my feet. "I never said he was my fucking *buddy*," I rasp. "I caught him trying to molest this girl, and I put him in *here*—" I gesture at the ER, "for three days. Echo told me something happened with Marcus, but she wouldn't tell me what exactly." I tumble backward, falling heavily into the chair.

"She wouldn't. She doesn't talk about it. She reported him; he got a week's suspension from school and football. That was it. And believe it or not, it was more than others in his position have gotten. She refused to leave her dorm room for two weeks straight. She nearly flunked out of three classes, missed a bunch of gigs, and lost about twenty pounds because she wouldn't eat. I had to—" He cuts off, stares between his feet, and then continues. "I had to break into her room and bribe her with shots of whiskey to get her to eat. She's always had a penchant for trying to drink her problems away, but never this bad.

She'd go on a bender for a few days, but she'd always snap out of it. I thought she'd snap out of this, too."

"She's been drinking, then?"

He laughs bitterly. "She hasn't been sober since she got back from Texas, Ben." He runs stiffened fingers through his hair. "We're close, I mean, I'm closer to her than pretty much anyone else in her life, but even I have only so much influence over her. I didn't even know what happened to her, at first. When her mom died, I mean. She just vanished. We were supposed to meet for drinks and she never showed up. Wouldn't answer her phone. Wouldn't return texts. So finally I threatened to report her missing if she didn't at least tell me what the fuck was going on. You know what I got from her?" He gives another dark, mirthless bark of laughter. "I got four words in a text message: 'Mom's dead. Stay there.'"

"So when shit gets heavy she shuts down."

"Exactly," Brayden says.

I shake my head slowly. "I guess I'm glad that it's not just me she shuts out, then."

"No, it's definitely not just you." Brayden glances at me sidelong. "She never said a word about you after she got back. Not till what she said earlier, on the stage, before she…yeah. She blamed it all on her mom dying. But there was something else, I just couldn't figure out what, and she wouldn't talk about it. Even to me, she even shut me out." He sighs, and it's part sob. "I shouldn't have left her alone. She was drinking so much, but I thought she'd snap out of it. I thought—I thought—"

I put a hand on his shoulder. "It's not your fault, Brayden. You can't *make* someone trust you."

He turns to me, clutches at me. It's awkward, because I'd thought he was straight, but the way he's wrapping his arms around me and crying on my shoulder doesn't feel that way, which has me baffled and uncomfortable. I pat his shoulder a few times until he lets go and moves away.

"Sorry, sorry." He sniffles, wipes at his eyes with his middle fingers. "I should have kept a better eye on her. I should have seen how bad it was. I should have done something. She's all I have, her and the rest of the band. My family disowned me after I came out as bi, and she never even flinched when I told her. She just accepted me as I am, even though we'd had our own little…whatever you want to call it. We had a thing when we first met, just so you know. That's long over, though."

I frown. "Wait, you and Echo…?"

He nods, his head tilted sideways, sniffling. "Yeah. One time, a few weeks after we met. She didn't know

I was bi. I told her afterward, and we were both like, yeah, we're better off as friends. And that's what it's been ever since. She didn't care, she just didn't want that for herself, you know? Which I get. It's not for everyone, but it works for me. Usually."

"You know, you've told me more about Echo in the last five minutes than I found out in the entire three days we spent together."

"That's not surprising. It's just how she is."

"It's a sucky way to be, if you're trying to get to know her," I say.

Brayden sighs. "Yeah, it really is." He glances at me. "You obviously care about her, so I'll tell you this, just…as an FYI, I suppose. She's not a long-term type of girl. She never has been, and I doubt she ever will be. She's been hurt too many times, in too many ways. She's my best friend, my family, basically. But she's not good with relationships of any kind. She just won't let herself ask for anything. She keeps everything locked inside and just…doesn't share."

"She cried. About her mom, with me."

"Damn, she did?" Brayden seems shocked. "I've never seen her cry. As we've covered, she shuts down. Gets wasted. Gets crazy, writes these raw, intense songs and sings the fuck out of 'em. That's how she gets it all out. The one thing she doesn't do is cry."

"After the funeral, I was leaving, and she just hijacked my cab. Got in and ordered the driver to take us to the nearest bar. And she got just…colossally shitfaced literally in a matter of minutes."

Brayden laughs. "Yeah, that's my girl. She can put away the whiskey like no one else. Especially when she's in a mood, you know?"

"Well, she was in a mood. She got to the point where she was just…gone. So I brought her back to my place. She got crazy, and tried…well, I'm sure you can guess. But eventually she passed out. And when she woke up, she just started…sobbing isn't even the right word. She just lost it. So, yeah. That's how we met."

"Your story has some gaps in it, my friend."

I shrug. "Not everything needs to be explained."

"True enough." He's leaning forward, elbows on his knees, wrists dangling loosely, his posture a strange, confusing mix of sexual orientation. Whatever, it's not like it matters to me, as long as he doesn't try to hit on me. He glances at me sideways. "Just be aware, whatever happens from here on out, that she may not ever open up, okay? I've known her for almost four years, and she still shuts me out."

"She never mentioned you. In Texas, I mean."

"Not surprising. She's a master at compartmentalizing." He doesn't seem upset that she never even referenced him once.

"I'm learning that."

We lapse into silence then, lost in our own thoughts. Hours pass. I send a vague message to my parents letting them know to not worry about me. I pace until my knee aches, and then I sit. Brayden paces, sits, paces. He answers a few messages on his phone, presumably from the other members of the band.

At some point in the small hours of the night, a doctor emerges from a hallway, and calls out, "Family of Echo Leveaux?"

Brayden and I both stand up; make our way over to him. "How is she?" Brayden asks.

"Are you immediate family?" the doctor asks.

"We're all she has," Brayden explains.

"I'm sorry, but I can't give out medical information to anyone except immediate family members."

Brayden paces away and tears at his hair, then returns. "Listen, she doesn't *have* any immediate family members! She has one set of grandparents, but they live in Texas and couldn't be here for days, if they make the trip at all. We are the closest thing to family she has right now, okay? Just…*please,* tell us how she is."

The doctor hesitates, his eyes flicking from mine to Brayden's and back. "All right. Well, she's doing okay, all things considered. She's breathing on her own, her heart seems fine, and initial scans make me optimistic that there won't be any lasting brain damage. You got her here in time, and that's what really counts. Much longer, and I don't think I'd be giving ya'll the same news."

He sighs and pinches the bridge of his nose before continuing. "She's resting for now, so you boys might as well go home and get some rest, come back in the morning. I've scheduled a psychological evaluation for...later this morning, I guess it is. I think I'm going to recommend detox at least, if not rehab. I'll have a referral for a mental health specialist for her, on discharge. She'll need someone, or both of you, preferably, to encourage her to seek the help she very clearly needs."

"She just lost her mother," Brayden explains. "And I doubt she'll cooperate with an evaluation. But we might as well give it a shot, right?"

"She intentionally overdosed on a significant amount of Vicodin and alcohol. That's called suicide, son." He shakes his head. "If she'll try it once, who's to say she won't try it again, when one of you isn't around to bring her in? She needs help."

"*I* know that, and *you* know that. But good luck convincing *her* of that." Brayden lets out a long, frustrated sigh. "When can I see her? I can try to talk to her."

"Tomorrow, late morning or early afternoon. We'll need to run some follow-up tests, and have her speak with an in-house psychiatrist."

"Okay, thank you, Doctor." The doctor turns and leaves, and Brayden rubs his face vigorously with both hands, then looks at me. "Can I get a ride from you? My Jeep is still at the bar."

"Sure. Come on."

I drive him back to the bar and drop him off beside his old red Wrangler. Before he gets out, he glances at me. In this moment, he looks young, small, and tired. "She'll be okay, right?"

I can't summon a smile. Don't even try. "I hope so. I really hope so."

I go home, and collapse facedown onto my bed. I hear my door creak, and I know it's Mom, checking on me. "I'm fine, Mom. I don't want to talk about it. A…friend had an…emergency."

"Is she okay?" Mom's voice is quiet, compassionate.

How does she know it's a her? I roll to my side and glance at her. "I don't know. Maybe."

"Being there for a friend who is going through a hard time is understandable, Benny," Mom says, perching on the edge of the bed beside me, trailing a hand over my forehead. "Just don't let it bring you down, okay?"

"Doing my best."

She smiles at me. "I know. Just…sometimes, we have to know when to walk away and let them find their own way."

"I can't walk away. Not again."

Mom nods, her eyes knowing. "Like I said, just… don't let it bring you down too, okay?"

"Okay."

I fall asleep and dream of sirens and ambulances, blood and vomit and hanging braids and Echo gasping, apologizing, Oz bleeding, a smoking, crumpled hood, Echo telling me goodbye, Kylie's face as I walk away…I dream of everything, of hell and pain and all the things that haunt me.

Waking up is a relief.

Fourteen: No Man Is an Island
Echo

WAKING UP CONSISTENTLY SUCKS. MORE MORNINGS than not, I loathe the moment consciousness floods through me. Waking up brings pain. Emotional pain, mental pain, physical pain.

I don't want to wake up. I keep my eyes closed and plead with whatever the fuck is out there—or isn't—to let me back under, to let me stay under where there's no pain.

But there's only waking up, my head throbbing, a viciously raw throat, a stabbing pain in my stomach. I'm dizzy, sore, confused, sluggish. I'm awake for a long time before anyone shows up to check on me. I use that time to try to remember what happened, why I'm in the hospital.

I remember being at home, drinking hard. Hating myself. Hating being me, hating my life, hating being awake. Wanting to sleep, just…sleep. Not think, not feel. I remember not caring that I had a gig. For the first time I can remember, I didn't want to sing, didn't want to perform. I just wanted to sleep.

I remember going to the bathroom and happening across a bottle of Vicodin Bray had left at my place, a while ago. I remember how I'd taken a Vic and then had a couple drinks, how tired I got, sleeping for twelve hours straight. If one pill and a couple drinks could do that…

Oh god.

I remember downing all of them, one by one, chasing them with the Beam. And then Bray showed up and physically dragged me to the gig. By which point I'd already finished the fifth, my second in two days. But he didn't know that, or that I'd taken the pills. It was all starting to hit me, I remember that, too. He dragged me to the show because he knows under most circumstances that getting on stage and singing it out will cure what ails me. Temporarily, at least.

I remember getting sleepy, so tired, being pulled under, feeling sick…

I thought I saw Ben, but I don't trust that memory.

A doctor sweeps into my hospital room, then. He's tall, dark-haired, and stern, anywhere from thirty to fifty years old. It's hard to tell, being clean-shaven with a youthful face, but his eyes are hard and tired. "Miss Leveaux."

"Doctor." I have no desire to talk to him, to hear his recriminations and faux-concern.

"How are you feeling?"

"Shitty."

He nods as if this is exactly how I should feel. "Well, I suppose this is to be expected, under the circumstances."

"Yeah? What the fuck do you know about my circumstances?" I sound hostile, because I feel hostile. I can feel him judging me, even before he opens his mouth.

"I know you recently lost your mother which, understandably, has led to some…emotional distress, you might say."

I just stare at him, knowing I should hold my tongue, because he's just doing his job. But does he have to be such a pompous dick about it?

"Emotional distress," I repeat. "Yeah, you could say that."

"And, sometimes, when we're under extreme duress, we may find ourselves making decisions that—"

"Don't lump yourself in with me, asshole. You don't know shit about me, and you don't know shit about my *emotional duress* or whatever the fuck you just said. When can I get out of here?"

He frowns at me, but doesn't seem fazed by my outburst or my profanity. "Well, we'll have to do a few tests to make sure you didn't do any lasting damage to yourself. Can you tell me how many pills you swallowed, and how much alcohol you drank?"

I sigh, and try not to snap at him. "I wasn't really counting the pills, but…nine or ten, I guess. As for how much I had to drink? That day? Or…?"

"I see. Yes, how much did you have to drink yesterday?"

"A fifth, or most of it. I don't remember. They're all starting to blur together at this point." No sense in lying about it, right?

"I see."

"You see, do you? You know what, I really don't think you *do* fucking *see*, Doctor."

"Loss affects us all differently, Miss Leveaux." He sets the chart down on his lap, clicks his slim silver pen closed, and regards me for a moment. "For example, when my wife passed away from breast cancer some years ago, I worked double and even triple shifts every single day for three months. I barely slept, barely ate.

Eventually the hospital director had to have me forcibly removed from the hospital. So you see, perhaps I do, after all, *see*. Just a little bit, at least."

"I'm sorry for your loss, Doctor. And maybe you do get it, but don't sit there and act like you get *me*, okay? Because you don't. No one does." Why am I saying this shit to him? He's not even a psychiatrist. He's just some ER doctor.

"You know, it's in times like these that I remember John Donne, who wrote in his seventeenth meditation that 'No man is an island.' People quote that a lot, but they always stop at that first part. The rest of it makes it all so much clearer, you see. You need the quote in its entirety: 'No man is an island, entire of itself; every man is a piece of the continent, a part of the main.' We're all a part of a whole, whether we want to be or not, whether we think we are or not. And, you know, the phrase 'for whom the bell tolls' that Hemingway made famous also comes from that same writing of Donne's."

The doctor leans back, crosses his legs at the ankle, and pokes at the corner of his mouth with his pen. The hardness of an ER doctor has faded, replaced by a softer and more introspective philosopher. "He opens the meditation with a bit of Latin: '*Nunc Lento Sonitu Dicunt, Morieris*', which translates to: 'Now this bell, tolling softly for another, says to me, Thou must die.' Donne then elucidates upon that phrase, saying, 'Perchance, he for whom this bell tolls may be so ill, as that he knows not it tolls for him.' It's all subjective, of course, but I've always taken this to mean that we often don't see what's right in front of us, we don't see our own afflictions for what they truly are. He writes much on affliction, Donne does, and how it not only glorifies God, but strengthens *us*. We often fail to see this, though, and we even more frequently, and sadly, fail to see the help that lies waiting for us, so close to hand. And I'm not speaking of God, Miss Leveaux. There is *always* help to be found. Donne's point in the bit about no man being an island is that we are not alone. We aren't each of us this disconnected and disconsolate dot of dirt in a sea of misery. We think we are, but it's just not true. 'Any man's death diminishes me,' Donne also writes, 'because I am involved in mankind, and therefore never send to know for whom the bell tolls; it tolls for thee.'"

I just stare at him, unable to process the sudden influx of seventeenth-century poetry, or whatever the hell. I just stare at him, because even though I refuse to show it or admit it, even to myself, his words have a profound effect on me. I swallow hard and keep my gaze level, even, keep my emotions tamped down.

"Thank you, Doctor." It's all I can manage.

He nods, prepares to stand up, and the philosopher has vanished, replaced by the brusque, efficient doctor. "Because you're classified as an attempted suicide, a psychiatric assessment is required before I can discharge you. Part of your discharge process will include referrals to qualified mental health professionals in the area. Seek help, Miss Leveaux. There is no embarrassment in needing help, every once in a while. It doesn't make you weak, it merely makes you human, just like the rest of us."

I say nothing, do nothing, and he leaves.

The evaluation is fairly standard, and I cooperate, if only so I can get out of this damn hospital. Seek help, he says. Right. It's not about weakness. That's what I didn't say to him. It's not about being afraid of being seen as weak, it's that help is a fallacy. An illusion. There is no help.

And I am an island. I always have been.

When the hospital shrink finally leaves, I sit in silence for a long, long time; it's unmitigated hell. Silence is my enemy. Where there's silence, there are endless thoughts, the cycle of guilt and grief and heartache and regret, all unending and spinning through me until I can't breathe or move or speak or get out from under the weight of it all. It's why

I drank, and it's why I took the pills. Not because I wanted to die. It wasn't about death, or ending it all. It was just about wanting to silence the noise, needing to stop the cycle in my head and my heart. I'm not suicidal. I'm just fucked up, and don't know how to fix it.

The door to my room swings open, and Brayden walks in. He's such a beautiful boy. Tall and slim and sleek, brown hair and such uniquely dark blue eyes, such killer fashion sensibility. He's always put together. Brayden's constant presence has been a reassurance to me in the past few years. He's always there, and he's always handsome and sophisticated, and so talented; those delicate, manicured hands of his can make a mandolin sing like an angel.

Yet, as he enters my hospital room, he's not put together. He has dark circles under his eyes, he's unshaven, and he's wearing the same clothes as yesterday. He looks haunted, exhausted.

He drags a chair over to my bedside, and he sits down, stares at me without speaking. When he does, his voice breaks, and his eyes waver, shine, fill with tears. "Fuck you, Echo Leveaux. *Fuck you* for doing that to me."

That is so not what I expected from him. "Bray, I—"

"You what? What can you say to me, Echo? After all we've been through, you…you try to *kill* yourself? What can you say to me? What can you *possibly* say that can erase what I just went through? Watching you collapse, watching you make a fool of yourself in front of a hundred and fifty people? Watching you vomit all over yourself, all over Ben? Watching you puke blood? Watching you—watching you stop breathing? How could you…how could you be so—so *fucking selfish?*" He shouts that last part so loudly I flinch backward, shocked and horrified. Brayden is not a loud or angry person, making this so, so much worse.

"That ride to the hospital…that was the longest ride of my life, Echo. You're all I have left. You *know* that. You *know* that! You were there when I told them, Echo. You—you heard what they said. 'No son of ours', they said. 'Never show your face here,' they said. And you heard it. I've never pushed you, Echo. I always let you have your space. I let you push me away when you're hurting. I let you drink yourself into a stupor because, god, I know how bad you need to do that sometimes, and I fucking get it. You can't trust anyone, and I *get* it. I don't trust anyone either, except you. Except now…can I even trust you anymore? I don't know. You—you fucking O.D. on *my* goddamn Vicodin? How could you?"

I get angry. "It's not about you, Brayden!" I shout.

"That's just your problem, Echo! You don't realize that it is about me!" He's shouting back. "You just don't see that there are people all around you who care, who want to be there for you, but you just won't let us! You don't see that all of us in the band love you! And you don't see that we have our own drama to deal with, no, you only see yours. Vance? His dad is an alcoholic, and beat him bloody every single day of his life until he finally got away. Atticus? His brother offed himself last year. But you didn't know that, did you? Because you're so sucked into your own head *all the fucking time!* Mim is the most normal of us, and she's so fucking insecure about herself that she dresses like a guy to disguise her body, and god only knows what happened to make her that way. Will does coke, did you know that? He snorts mountains of the shit. He's gonna be the next one to O.D., I'm guessing, which is just *super*. And me? The one who can't figure out if he likes girls or boys better? My parents disowned me, and my brother hates me because his best friend fell in love with me, his *male* best friend, and we won't even go into my sister.

"Didn't know *any* of that, did you? And oh, wait! There's Ben, who you didn't fucking tell me about! Ben, who sat out in that waiting room for *six hours,* who you vomited on, who was fucking sobbing over you. I don't even know what the deal is there, but I can guess. He likes you, but you just can't have that, so you push him away because *god forbid* you give anyone a chance. God forbid you let anyone in, even a little bit. Yeah, I've been hurt and betrayed and cheated on too, and that's by guys *and* girls, and I still take a chance on people. But you…oh no. You just shut us all out, and when it's all too much, instead of letting us help you, you pop a bunch of Vicodin and wash it all down with a bottle of whiskey. Because that's better than *trusting* me, or Ben, or anyone, apparently. But yeah, you're right. It's not about me, is it?"

He stands up, moves toward the door. "I love you, Echo. I want to be there for you. I have been, and I will be. But I will *not* sit by and watch you do this to yourself. This is your last chance with me, babe. Do this again, and I'm gone. And if I go, so will the band. It's not an ultimatum, or a threat. It's just…the facts." He gives me one last sad glance. "Get help, Echo."

And then he's gone without a goodbye or a backward glance, and I'm trying to cry, but I just can't, because it's all stuck inside me. Just…stuck.

Moments later—or maybe it's minutes, or even hours—the door opens again, and Ben comes in. I groan and slide down to the horizontal, cover my face with the thin white scratchy blanket. "It is you," I say. "I was hoping you were a hallucination."

"Wow. What a welcome." He sounds bitter, unsurprisingly.

"I don't want you to see me like this."

"Too late. I've already seen you at your worst, Echo, or did you forget how we met?"

I'm not done being self-destructive, clearly, judging by my next words. "Go away, Ben."

"So it's like that, is it?"

I shake my head. "No, I—" I fight a sob. "You deserve better than this, Ben. I—I regret how I ended things. But…I just…I need some time, okay? I need—I need to get—" It's too hard to even finish. It's all a hot wet hard knot in my throat, Brayden's righteous, justified anger, my embarrassment, my regret, my guilt, it's all too much.

"Okay, Echo. It's fine. I get it." He stands up, and I notice he has a new cane, a polished length of shiny brown wood with a curving silver handle.

I reach for him, grab at his arm, desperate to make him understand. "No, Ben, please, just wait a second."

"You just told me to go away, that you need time—"

"But I'm not…I'm not pushing you away, okay? I just—I fucked everything up. I'm a mess, an awful shitty mess, and I want to—clean myself up, I guess. I don't want you to go away, not forever. I just want you to see me when I have something to offer besides..." I choke on my words, my tears, "besides what I am right now."

"But Echo, don't you get it? I care about who you are right now, regardless of what you think you have to offer or not."

"That's because you're a better person than I am." I breathe slowly and deeply in an attempt to sound halfway intelligible. "Maybe this is me still being selfish, but I don't want you to be with me when I'm like this. I want better for you from me, for myself. God, that doesn't even make any sense. It sounded better in my head."

"No, I get it." He grabs my hand, his big, rough, tanned palm engulfing mine. "I'm here, though, okay?"

"You'll wait?" I pull at him, wanting his proximity, now that he's here and he's real and he doesn't seem to hate me. "You'll wait for me?"

He nods. "I'll wait."

I gaze up at him. I feel so needy, all of a sudden. Like all the years of holding myself rigidly strong and never needing anyone have left me empty inside and hungry for whatever I can get.

"Kiss me?" I ask, feeling small and hopeful.

He stares at me for a long moment, and then his brows draw down and his expression shifts to reflect some inner pain. "No, Echo. See, I'm selfish too. I want all of you. I don't just want one kiss because you feel bad about yourself."

He crouches at my bedside, and I roll to face him, and he has both of my hands in his. Tears stream down my face. "Ben—"

He ignores me and keeps talking. "I want more than one kiss. I want more than one *night,* more than one tumble in the sheets."

"But I don't know how—"

"It's simple, Echo. You just have to learn how to be totally vulnerable, that's all."

I laugh. "Is that all? Just bare all my secrets, just like that? Just...be totally vulnerable?"

"That's all."

I sniff and roll onto my back, stare at the ceiling through blurry, red-rimmed eyes. "Let me just rip my chest open real quick, then." I say it with a laugh, but the laugh turns to a sob, and then I'm sobbing hard, and then I have to twist to the side so he doesn't see how terrified I am. I'm crying because it's impossible, because I just don't know how to do what he wants.

"Do it, Echo. Rip your chest open, and let me in. Let me see you bleed. I can't promise I can make it all okay, because I can't. But I can promise to be there when it's not."

I look at him over my shoulder, my body still facing away, and my hair obscures my vision, so I don't see him coming, I smell him first—soap, shampoo, cologne, and that otherness of Ben-scent—and then I feel him, an all-consuming presence over me, fingertips brushing my hair away, hand cupping under my neck and lifting my head, and his lips touch mine softly, briefly, gently.

It's not a kiss; it's a promise of kisses to come.

He goes, then, and I let him go, even though I want to scream and cling to him and cry and beg him to carry me away and wrap us back up in that bubble, where nothing mattered and nothing hurt.

He goes, and I need whiskey with a vicious desperation that has me clawing at the sheets.

And that's when I know I have a problem.

A lot has happened in the last two weeks and while I still don't completely have my shit together, at least I know it and I'm trying to do something about it. Bray is sitting next to me on the couch, shirtless, hair messy, eyeliner from the night before smeared across his eyelids. He's in a "gay phase", as he puts it, which means he borrows my skirts and wears my makeup—poorly applied, usually, but whatever. Maybe I should give him makeup lessons. He has a bird tattooed on his chest, on the left side, over his heart. It's a lark, he once told me, but wouldn't explain its meaning. It's a gorgeous tattoo, done life-size in photorealistic detail and color. The lark is perched on a branch, crest raised, mouth open to sing, wings spread as it prepares to take flight.

He leans forward, touches the record button on the GoPro that faces us, set up on a tripod. "Hey, hey, ya'll. I'm Brayden and this Echo, *ob*viously. Since Echo the Stars is on temporary hiatus, we know all ya'll need your fix of Echo's singing, and possibly my magical mandolin. So, here we are. This is a personal project, I should probably point out. No filters, no polish, just Echo and I as we are. I haven't even slept yet, and it's six a.m. I'm still wearing last night's makeup, and I lost my shirt at some point, but I don't care. We're just gonna make some music and put it out there. This is for us. And hopefully, ya'll will like it, too."

I glance at him. "Bray-bay?"

"Yes, my dear?"

"You're rambling. Shut up and play your mandolin."

He sticks his tongue out at me. "Meanie-head. But alas, you're right. Without further ado…" He flexes the fingers on his chord-hand, closes his eyes and ducks his head, and then begins strumming a slow, mournful melody.

I sing:

"Forgive me, forgive me…forgive me,
But I just can't get those words out,
Those two little words, can't set 'em free,
Forgive me, forgive me, forgive me,
I should be able to say it, should be easy,
But those words, they get stuck
And anyway it's not like you give a fuck
If I say I'm sorry, they're just words, two little words,
That mean so little,
Too little, too late,
And they just can't erase the hate I pile on myself,
Can't bury the guilt I keep on my shelf,
Can't bring down these walls,
Can't tear down these halls,
Even if I beg you on bended knee,
Forgive me, forgive me,
Forgive me,
I should be able to say it,
But those words just get stuck,
And anyway it's not like you give a fuck,

And it's just my luck,
You'd forgive me, you'd forgive me
Like it's just that easy,
Because we all know the truth,
We all know the hardest part,
The thing that's really an art,
Is when I say forgive me, forgive me,
Forgive me,
Is to say it to myself,
To take the guilt off the shelf,
To bring down my walls,
To tear down the halls,
To beg myself, to plead with my own soul,
Forgive me, forgive me, forgive me."

"That was, obviously, a song called 'Forgive Me'." Brayden tilts his mandolin so the rounded bottom rests on his thighs, leans his chin on the edge of the headstock, and then gazes at me sidelong. "And Echo? Just so you know, *I* forgive you."

My chin wavers, and I try to smile, and then he stops the recording and pulls me into a hug. "Thanks, Bray."

"Love you, babes." He inclines toward me, kisses me on the temple. "I've gotta crash. Be good, you."

He settles his mandolin in its case, clips the latches closed, carries it to his bedroom and closes the door behind himself.

We're sharing an apartment, Brayden and I. The girls I was living with were no good for me to be around. Really, the only thing we had in common was partying and I'm determined to keep away from that lifestyle. Bray's lease was up, so we decided to get a place together. He keeps an eye on me, making sure I go to my appointments with Dr. Pruitt at the counseling office, and makes sure I don't do anything stupid. This way, we can make music together all the time. The other kids in the band agreed that we needed a hiatus.

That *I* needed a hiatus.

It's been two months since I O.D.'d, and I've exchanged a few texts with Ben, but I haven't seen him. I don't know what he's doing. Finishing his degree, I guess. Good for him.

I'm in bed now, and it's 3 a.m., and I'm listening to "3 A.M." by Gregory Alan Isakov. My phone buzzes in my hands and the gray box pops up over the Pandora app, with Ben's words, and his name as he saved it—Benji:

Just wanted you to know, I'm still waiting for you.

I stare at the screen for a long, long time before my fingers begin typing out a reply: *And just so YOU know, I'm still working on things. Keep waiting. PLZ?*

As long as I need to.

Promise?

Promise.

The question for me becomes: when *will* I be ready? Will it ever happen? Because I still don't know how to be what he wants me to be. I'm not even sure what he wants. Exclusivity? A long-term relationship? To be, what? Lovers? Is that a term monogamous types still use? I don't know. I've never done that.

And I have so many fears: If he knew my history, in terms of sex, would he still want me? I mean, let's face it, I'm kind of a slut. It's a self-appointed and accepted label. The first time a guy called me that, I didn't hit him, didn't slap him, didn't walk out. I sat back and thought about it, and then nodded and agreed with him. *Yeah,* I said. *I guess I am, aren't I? And what does that make you?* A slut-fucker. Not a good thing, I'm thinking now.

Is that what Ben wants? What he deserves? I mean, yeah, I'm good at sex. He likes what I've got going on, obviously, but if he knew how many have been there before him, would he still feel the same way?

My bedroom door opens and Brayden sticks his head in. "You think too damn loud, girl. You may never be ready to love that boy. But you'll never know unless you try."

I stare at his silhouette. "Was I talking out loud?"

"No, I just know what you're thinking. I mean, it's kind of obvious." He blows me a kiss. "Now, shut off your brain and go to sleep."

I blow a raspberry at him. "I wouldn't be up at three in the fucking morning if I could do that, Bray-bay."

"I know. But try."

"Yeah, yeah." I wave him away, and he closes the door.

I stare at my phone for a while longer. *You still up?* I text him.

Yup. Why?

You know where Fannie Mae Dees Park is?

Yeah...?

Meet me there.

When?

Now?

Be there in 10.

I get out of bed, my hands shaking, heart palpitating, and rinse off in the shower. I brush my hair till it shines and leave it loose, brush my teeth, put on some deodorant and perfume, and then slip into a sleeveless white full-length dress, no bra, no panties. I step into sandals, stuff my phone in my purse, and head toward the door.

Brayden is sitting on the couch, facing the coffee table, wearing nothing but a black miniskirt. It just looks so *weird*. He's really embracing this side of himself, apparently, and good for him. I love him regardless, and I'm proud of his fearlessness, but... it's just weird. He's talked about being bisexual, and I've met a few of the guys he's "dated", but I've never seen any actual hard proof that he's actually *done* anything to speak of...in that way, I mean. He's always been impeccably dressed, a little too well dressed, really, which was my first indicator. But he was always dressed like a *guy*. And a partially gay guy, sure, in pants and shirts and boots and scarves, mostly. This Bray that wears my skirts and puts on makeup is...a little hard to get used to.

As I pass him by, I get a look at what he's doing: rolling a joint. I stop and stare. "I didn't know you smoked pot, Brayden."

He starts, gasps, and claps a hand over the lark adorning his chest. "Jesus, Echo. You scared me." He shrugs. "I used to. I stopped for a while."

"Oh. Um, okay."

He licks the paper and seals the joint, then turns on the couch to glance at me. "Is it a problem?"

It's my turn to shrug. "No, I guess not."

"You want some?"

I almost do, but I hesitate. I think about Ben, waiting for me. "No, thanks. Probably not a good idea for me."

He blinks at me, owlishly. "No, I guess it wouldn't be. Sorry." He then takes in my appearance. "Nice dress. I'd rethink going braless, though. Where are you off to?"

"Meeting Ben."

"At three in the morning?"

"I'm awake, he's awake and, like you said, I'll never know unless I try." I lift my tits through the thin white cotton and let them fall. "And besides, I like how I look without a bra. It feels nice. Freeing."

He nods and shrugs. "Okay, then. Just...don't run. You might smack yourself in the face with those puppies."

I lean across the couch and smack him on the back of the head. "Shut up, weirdo."

"I'm not weird. I'm just...exploring myself."

"You're wearing my miniskirt."

"So?"

"It's weird," I say. "And...I'm not sure I want to know the answer to this, but what are you wearing underneath it?"

"You don't want to know."

I close my eyes and shake my head. "No, you know what? Forget I asked. Just wash it and put it back when you're done."

"Sure thing, babes." He blows me a kiss. "Go get him, tiger."

"Rawr." I make claws with my fingers, and then leave Brayden to his marijuana.

I feel hopeful as I walk to the park; hopeful, yes, but also shaking with fear, and nearly paralyzed with doubt.

Fifteen: Giving In
Ben

I'm sitting on top of a picnic table under the gazebo at Fannie Mae Dees Park. It's warm out despite the hour, and still. Quiet. There's a playground not far away, with a stone dragon diving into the earth and remerging, painted a dozen different colors.

I wonder what's going to happen, what Echo will be like, what she'll say, where this will go. I can't even begin to guess. I know she's doing better. I've watched her and Bray's YouTube music videos, which they post with prolific frequency. They're more like musical video journals, though, than a typical music video. The lyrics Echo sings are painfully honest, discussing the nature of pain, the problem of addiction, discussing her mother's death and how she's having such a hard time dealing with it. She holds absolutely nothing back; it's heartbreakingly courageous and breathtakingly daring.

I don't hear her approach. I feel the picnic table shift and creak, and then she's sitting beside me. I take a deep breath, eyes closed, praying and hoping and not daring to hope. And then I look at her, and my heart stops, lurches in my chest, and I'm struck dumb.

She's wearing a floor-length white dress held up by thin, nearly-invisible straps. It falls to her feet, clings to her curves. The material is bunched around her knees so the hem doesn't catch on her sandals, and the cotton is pinched between her thighs, cupping the V of her core, clinging to her flat stomach and hugging her ribs. Her breasts bulge against the fabric, pulling it taut, making it erotically apparent that she's not wearing a bra. I can see the outline of her nipples and a hint of the darker circle of her areolae. My gaze dips back to the apex of her thighs, and I'm pretty sure she's not wearing anything down there either. Her blonde hair is loose around her shoulders and face, thick and wheat-golden and glistening, as if she just brushed it. She smells clean, freshly showered, with a hint of something citrus.

"You look incredible, Echo," I say.

She ducks her head and smiles. "Thanks." She nudges me with her shoulder. "You're just saying that because I didn't put on a bra."

"Or underwear." I curl my arm around her shoulders and pull her against me. "But no, as much as I do enjoy that particular view, it's you. *You* are beautiful." I sense we have a serious conversation coming, and force myself to put my need for her on a chain, keep my lust reined in.

"Thank you." She rests her head on my shoulder for a moment, and then pulls away. "So, I was waiting to see you until I felt...ready. But Brayden informed me that I might not ever feel ready, and I realized he was right. I owe it to you to tell you that I'm—I'm not sure I can ever be what you deserve, Ben. I'm not sure I know how to be the kind of girl you want. But...I want to be. I want to at least try."

"Echo, how do you not understand? Just be you. That's all I want. And as for what I deserve? That's horseshit. No, not even that, it's...*what I deserve* isn't even a real thing. What I deserve is what I want. And I want you."

"You make it seem so easy."

"Well, it is. Or, it's simple, at least. Maybe not easy. But sometimes the hardest things are the simplest."

She pulls the white cotton of her dress up around her knees, baring her calves, and a pair of strappy white sandals. She's silent for a while, and I wait for her to speak. "My father is French. He's a musician, a really amazingly talented one, too. He and my mom met at Juilliard. He was there on a violin scholarship and, from what my mom told me, he barely spoke any English. He was a wizard with the violin, though, and gorgeous, with a sexy accent and all that. Well, they fell in love, and...she was ice-skating with him when she fell and broke her ankle and messed up her Achilles tendon. He stayed with her, took care of her, supported her, and it seemed like they were just...destined to be together.

"After my mom officially withdrew from Juilliard, she and my father got married. They were both not even twenty, at the time. And...Mom got pregnant within weeks and had me nine months later. And he stayed around. They lived in New York, and Mom started going to school for nursing at night while Dad took care of me. And then, one day Mom came home from class late one night. I was in my crib, and our neighbor was sitting on the couch, watching TV. My dad was nowhere to be found. His things were gone, all of his clothes, his violin, and the money they'd saved. All of it. He didn't leave a note, and she never saw him again. He withdrew from Juilliard without any notice, mid-semester. Went back to France, apparently. Just...left. Cleaned Mom out, like he took every single dollar they had and even stole some of her jewelry."

Echo shifts on the bench, staring at her feet. "Mom moved back to Texas where she'd grown up, lived with Grandma and Grandpa, transferred to a community college and got her nursing degree. She never had the money to get a divorce, and by the time she did have enough money there didn't seem to be any point, because it had been years and he never sent a letter or anything, never made contact. Jean-Luc Leveaux. That's his name. I found him, actually, my senior year of high school. He lives in Paris. He's remarried, with three other kids. Plays for the *Orchestre de Paris*. I even sent him a letter, and a picture of myself. I look like him, enough that it's clear I'm his daughter."

"Did he write you back?"

She shakes her head. "No. But I'd already been accepted to Belmont by then, and I got a notice saying my entire tuition had been paid for up front, all four years worth. No letter, no explanation. Mom wanted me to give it back, but...how do you do that? He'd had them calculate how much my entire degree would be and sent a check, apparently. There was no way to undo it, and besides, how do you turn down free college?

"That was another part of what Mom and I disagreed on. She was still so angry, so hurt, and so bitter about him, she wanted me to switch schools, or tell them to apply it to someone else's tuition, or anything, *anything* other than accept a single thing from him. But I went anyway, and I don't think she ever forgave me for it. She didn't want me to go there in the first place so that, on top of what she saw as a betrayal…? She wouldn't come with me for my orientation. I moved here by myself."

"Damn." I shake my head. "It's hard to reconcile that with what I knew about Cheyenne."

"I know. She was always so level-headed and kind and loving, and until that we never argued about anything, ever. That's what made it so hard. I didn't know how to be mad at her; I just wanted to forget it all, to move on. I just wanted her to…to be proud of me. To see how amazing Echo the Stars is. To just…get over it. But she couldn't. And then she died, and I never got to say goodbye, never got to—" She breaks off and puts her face in her hands, shudders, shakes, weeps.

I pull her against me. "Ssshhh. Echo, I know. I know. I'm so sorry."

She cries for a moment, and then straightens up and wipes at her eyes. "I think that's something I'll never get over—that she died and the last words we had were in anger." She sniffs, wipes her eyes again. "I think I'm also a lot more angry at my dad than I've ever realized. I've been talking to a therapist at school, and this is something we've just started touching on. He abandoned me. My dad, I mean. I never knew him, never saw a picture of him or knew his name, not until I was a teenager. Mom just never talked about him. I asked, when I was…six? And then again when I was eight, and then ten, and twelve, and she just said it wasn't a topic she was willing to talk about. Finally, when I was fourteen, I refused to leave her alone until she told me *something*. I pestered her for weeks about it. Wrote her notes and letters, left them in her purse and in her gym bag, on the fridge, written in lipstick on the bathroom mirror. I never left her alone about it. I refused to eat for three days, too. That was what broke her, eventually, because I refused to eat. She tried to force-feed me, and that…didn't go well. We both ended up covered in food, wrestling on the kitchen floor, laughing our asses off, and then she was crying, and told me the whole story. I was fourteen, almost fifteen when she told me."

"Damn. She *really* didn't want to talk about it, huh?" I try to insert some humor, but it falls flat.

Echo shakes her head. "No, she didn't. She never got over it. Or over him. And neither did I. He left us, just…walked out without looking back. I was just a baby, and Mom was…so young, and she loved him so much. I could hear it in her voice when she told me about him. The effect that his abandonment has had on me, to this day is…something I'm still uncovering."

"Like what?" I ask. I want to delve deep while she's so unexpectedly opening up.

"Like…god, *everything*. It's a large part of the way I am. The one man that was supposed to love me and be there for me…just walked away. Growing up, I always wondered why my father wasn't around. I invented stories, like girls do about that kind of thing. I think his abandonment instilled in me very early on this innate distrust of men. This just…instinctive suspicion that if my own father would do that, then so would other guys. It also made me needy for male attention. Mom never dated again. Not once that I ever knew of. I told you that, I think. Well, I grew up never having a guy around, except Grandpa, and God bless him, but he's a cranky old farmer. Gruff, and not real affectionate. The only sign of affection he's ever shown is calling me 'sweet-pea.' And we didn't see them a whole lot. Mom worked a ton, and they were busy with the farm. So there was Grandpa, but

I wouldn't really call him a father figure." She pinches her dress, twists the fabric, lets it go, pinches and twists again. "So I started looking for male attention pretty young, is what I'm getting at. I had my first kiss at eleven, started messing around with seventh and eighth grade boys at twelve. Lost my virginity at thirteen to a high school freshman. In his defense, he didn't know I was thirteen. I told him I was fourteen, and he'd only just turned fifteen. It was downhill from there."

"Thirteen. That's…early." It's all I can say. I don't even know what I'm supposed to think.

"Yeah. By high school I already had a reputation for being…easy." She glances at me, and I see a hint of something wet in her eyes, but her posture is closed off, so I just let her talk. "And I was. All through high school, I had a different boyfriend every few weeks. They knew it was only about one thing, and they never tried to pretend it was anything but sex. Except Steven Diller. He really thought he was in love with me. He wanted to believe my reputation was all just nasty rumors, bless his heart. He was a cute, sweet, earnest kid. I popped his cherry in the back of his soccer-mom minivan, and I think that was when he realized the truth about me. He wasn't trying to be hurtful, I get that now and I got it back then, too, but the fact that I popped his cherry and then he just dumped me…that hurt. More than I thought it would. Before that he was so sweet and considerate and wouldn't hear bad talk about me. He defended me to the point of being picked on for it. Until I fucked him, and he realized I really *was* a skank, and then he just dumped me like a bad habit. He was just a naïve kid, but it still hurt." She lets out a breath, tents her fingers over her mouth and nose.

"You don't owe me any explanations, Echo—" I start.

"I do, though. You want to be with me? You think you care about me, or whatever? Then you need to know what you're signing on for."

"Where was your mom during all this?" I can't help asking. "Didn't she know?"

Echo laughs through a bitter sob. "She was a single mom just trying to make ends meet. She was working sixty hours a week and going to night school, first to get her RN, and then to get her physical therapy degree. I think she knew, but she didn't know what she could do about it. I was on birth control by fourteen, so I think she did know, but…she never did anything to stop it. She's…she was my mom, and I loved her—love her? I don't know—but I feel like I hold her a little responsible for how I am, you know?

I can't blame it all on Dad leaving me. Mom didn't do anything to try to curb my promiscuity. I mean, in the end, it's all me, though. It's my choice to be this way. I put it in the present tense, because it's how I still am. Not since—not since I met you. I haven't been with anyone since I met you. You have to believe that. But up until I met you in Texas, I was…I *am*—" She halts, takes a deep breath and lets it out, and then pivots on the tabletop to look me in the eye. "I've always been kind of a slut, Ben. Let's call a spade a spade, here. Just in the interest of full disclosure, I guess. But after what happened with Marcus, I stopped even trying to pretend to date. I just embraced the one-night stand mentality, I guess.

"I thought Marcus was nice. I thought he…well, I'd heard rumors, but he was always really sweet with me, until we went to that party. He got me super drunk and dragged me up to a dark, empty room, and he put his—his hand over my mouth and—I couldn't stop him. I thought it was my fault at first. I'd teased him. He knew my reputation, but I cock-teased him. I wouldn't put out right away, just to—to play with him, I guess. I don't know. I thought it would be fun. I don't know. I just…after it happened, I got even more messed up in the head. Bray finally got through to me and helped me see it wasn't my fault. Even if I had been a cock-tease, it didn't justify what he did." She stifles a sob. "God, Bray has saved me so many times."

"Shit, Echo. Just…shit." I don't know what else to say.

She nods, lets out a slow, shaky breath. "So there it is." She stands up, rolls her shoulders, and drags her hands through her hair, pulling it back over her shoulders, straightens her dress.

And then she starts to walk away.

"Echo? Where are you going?"

"Now you know the truth about me. And you're…*good*. You were a virgin until you met me. So you and I, we're just not—"

I've caught up to her, and I grab her by the shoulders, spin her around, pull her against me.

I kiss her. I capture her face in both of my hands, cup her cheeks and feel the wetness of tears, pull her close and feel the soft press of her breasts against my chest and her hips bumping against mine, and I kiss her. My lips slide boldly across hers, feel the plump softness and slight moisture of her lips, and then her mouth opens and her tongue scrapes over my teeth and finds my tongue, traces my lips. Her hands are pinned between our bodies, and her fingers dig into my shirt, they bunch and twist the fabric until she's got double-fistfuls, and she's pulling at me, lifting up on her toes and gasping into the kiss.

And then she breaks away with a sob, lowering herself slowly, eyes wet, shimmering, hands still fisted in my shirt. "Ben…" She lets go of my shirt and smooths it with her palms. "Didn't you hear anything I just said?"

I catch her wrists. "Every word, Echo. And I know what you're doing."

She frowns up at me. "What am I doing?"

"You're still pushing me away, this time with the truth. Or with what you think will scare me away." I refuse to let her go when she tries to free her hands. "And it's not going to work."

"You said you didn't know anything about me, and Brayden told me I push people away and shut them out, so I was just…trying to be open."

"Yeah, I'll buy that. But you're scared shitless, Echo. I can see it, I can hear it, and I can feel it. Your instinctive reaction is to push."

"How am I pushing, Ben? I'm just telling you the truth." She jerks, but I keep a grip on her wrists. "Let go, Ben!"

"The truth? Maybe. But you clearly thought that if I knew your history, it would push me away. It's not working."

"So you don't care?"

"About what?"

She finally rotates her wrists hard and fast, breaking my hold on her, and backs away. "That I'm a—"

I cut in over her. "No, Echo, I don't. Why should it matter to me how many sexual partners you've had? Is that supposed to be a turn-off to me? Is it supposed to scare me? Make me jealous?"

"Yes! To anyone with a lick of common sense, yes!" she shouts.

"Then I'm clearly lacking in sense." I follow her as she backs away from me. "Echo, stop trying to get away from me and fucking listen, okay? I like you. I like who you are. I liked who you were in Texas, when I didn't know a damn thing about you except your name. I liked you before I knew you were this—this insanely talented musician, before I heard you sing, before I heard the things you write about. I liked you before I met Brayden, your very confusing friend. I liked who you were before you had a nervous breakdown or whatever that was, and I *still* like you now. More, even, because you woman-ed up and handled your shit, and I respect that. I respect you as an artist, and when Kylie Calloway is your best friend, you learn a bit about music, just by the process of osmosis or whatever."

"Kylie Calloway?" Echo repeats. "That's the best friend you fell in love with?"

I nod. "Yeah, why?"

"I've seen her and Oz play, and they're incredible. I've had a couple classes with her, actually. She's wicked talented."

I sigh. "Yeah, she is. And so is Oz."

"And Oz, her husband, he's your cousin, right?"

I shrug. "I guess so. I'm still working on that part." I cup the back of her neck. "Quit trying to change the subject."

"I'm not." She's frozen under my touch, gazing up at me, eyes wide and wavering and fearful and hopeful. "I just…I don't get how you can just not care that I've been with so many guys I can't count them on both hands, or even both hands and feet."

"We've all got our journeys, Echo. I can't change who you are, I can't change where your life has taken you, or the choices you've made. Is knowing you've been with however many other guys, like…I don't know—something I feel great about? No, if you want honesty. I really don't know how I feel about it. A little uncomfortable I guess, but mostly jealous. I want you all to myself. But does it make me care for you any less? No. Does it make me think less of you as a person? No."

She tries to look away, but I tilt her chin up with a forefinger so she's looking at me, so she sees my honesty, my vulnerability. "All of that, your past… Echo, it's part of who you are. You can't pick and choose which parts of a person you love, Echo. You love the whole person, or no part of them. Good and bad, all of it."

"Don't play with me, Ben." She backs away, shrugging off my touch, and stabs at me with her finger. "*Don't* say shit you don't mean, don't—don't make promises you can't keep. Just…*don't*."

"Why are you getting defensive, Echo? What did I say to make you angry?" I stand still, a foot away from her, hands at my sides.

She turns away, crosses her arms under her breasts. "*Love,* Ben. You said 'which parts of a person you *love.*' Using that word, it's…just cruel. How can you say that to me? How can you act like you could— like you could…" her shoulders shake, and she has to gasp for breath, "like you could love me?"

"How can *you* act like I couldn't possibly love you? Is it so far-fetched? So impossible?"

"Yes!"

"Why?"

"Because—I don't know! It just is! You shouldn't."

I move up behind her, stand with my front flush against her back. Wrap my arms around her waist, whisper in her ears. "But I do. Or, I'm falling that way, at least. Why is it so hard for you to let anyone get close?"

"Because I'm afraid, Ben! My dad left before he even knew me! I know it's not rational, I know logically that it didn't have anything to do with me, but I can't change how I feel about it! I've tried, I've fucking tried, and I can't—I just can't shake it. No guy's ever wanted me except for sex. No one's even tried, it's just always been...fuck once and done. Ever since I was a kid, I just wanted someone to *see* me. To—to *want* me. Even Mom, god, I loved her so fucking much, but she was always working. And it sometimes felt like—like working was more important than...me."

She collapses to the ground, sitting down hard on the concrete of the pathway, her shoulders shaking with silent sobs, arms wrapped around her drawn-up knees. "It feels like such a betrayal of her memory to say this, but...I've always felt deep down like maybe she resented me, or blamed me for Dad leaving, or...that she just couldn't love me as much as she should've. Why would she let me sleep around as much as I did and never try to stop me? Why didn't she care enough to stop me? And if she didn't love me that much, my own mother, the only person I've ever loved, ever really—the only person that's ever been consistent in my life? How could anyone else love me?

And you know what? No one ever has."

"Maybe because all the guys you've been with, you picked them because you knew deep down they wouldn't even try, because that was easier than having them leave? I don't know, I'm just guessing. I don't know, Echo.

"I don't have any answers to all these questions. I'm not a psychiatrist or a therapist or whatever. I can't fix you and I can't solve all those lingering issues, and I'm not gonna try to fix you, or even say you *need* fixing, because to me, Echo, you are who you are, *right now.* And that's the person I can't seem to stop thinking about, can't seem to stop wanting to be around. From the moment I met you, I've just been…drawn to you. Attracted to you physically, yes, and that in fucking spades. But I'm attracted to *who you are,* Echo. I've seen you at your worst, and I'm still here, waiting for you to stop fighting this, to stop fighting me, to stop fighting *us* and just let yourself be. Let yourself have what *you* want."

"I don't *know* what I want!"

"Bullshit." I pull her to her feet, wrap her in in my arms, and she looks up at me. I can see hope finally shining through the fear. "You want what everyone wants: love, acceptance, belonging. To be taken care of."

"And you can give me that?" Her palms rest flat on my chest, and her eyes are bright despite the skepticism in her voice.

"I can sure as hell try," I tell her, gazing down at her, into her dark, damp brown eyes.

"Then I guess…" She inhales deeply, lets it out slowly, and then rests her cheek against my chest, melting into my arms. "I guess I can try to let you."

I curl my arms around her waist and we stand there for who knows how long, just holding each other.

Eventually she props her chin on my chest, her hands on the backs of my shoulders, and her eyes find mine. "Now what?"

I shrug. "I don't know. This is new for me, too."

"How about you take me home? I have a door that closes, and I'm sure Brayden can take a hint…"

My hands wander down her back, and I finally loosen the chain reining in my libido, a little. "That sounds like a great idea."

Her hands circle and graze lower down my back, until they rest just above the waistband of my basketball shorts. "Yeah?"

"Yeah. You're killing me in that dress, Echo. It's been hard to stay focused."

"Well then take me home, and you can take it off me, and see where that leads." She digs under my shirt and touches my skin, tracing circles on my skin with her palms.

"Echo, babe. We both know exactly where it'll lead."

"Oh yeah? Where?" She glances up at me, her gaze coy.

I feel my skin heat and my crotch tighten. "With you naked beneath me and screaming my name."

"Is that so?" She slides her soft warm hands under the elastic of my shorts and cups my ass.

"That's so." I take her hand and lead her toward my Silverado.

It's silent as we drive and the air is tense with charged sexuality. The only words spoken are Echo directing me the few short—yet still far too many— blocks to her apartment building. I find a parking spot, and Echo is out of the cab before I've got the truck turned off, grabbing my hand and leading me to a nondescript, unmarked doorway sandwiched between a bistro and a head shop, dragging me up a narrow flight of stairs to a small landing with a single doorway on the left-hand side. She digs in her purse and produces a single key on a Belmont lanyard, and unlocks it. The door opens to a wide living room, the back of a battered, tattered, faded black leather couch facing the doorway, a matching loveseat on one side and an arm chair and ottoman on the other, a glass-topped, low wooden coffee table in the middle. A GoPro is set up on a short tripod on the coffee table, facing the couch, and I recognize the setting as the location where Echo and Brayden record their videos. To the right is a kitchen separated from the living room by a huge butcher's block island. Opposite is a bathroom between two doors that lead to the bedrooms; one door is open, showing a messy bed with jeans, T-shirts, underwear and boots scattered across the floor, making it Brayden's room; the other door, Echo's, is pulled closed.

There's a faint, acrid, almost sweet smell to the air, which I belatedly identify as the scent of pot. Brayden's head pokes up from where he'd been lying on the couch, out of sight. He has a joint in his mouth, the cherry lit, smoke curling in thin gray tendrils around his face.

"Oh. Hey, you two. Get it all worked out, did you?" His voice is thick and slow, muddled, sleepy.

Echo lets go of my hand and moves to the back of the couch, brushes a wayward lock of brown hair away from Brayden's face. "Bray? Are you okay? For real?"

He flops back down onto the couch, pinching the joint between a thumb and forefinger and staring at it as he sucks in a mouthful, inhales and holds it, and then blows out a series of smoke rings. "Fine, babe.

Just fine."

"And I call bullshit, Bray-bay."

"Just personal drama, sweetheart. If it gets to a point where I need to talk about it, you'll be the first one I come to. For now, I just need to brood on it, okay?" He shifts to a sitting position, joint clamped in the corner of his mouth, eyes narrowed against the smoke. He grabs his ashtray, the baggie of pot, the pack of papers and the lighter, and moves toward his bedroom. "Something tells me it's time for little old me to get scarce and turn on some music."

His door closes behind him, there's a moment of silence, and then the music starts. It's a quirky folk duo, guitar and cello and a distinctive male singer. Echo listens for a moment, staring at the door, then shouts, "Who is this playing, Brayden?"

He sticks his head out. "Brown Bird. The song is 'Ebb & Flow'. They're totally amazing, but epically tragic."

"Why tragic?" Echo asks.

"The lead singer died of leukemia after they'd made only five or six albums." He gestures to himself and then Echo. "We should cover them, some-day." And then he closes his door again, somewhat abruptly.

She stares at the door as if still seeing him.

"Something's up with him. He's not usually so broody, and I've never seen him smoke pot before. He doesn't even drink all that much, now that I think about it."

I pivot around in front of her, so I'm in her line of sight. "Like he said, he'll talk to you about it when he's ready."

She ducks her head. "I haven't been a very good friend to him. To anyone in the band, really. I've been so self-absorbed."

"Now you know, and you can remedy that. But not this very second." I rest my hands on her hips, dig my fingers through the thin white cotton dress into her flesh.

She takes a deep breath and lets it out, then looks up at me, eyes wide. "No, not right now."

"Show me your room," I whisper to her.

She steps into me, and I walk backward. Her hands rest on my chest, slide downward, and curl into the lower hem of my Commodores T-shirt. Her eyes are bright and her breath is coming deep and slow, a smile of anticipation curving her lips. The tips of her breasts poke against her dress, and the material is just thin enough that I almost make out a tantalizing glimpse of her areolae and the hardening buds of her nipples. My hands caress up from her hips to cup and lift and release her heavy boobs, and her breath catches when I scrape my thumbs over her tautened nipples.

I bump up against her door, and she's crashing into me, tits flattening between us, her mouth finds mine, hot and hungry. Her lips slant across mine, her tongue slashes between my lips and her hands slip under my shorts to graze my hips and then cup my ass, and I'm gasping into her kiss, stunned momentarily by the sudden assault of her kiss, her tooth-paste-fresh mouth, her hands clawing at my backside, her body hot and soft against mine.

I'm stunned into letting her lead for all of thirty seconds, and then my ravenous need awakens, and I take charge. I reach behind me and twist the door-knob and we both go stumbling backwards, caught off-balance. Echo tumbles against me, and I catch her, lift her. Her legs go around my waist, and I push her dress up around her hips, gasping at the vise grip of her thighs, inhaling the musky aroma of her desire. She wraps one arm around my neck and shoves the door closed with the other, and then she's leaning back in my arms, clamping down hard with her legs to keep her weight supported as she lets go and jerks at my shirt. I cup her ass with both hands, gripping and kneading the generous, supple flesh, and then raise my arms over my head as she peels my shirt off and tosses it across the room.

Then her hands are on me, all over me, as is her

mouth, clawing and palming and kissing and licking my skin wherever she can reach. I trip over a shoe, regain my balance and pivot, set Echo down on her feet. She reaches for my shorts, but I capture her wrists, a smile on my lips.

I've missed her so much and waited for so long. It feels like a lifetime, but it is really somewhere around two months. I spent those two months in class and working out like a madman, exercising my knee until I was as close to normal as I could be. Now I can walk normally without the cane, and I can even jog for a half a mile or so.

I've missed her, spent every waking moment waiting for a call or a text, trying not to think about her and failing miserably. I'd wake up at night, horny and rock hard, dreaming of her, aching for her. Once I even woke up having made a mess of myself from an erotic dream of her mouth on me, and her hands on me, and her eyes needy for me.

And now I have her, now she's here and wants me not just for sex but for a potential us? There will be no rushing in my claiming of her.

I move her hands behind her back and pinion them with one hand, standing close so she has to stare up at me, hair draped across one shoulder to hang over her left breast. I use my other hand to slide the skinny white strap of her dress down over one shoulder. Her lips part and her eyes fix on mine, wide and waiting, and her nostrils flare, and her nipples tighten to diamond-hard buds against my chest. I slide the other strap off, and the dress slithers downward, baring mile after mile of lush skin and taut curves. The dress is halted in its slide by the press of my hips against hers and by the grip of my hand around her wrists. Her tits are bared to me, begging for my mouth.

I release her hands and step away from her. The white dress pools at her feet, and she's naked in front of me. I don't move to touch her, kiss her or take her in my arms. I only stare at her for a long moment, drinking in her beauty, her golden skin and her glossy honey-blond hair, her heavy breasts and her bell-curve hips and plump, firm ass, her long legs and her hands, her hands, trembling at her sides.

And her liquid brown eyes, staring at me expectantly. "Benji?" she asks, and my name is a plea on her lips.

"Oh god, Echo, you are…so lovely, so perfect. I just want to look at you for a moment."

"I need you, Ben. Please."

I take a step toward her so our bodies are nearly touching, but not quite. The taut tips of her tits graze the skin of my chest. "Please what, Echo?"

"Make love to me?" Her voice is small but firm,

her eyes wide and clear and hot with need.

I let a smile curve my lips. "I'm going to do so much more than that, Echo." I close the inch between us, press my body against hers, let the rigid bulge of my erection behind my shorts communicate my need for her.

I palm her hips and kiss her throat, bend and kiss the valley between her perfect breasts, move to my knees and cup the backs of her thighs and her ass, kiss the dip between hip and core. She gasps and buries her fingers in my hair, and I gaze up at her, and then nudge her thighs apart and prepare to worship her.

Sixteen: Newborn Love: River of Passion
Echo

I CAN'T BREATHE, CAN'T MOVE, CAN ONLY CLUTCH AT his hair and gasp for breath. I can only try to remain upright and swallow past the hammering of my pulse in my throat and chest.

My Ben, my Benji, he's on his knees in front of me, both hands curved against the bubble of my ass. I'm standing with my feet wide apart, spine arched inward, head hanging back on my shoulders, trying not to scream as he laps at my core. Screaming isn't possible, I realize, because I'm totally breathless. But I need to scream, *need to,* because I haven't felt his touch in so long, haven't felt this good in… ever. I haven't even touched myself since I came back from Texas. The last orgasm I had, Ben gave me. I'm swollen with heated need, aching with the pressure of built-up desire, because even through my guilt and grief and drunken wallowing, I needed Ben, wanted him. If I wasn't fighting tears or trying to keep myself coherent despite the whiskey, I was dreaming of him and aching for his touch. And now I have him here and I have his touch and I won't ever ever, ever let him go. God, my fucking god, no, I'll never let him stop touching me. I won't let him get dressed, even. I'll keep him naked forever, oh yes, I'll keep his huge muscled frame close and his hot skin bare, and his hard thick cock buried inside me…but right now all I want, all I need, all I can even conceive of is his talented hungry mouth eating me out like he's never tasted anything so delicious as my quivering, quaking folds. I'm so greedy for this, aching for this. I cup his head and press him closer, grind my hips to get his tongue deeper into my opening, harder against my swollen clit.

I hear words pouring out of me, and don't even try to edit them. "Oh yeah, Ben, don't stop! Eat me, Ben, eat my pussy…oh god it's good, so good…yes, yes!…oh fucking yes!"

He growls and his tongue swipes up my pussy, and I jerk as the tip of his tongue swats at my clit, and I nearly buckle when his lips close around that sensitive, delicate, needy little bundle of flesh and nerves and sucks and his tongue swirls around it. And just like that, within moments of his mouth latching onto me I'm ready to come, ready to explode around his mouth, and he knows it, feels it, hears it.

And he abruptly quits all contact with my pussy, stands up and ignores my wordless wail of protest. I reach for him, but he grabs my hands in both of his and spins me in a circle so I'm facing away from him. I gasp in shock when he shoves his big body up against mine, pressing the thick ridge of his cock between the globes of my ass, and his hands cup my tits, grasping roughly and thumbing my nipples until I wince and gasp and my knees dip. He's all over me, all around me, huge and hot behind me. His mouth is on the ridge of my shoulder and now at my neck, and then at my throat, and I tilt my head to bare my throat for him. He accepts my offering, and his mouth sucks at my throat, and his hips grind against me. I whimper and writhe my ass against his cock, needing pressure, needing touch, my folds are aching and my clit is throbbing and I'm fading away from the edge of orgasm and I could scream from the desperate need to fall over that edge.

He has my hands imprisoned in one of his, held in front of my body so I can't reach for him, can't try to get his shorts off like I want to. I need him as bare as I am, need all of his skin naked against mine. But he's got me in his thrall, and I don't dare fight him for fear he'll refuse to let me come. I hold utterly still as his free hand steals down my belly and slips over my core, cups my pussy; I don't even breathe as his middle finger penetrates my folds and delves into me, and I don't dare even breathe as his palm presses against my clit. I'm paralyzed, needing this so badly it's all that exists. He adds a second finger, his ring finger, and he's knuckle-deep inside me, pinky and index finger lying along my inner thighs, thumb tucked in. His fingers reach in and up and curl, scrape, withdraw, slide in, and my pent-up breath explodes out of me in a groaning sigh when I feel the hot wire of orgasm go taut and white-hot. His fingers pinch my nipples, one and then the other, and I feel the tug in my belly and in my core. His mouth rasps against my throat, his teeth nip at my delicate skin, and his hips move, sliding his fabric-covered cock between my ass-cheeks.

"Ben..." I gasp, wanting to beg him to...I don't even know what I want more, to come, to feel his naked cock against me, to feel him inside me? All of that, all at once. But I can't get words out and so I just let him have his way.

His way, it turns out, is to finger-fuck me until I'm riding his hand, dipping at the knees and spreading my feet apart to get his fingers deeper and growling like an animal and writhing on his hand as he digs his fingers up and in and curls them and presses the heel of his palm against my clit.

"I'm gonna—oh god, oh god, oh fucking god—Ben, Jesus Ben…please don't stop please don't stop please let me come let me come—" I sound breathless and wanton and I'm begging shamelessly.

My thighs clench together and quake as my climax begins to wash over me, and I'm right there, teetering on the edge.

And his fingers are gone. I do scream now and turn to slap him or claw at him or attack him somehow, but he's got his hands on my face and he's kissing the living shit out of me, kissing the breath right out of my lungs until I *have* to break away.

His eyes are blazing hot, deep brown and dark with fiery need. He hooks his thumbs in his shorts and tugs them down until the V is bared and the head of his cock is bared. I reach for him, need to feel him, ready to do literally anything he asks to make him push me over that razor's edge. But he knocks my hand away, grabs both my wrists in his strong fingers. His shorts are still halfway on, half of his huge dick bared to my view, and I can't look away from it, wanting it, to touch it or lick it or feel it inside me.

I'm feral with need, and he knows it. He's engineered my desire to this boiling point, and he's got me where he wants me.

And then, with a slow smile, he pulls his shorts back up. "Are you close, Echo?"

I nod and tug at his hold on my wrists. "God yes, so close."

"You want to come, don't you?" His voice is low and husky and demanding.

"So bad, Benji."

"Take my shorts off for me," he orders.

I like this commanding Ben, this take-charge Ben. I grin hungrily and sigh as I fall to my knees in front of him, slowly peel his shorts away from his body and slide them down to expose his cock, standing rigid against his belly, straining and beautiful, a dot of moisture at the tip. He steps out of his shorts and I toss them aside, glance up at him for instructions. He just smiles at me, and so I wrap both hands around him and put the bulbous head that protrudes over my upper fist into my mouth, and then slide one fist down his length and then the other, and then sink lower and take his cock into my throat until I nearly gag, and then pull away and glance up at him, wiping my saliva and his pre-come off my lips with the back of my wrist.

I bend to take him into my mouth again, but he threads his fingers into my hair over my ears, gently guides me to my feet. His mouth crashes against mine, and once again he kisses me senseless, his tongue tangling against mine and his lips scouring my mouth and I melt against him, let my hands roam his body with desperate hunger while his do the same.

He breaks the kiss, stares into my eyes, and the ferocity in his gaze tells me it's over. No more playing around, no more teasing.

I'm right, so wonderfully right.

He spins me in place, his big hands rough on my hips as he turns me to face the bed, and now his saliva-slick cock is nestled naked against my ass. I gasp in shock when he gathers my hair into a sheaf and wraps it around his fist in a gentle but firm grip, and then whimper in pleased surprise when he bends me over the bed, pushing me down. I press my cheek to the sheet at the edge of the mattress and watch as he caresses a palm down my spine. I'm breathing hard, anticipating. His hand releases my hair and both palms cup my ass cheeks, and then he reaches between my thighs and traces my opening, dips two fingers into my wetness and steps closer to me. I slip a hand between my legs and reach for him, grasp his hard slick shaft and guide him into me. As soon as he's in, he groans in relief. One palm traces up my spine and back down, coming to rest on my ass. I spread my legs wide and brace against the bed, and then with a drawn-out moan of bliss, Ben drives deep into me.

I whimper breathlessly as he fills me, and then I'm shrieking as he pulls back and slams home. I fist my hands into the sheet and push back into his thrusts, growl as his hands grip my hips and pull. Oh god, this is good. So good. He's taking me, claiming me, and I've never loved anything so much, never wanted in all my life for anything to never stop as much as I want this to just continue forever, this feeling of fullness and this knowledge that this man is mine and I'm his and I can give him exactly what he wants. What I want to give him, what I've never given anyone in all my life? Submission. I've always guided things; I've always been in control. I've always taken what I wanted because a guy's needs in this kind of thing are simple. It won't take long, never does. So to make sure I get what I need, I've always been in charge.

And after Marcus—I couldn't let anyone have control over me, couldn't bear to be vulnerable for even a second.

But with Ben, it's as easy as breathing. I'm safe with him. I can let myself need him. I can unleash a lifetime's worth of vulnerability onto him, and know that it's safe and sheltered.

There's no more room for thought, no more space for rumination. There's only fullness, only the slick wet slide of his huge cock inside me, the caress of his palms over my back and over the swell of my hips and around the taut curve of my ass, and then those same curves of my ass are pressed flat as he buries himself deep.

"Ben...Ben...?" It's a plea, but I'm not sure for what.

"Yeah, baby? Talk to me."

"More...just more of you."

"You've got all of me, Echo."

I can only shake my head, because it's not enough, this slow and gentle gliding of his body is not enough. "Harder." It's all the sense I can make, but he gets it, I think.

He leans over me and kisses the very center of my back, and then grabs my hair in his hand and the creased curve of my bent hip in the other, and he uses both for leverage to fuck me deep and hard so my ass jiggles against him, and I gasp as he pierces me, and I nearly come from that one slapping thrust.

"Again!" I gasp.

"You want it like that, Echo?" he growls, buried deep, teeth clenched, and I can feel him shaking behind me, and I know he's close, too.

"God, yes. Fuck me so hard, Ben. Be rough. I can take it. I want it." And god, that is the deepest truth I possess.

Since I've always been in charge of the sex I've had before, I've never given a guy free rein to do what he wants, how he wants. With Ben, I feel so free, I feel like I can just let go, and I can allow myself to have what I want, to want the deepest secrets inside me. I have a feeling Ben is going to plumb those depths and give me things I didn't even know I wanted.

He groans and tightens his grip on my hair, pulls my head back, and I plant my palms on the bed and lift up, spine arched, belly pressed into the bed, feet flat and ass high. I push back with my hands, lunging into his next thrust.

"Don't move, Echo," he groans. "Just hold still and let me fuck you."

I duck my head between my arms and gaze down the length of my body, and the view is pretty incredible. I can see between my dangling, swaying tits to where we're joined, and I can see a hint of his cock sliding out, glistening wetly, and then I'm growling between clenched teeth and I'm rocked forward and I keep watching our joining, watch his dick bury into me, and now there's his taut heavy balls and he's impaled in me to the hilt, so those balls of his smack against my flesh.

Oh, Jesus. I've never wanted to watch this, before. But now I want to see it all. I want to see my folds stretched thin to accommodate this massive grinding pulsing girth and I want to see even inside so I can see his cock spit his load into me, and I want to watch his face when he comes and I want to watch my own when I come…

Which is right now, oh fuck oh fuck…I scream breathlessly and grip the bed and force my eyes open so I can watch his cock slide in, withdraw, slide in, watch his sac sway heavy and slap my skin. I'm torn apart, a live wire is piercing my core and connecting to my every nerve ending, and my core gushes heat and clamps down and the built-up pressure explodes, and I'm crying, sobbing, and my entire body is trembling and shaking and being rocked forward by powerful, unrelenting thrusts.

And now he's faltering with his cock deep, shaking, grinding, and I feel him tensing, feel his balls tighten. He takes both of my hips in his big strong hands and lifts me off the ground and jerks me back against his body, sets me down on my tip-toes and then pulls me backward, and I'm nothing but putty in his hands, gasping crying sobbing begging wet clay for him to shape.

"Oh…fuck…Echo…" he gasps, pulling back and thrusting again deep and hard so my body jolts forward and a spear of bliss tears through me, ecstasy so potent it hurts.

"Come, Benji. Come in me," I beg, breathless, "or come on me, do what you want Ben, take me, fuck me, use me."

"How about I love you forever?" he says, and taunts me with sudden shallow thrusts.

"God yes, I want that, and I want to love you forever too...but Ben?"

"Yeah, Echo?"

"Shut up and let me feel you come."

"I don't want it to end. I want this to last forever."

But now I'm so hypersensitive from having just come, so limp and so sated that I can't take another thrust, can't take another slap of his body against mine, and I just want to touch him and feel him and accept the wet thick heat of his come wherever I can get it, but I simply cannot take another pounding fuck of his body. That's a problem I've never had before.

Ben lets me push him away and stands shakily as I twist and collapse backward to sit on the edge of the bed, staring in awe at his wet gleaming cock as it sways proudly before me, and he's shaking, gasping, groaning, his muscles stand hard and tensed. I take his cock in my hands and caress his length slowly. He shoves his hips forward, fucking into my grip. His eyes stay hot on mine, and I lean forward and wrap my lips around his head and suck once, gently, and then extend my tongue to lick my essence off his taut dusky flesh, tasting my musk and his salt, and then I swirl my tongue around the head, pump my hands gently and slowly and teasingly soft around his base. He groans, sways in front of me, about to collapse, about to explode.

I'm watching him, tilting my head to one side so I keep his cock in my mouth and still see him at the same time, and I feel his gaze like the heat of fire on my skin. I cup my hand over his balls, squeeze and massage them until he groans, and then I feel his body tighten to coiled-serpent tautness. I keep my eyes on his, arch my back, squeeze his shaft and stroke his length hard and fast now, watching him, watching him watch me. I pull his cock downward and he fucks into my grip.

I lick the head, slide the flat of my tongue over the very tip of him to taste his readiness. "Come on me, Ben. Come all over me."

"Fuck, Echo, Jesus, I'm coming…"

And he is, ohmyfuckinggod, he's shooting a thick wet white flood of come. It hits my lips first, and I lick it away, and it trickles down my throat both inside and out, and he's stilled with his hips flexed as I massage his taut heavy tensing balls and finger his taint and pump his considerable length, stroke all the glorious dark seed-spitting inches of his beautiful cock. He groans wordlessly as his dick twitches in my hand and then another stream leaves him and sloshes onto my chest and down between my tits, and I angle my torso so his seed spills in dripping rivulets on each of my tits and over my nipples and down my stomach and he's watching with heavy-lidded eyes.

And then, as he flexes and thrusts again, I tongue his head and wrap my lips around his thickness and take him down my throat, angle my head and body so I can take him until he's fucking my throat and coming one more time. I back away and let him send a mouthful of come onto my tongue and swallow it and suck until he's gasping and cursing and pulling away.

He collapses onto the bed beside me, and I lie back beside him, his come cooling on my skin.

Ben pulls me to lie on his chest. "Holy shit, Echo."

"Holy shit, Ben," I agree.

His voice is a low, sated, pleased rumble under my ear. "I've dreamed about fucking you like that for so long. I literally dreamed about it, having your ass spread out for me as I take you from behind…"

"Did it feel as good as you dreamed?" I ask.

"Jesus, Echo…better, so much better," he says, cradling me to him, cupping my hip in his warm, strong hand.

He rests for a moment like that, and then sits up, scans my room, and spies the towel on the floor from my shower, and retrieves it. Gently, carefully, lovingly, he cleans the mess off my skin, folding and re-folding the towel and wiping until I'm clean.

And then he cradles me in his arms and settles us on the bed, my head on his chest and his heartbeat in my ear, and covers us with the blankets.

Within seconds, we're both asleep.

I wake up with sunlight on my skin, Ben's hand on my hip, and a screaming bladder. I worm out from under Ben's touch and creep naked out of the room and into the bathroom. When I'm done, I discover that Brayden left a note explaining that he'd left early in the morning, knowing we'd want privacy, and to call him when it was safe to come back.

I grin, knowing it'll be awhile.

When I close my bedroom door behind me, Ben is awake and watching me, the blanket draped over his hips. I stop at the foot of the bed, admiring his gorgeous frame, the heavy muscles and the dark olive skin, the hungry heat in his brown eyes and how his messy black hair hangs over his forehead. I trace his pecs with my eyes and the V-cut where his abs disappear under the sheet. His biceps are thick and his hands are curled loosely where he has them tucked behind his head. He is, in short, utterly gorgeous, and all mine. I crawl onto the bed and paw away the sheet to bare his erection. I prowl up his body until I'm straddling him, and I curl my arms around his neck and clutch him to kiss him dizzy. His hands go to my skin, down my waist and my back to cup my ass and I wiggle against his touch, push my ass back into his hands. He grips my butt in his strong hands and caresses it until I'm ready to purr. I stretch like a cat, tensing every muscle, and then I settle myself on him, my thighs around his waist, shins to the bed, face buried in the side of his neck, his nose in my hair. His hands refuse to relinquish their hold on my ass, and I don't want him to.

In fact…

I touch my lips to his ear. "Hey, Benji-boy?"

"My love?"

I pull back to stare at him, momentarily stunned by the easy way he said that, and by the way my heart squeezed—but in utter inexpressible joy, rather than fear.

I reclaim my thoughts, and writhe against his hold on my ass. "I like this."

"Me too."

I bite his earlobe, and then whisper, "But I want more."

"More, how?" he asks, but his fingertips slide closer to the crease between my globes.

"Like that. Yeah, baby." I try the endearment on for size; having never even pretended to love a guy before, I'm a stranger to lovey-dovey terms. I nibble at his shoulder and try to keep myself totally relaxed as his hands explore where I've never let a man go before. Finally, he gently tugs one of my cheeks aside and traces the gap. "Oh god, yeah, oh yeah, that's where I want your touch, Benji-boy."

He finds my rear opening with a finger and presses lightly. "Here?"

I moan, long and breathless. "Uh-huh."

"You're sure?"

"Gently, baby. You're the first and…the—the only one to ever touch me there." I bury my face against his chest and claw my fingers against his shoulders.

With one hand he spreads me apart, and with the other he gently, slowly presses a thick finger to the tight knot. "This feel good, Echo?"

"Jesus…yes!" I gasp, when he presses just so, and now I'm penetrated. Just a sliver of the tip of his finger, but penetrated where I've never been touched, the one place I'm still virgin for my man.

"Touch your pussy, Echo."

I obey him immediately because fuck yes, that's what I need. He doesn't move, just waits for me to press my fingers to my throbbing button, and I inhale a gasp because all of me tenses, and then rockets explode inside me, and I feel myself clench around his fingertip, I feel wetness smear out of my pussy, and my nipples pebble against his chest. There's only one thing missing, now: I shift my hips and slide downward, and he's inside me, his thick shaft piercing my folds, and now I'm aching with fullness. I draw my legs closer to my torso, and seat myself on him, impaled by him. He's balls-deep in me now, and I wrap one hand around his neck and we both strain to press our mouths together, kissing each other's breath away.

"More…" I gasp.

He wiggles his finger, and I involuntarily clamp down around him, but he's up to the first knuckle of his finger and my breath has left me. I'm so stretched and filled that the universe has been reduced to the pulsating tightness of my body.

God, I ache so beautifully.

He holds still, and so I do I, letting myself grow accustomed to this new and delicious sensation. I've heard and read how good this can feel if done right, but I never believed it. Until now. This…oh yes, this is going to be something Ben and I explore and push the boundaries of; it's a new favorite thing, I think.

For now, I'm content to roll my hips and feel the finger inside me back there, and let myself growl like a lioness with how incredible I feel right now. I lie on him, draped on him, his body a solid sheltering mountain beneath me, supporting me and taking my weight easily.

I have to move. God, now the need is a fierce burn inside me, sudden and sun-hot. I press my lips to his chest over his heart. "Don't move, Benji-baby," I murmur, and roll my hips.

Oh, oh fuck yes. Oh hell is that good. His cock slides between the stretched lips of my pussy and his finger stimulates me back there, making me feel over-full in a dirty, naughty, perfect way. I like being bad. I like being his dirty girl.

As if reading my mind, Ben's lips move at my ear. "You're my dirty girl, huh, Echo? You like this, don't you? You like being kinky."

"God, yes. I'm so bad, Ben."

The hand cupping my ass lets go, caresses the globe, and then smacks my cheek with a sharp slap. "So bad."

I shriek out loud, because the slap shocked me and I almost didn't notice when his finger slid deeper, but now, oh now, my ass stings and I ache with the full-ness of double-penetration. He smooths a hand over the stinging flesh of my backside, and then slaps the other cheek, and I shriek again, breathless, because now he's in me to the second knuckle. It almost hurts, but doesn't. Or if it does, it's a hurt I can't get enough of.

"Again," I groan through gritted teeth, sliding my pussy up and down his length.

So he slaps my ass again, and it stings so per-fectly, and he pierces deeper, and he does it again on the other side, and now his knuckles crush into the plump muscle and skin of my ass. He can't go any deeper, and I'm growling in my throat at the sensa-tion, feeling dirty and fierce and primal and desperate for motion.

Ben's cock throbs inside me, and I know he's ach-ing with need. So I roll my fingertips against my clit, having forgotten momentarily to touch myself like I was supposed to, and when I do feel the press of my fingers against my swollen flesh, I have to breathe out a curse at the lightning that hits me.

"Oh fuck," I whisper, and grind my hips on his. "Oh fuck. Oh fuck."

"You feel so good, Echo. Jesus, you feel so good I can't take it."

"You don't even know, Ben. You just don't even know." I'm moving so gently it's hardly even a motion, just a whisper of skin against skin. "Just hold still and let me fuck you, Ben."

"Anything for you."

"You're my anything. My everything." I don't know where this is coming from, only that it's true, and that somehow the intimacy of this moment, the way he's touching me, the way he's so fully inside of me on so many levels has raw truth spewing out of my mouth. "I'm going to scream when I come, Ben. I'm going to scream, and it's going to be your name."

I slide my mouth across his, but I'm too full of him to kiss, I can only hold my lips against his and breathe as I start to move in earnest now, pushing upward, and then sliding downward, feeling him glide in and out of my pussy, and I gasp with each motion. It starts out slow, and his hand follows my movements, keeping his finger inserted in me. I drag my mouth away from his and press my lips to his chest, stutter them across his skin until I find the flat of his nipple and I lick him, then nip him hard enough to elicit a curse and a jerk that has him crushing deep into me. I bite his other nipple, then, just to get that same curse-and-jerk, and lick it to soothe the sting. My hips are gyrating now, and he's moving with me, and it's like the universe itself has been compacted down to an intricate, impossible knot inside me, the heat of all the stars going nova all at once burning low in my belly, making my core ache and my lungs heave helplessly and my heart slam like a tribal drum.

I'm moving hard and fast along his body now, hovering over him with my hands on his chest, not needing to touch myself to be on the edge of climax, but it's not a climax, it's the apex of all sensation, it's orgasm times love times infinity. His groaning and mine harmonize, our bodies move and meet in sinuous waves, and we're lost in each other, shouting and cursing, and it's music, we're a symphony together.

And then he sneaks a hand between our bodies and finds my clit with his fingers, strums my clit and I snap like an over-tightened guitar string.

"*BEN!*" I scream, shrill and breathless.

"I'm right there with you, Echo, oh god, I'm coming too, coming so hard," he growls.

Everything narrows down to the infinitesimal instant when I come and he comes, and it's a moment of perfect unity, our eyes locked, our bodies merged.

His finger is pushing in and pulling out, mirroring the action of our joining, and I'm coming apart, thrashing on top of him, screaming wordlessly, crashing down onto him hard again and again, and he's moving and thrusting up into me, and I feel him explode inside me, feel the hot gush of his release, and the universe that was within me is expanding out of my pores, fire in my veins and heat in my blood and I can only scream through gnashing teeth, biting his skin until he grunts.

We come, and we come, and we come. It's a never-ending tsunami of ecstasy bashing through us.

When it's over, I cradle his handsome, sexy face in my palms and stare down into his deep brown eyes. "I love you, Ben." I whisper it, breathless. What just happened between us, it dragged the truth out of me. Wrenched it free from deep down. And now that I've said it, the phrase pours out of me. I'm sobbing it over and over again, overcome by how truly I mean it, by how deeply I feel it. "I love you, I love you...I love you, oh Ben, I love you so much, Ben."

His mouth finds mine, and his lips tremble and I taste tears, his or mine or both I neither know nor care. "I love you so fucking much, Echo."

I can take no more, so I reach back and tug at his hand. He understands, and gently, so gently pulls his hand free. I gasp at the shocking emptiness I feel.

Ben rises, washes his hands and gets a clean towel from the bathroom, returns to clean me.

When he's done, he lies back down beside me where I'm collapsed facedown on the bed, trying to put my body back together again.

I grin at him. "Good morning."

He laughs at the utter absurdity of the greeting, at the *non sequitur* of saying such a thing after what we just did. "Good morning."

"I love you," I say, just to see if I can say it again, now that we're not in the throes of the most intense sex I've ever had. I grin, because I can, and it feels good to say it. "We should start every morning like that."

"With my finger in your ass?"

"Or your cock."

His gaze heats. "You want my cock in your ass?"

"Oh, it's happening. We may have to work up to it, but it's *so* happening."

"Let's go back to the part where you love me."

"Yes, let's," I agree.

He takes my hands and draws me to himself. I'm dragged up and up until I'm sitting on his lap, curled on him, my head against his chest, his palm on my hair, the other on my hip. And oh…oh, being held like this? After such a wrenching, wracking orgasm and such a fierce and explosive epiphany of love, being wrapped up in this man is just too much. So perfectly, beautifully, too much.

I can only weep, deep wracking sobs that Ben doesn't question. He just holds me through it until I can twist my head to peer up at him. "I love you with all that I am, Ben Dorsey." I palm his cheek and whisper this against his mouth. "It's crazy. It's like one second I was falling, and then now I'm just...I'm there. It's love so big it hurts, so much it's scary. So big, so much, all at once."

He rolls with me, pressing me with a delicate gentleness to the mattress, hovering over me. He's huge and beautiful and broad, all dusky skin and sleek muscles and bright eyes that breathe with potent love. "You can fall, Echo. I'll catch you. Because I'm falling too, and I need you to catch me, too."

"Now and forever, come what may," I tell him.

And when we join again, it's slow and with all the fragility of newborn love, each of us shaky as a newly birthed foal. My heart gallops as we move together, wrapped up in him, tangled up in him, loved by him, loving him back with a heart freshly opened to the long-pent-up and long-building well of passion that flows free like white raging river water from a burst dam.

When we come together, it's with whispers, mine and his weaving together and overlapping: *"I love you, I love you—god, I love you..."*

Seventeen: Falling Away
Ben
One year later

THE THUNDER OF HOMETOWN APPLAUSE IS DEAFENING. I stand backstage, watching as Echo the Stars takes the stage for their first live performance since Echo's incident, now almost a year and a half ago. They're signed with Calloway Music, Kylie's parents' label, and with the Calloways producing and guiding and honing them, Echo the Stars have found a sound that people all over the country are clamoring for. In that time, they cut their first EP, *Miles To Your Door,* followed less than six months later by a full-length album, *Sweet Refrain.* They've put up a slew of YouTube videos as a band, and Brayden and Echo continue their stripped-down duet journal-videos, but the band hasn't appeared live until tonight. This performance takes place as the opening act, preceding Oz and Kylie—who now perform under the moniker O+K—then the Harris Mountain Boys, and then Colt and Nell themselves.

The applause reaches a crescendo as the band settles in with their instruments, Atticus getting comfortable on his stool and twirling his drumsticks, Will picking up a dobro from the side-by-side stands holding that instrument, a banjo, and an electric guitar. Mim brings her bass to an upright position and settles it against her ample chest while Vance cradles his fiddle under his chin, propping it there and adjusting the tuning. Echo is absent from the stage, but she's standing in the wings, waiting until the crowd is screaming and howling and whistling.

Brayden stands tall and lanky at center stage, hooks the strap of his mandolin over his shoulder and clips it, adjusts the angle, and then reaches over to the microphone beside him. "What's up, ya'll?" he shouts. The crowd shrieks, and Brayden glances around the stage at each of the members. "Wait a second, wait a second. Someone's missing." He grins and glances at Echo, clearly stoked and ready to jam.

"Echo!" comes the response from the crowd. "ECHO!"

My girl is giddy, beaming, bouncing on her toes. The house lights and the stage lights go black, and

Echo trots out on stage in darkness, takes her place at the microphone. Atticus hammers a thudding beat with his kick drum—*BOOM...BOOM....BOOM*—and then Brayden picks a delicate, intricate melody that loops and dips and swirls around the beat for several seconds. Vance saws a long, low note which is mirrored by the deep, throaty, mellow note of Mim pulling a bow across the strings of her upright bass and then, lastly, Will sends a bent and wavering high note from his dobro to finalize the weaving, interlocking melody. The audience is screaming nonstop now, and they only go silent when the stage lights come on, bathing each member in a spotlight, Brayden and Echo sharing a pool of light and the microphone.

Echo's voice lifts into the air, rises and washes over the packed auditorium, a dulcet and magical note that carries and carries, looped through a digital effect for several more measures.

And then the note dies and she sings, harmonized every few lines by Brayden and Mim:

> *"An instant, oh just a single fragment*
> *Is all it takes to turn my long lament*
> *Into a song of dizzy joy,*
> *To shake the sorrow from my bones*
> *And know that I am not alone.*
> *An instant, oh just a single glance*

Just a single touch, by chance,
And I know I'm not alone.
All the sorrow, love of mine,
Oh, you take it all away,
You send it with the wind,
All the sorrow, love of mine,
All the sadness, oh, all the guilt,
The tower of my solitude,
It's falling, falling, falling away.
An instant, oh, just a single fragment
Is all it takes to turn my long lament
Into a song of love,
To shake the sorrow from my bones,
And know that I am not alone.
An instant, oh, just a single kiss
And I'm raptured, oh, oh, I'm drowning in your bliss,
My senses drown in the brown of your eyes
And oh, all the history is buried by our sighs,
All the sorrow and oh, all the guilt,
It's all pulled down, down with all the walls I built,
It's falling, falling, falling away,
Love of mine, oh
Love of mine, oh,
I'm falling, falling away, away,
I'm sinking into you, oh, and I'll forever stay,
So take me now and lay me down,

Fall with me, oh,
Sing with me, sigh with me, lie with me,
Because it's you and only you,
Whose kiss, whose touch, whose love,
Who with a single word, oh, a single glance,
Can change the vagaries of chance,
Can sweep me up and make me dance,
Can shake the sorrow from my bones,
Show me that I'm not alone,
With just an instant, oh,
With just a kiss and I know,
It's going to be okay, oh, going to be okay,
Because
We're falling, falling, falling away."

The band jams for a couple minutes after the harmonized vocals fall away, Echo dancing at the mic, swaying and nodding and turning to watch her friends as they play, and then all the instruments drop out one by one, in reverse order of how they came in, until it's just Atticus slamming his kick drum, and then the stage lights drop and the crowd is howling in the darkness. The lights come back up to reveal Brayden and Echo hugging, laughing, and then Echo grabs the mic off the stand.

"It's so good to be back on stage. It's been a long time, feels like a lifetime in a lot of ways, actually."

She turns to glance at me, smiling, and then returns her attention to the audience. "So much has changed for me since the last time Echo the Stars performed live. Everything, really. Me, most of all. I found love, you see. What happened is…I woke up, and I looked around me. I had to hit bottom, and hit it hard enough to shake me before I was ready to see what's around me." She turns and points at each of the band members. "These guys, my family. Atticus, Vance—" Her voice drops and she says the next name with a dramatic flair, "William Wolf…my girl Mim, sweet, beautiful Memphis, and of course, my best friend, my brother-in-arms, Brayden. They've all been there for me all along, I was just…I had my head too far up my own ass to see it. Guys…? I see it now. So thanks."

She points at me, smiles, crooks her finger at me. I shake my head.

Echo turns to the crowd. "Ya'll want to meet the other reason I'm up here? The person who has been most instrumental in helping me wake up to the beauty of life?" She strides across the stage and grabs my arm, pulls at me. I resist, but I go with her because I can't deny her anything. She hauls me front and center, beneath the spotlight. Brayden rests his hand on my shoulder and leans against me, and Echo hooks her arm around my waist on the other side of me, rests her cheek against my chest, and speaks into the microphone. "Isn't he gorgeous? Yeah, you have no idea. He's the reason I'm here. I think if it hadn't been for my man Ben, I wouldn't be here. I'd have drunk myself to death. Ben and Brayden, both of them, are amazing. I quit drinking, by the way. Thirteen months, not a drop."

I stare out at the crowd, and for a moment or two, I see what Echo sees when she's up here, what Kylie and Oz see, what Colt and Nell see: thousands of faces grinning and cheering, hands raised, cell phones flashing, a sea of humanity and noise. It's exhilarating.

I'm tempted to spin around right now and drop to my knee, pull out the ring I've had with me for weeks. But I don't. Yeah, I've seen Colt and Nell's proposal video, and even Oz and Kylie's. Those proposals are cute and romantic and whatever. But it's not me, and it's not us. When it comes down to it, I'm a more traditional guy. I've got a plan and I'm going to stick to it; I'm just waiting on some official news.

I let the moment pass, and when Echo turns to me, I cup her face in both hands and kiss her until the crowd starts whistling and Brayden makes an amused yet disgusted sound. I laugh, and make my way off-stage, where I watch the rest of their set. When they're done, I help the band tear down their gear and load it into the back of the semi trailer waiting to take them to the first stop of the tour, in Memphis. By the time all that's done, The Harris Mountain Boys are jamming onstage, and the band and I cluster off-stage and watch.

I finally catch a moment alone with Echo, deep in the shadows backstage. I pin her to the cinder-block wall and kiss her breathless. "I'm proud of you, Echo," I tell her. "And I love you."

She stares up at me. "I was sure you were gonna propose there, for a second."

"Disappointed?" I ask.

She shakes her head. "No. I would have said yes, but…"

"It's not us."

She grins and kisses my jaw. "No, it's not. I'm glad you know me well enough to know that."

"I'm a traditional guy, when it comes right down to it."

Her eyes light up. "So you *are* planning to propose, then?"

I shrug with false nonchalance. "I can neither confirm nor deny the substance of any rumors you may have heard."

"You are! You so are!"

"Someday," I tell her, and touch my lips to her neck, and then tug aside the scoop neck of her sundress and kiss the slope of her breast, sucking hard enough to leave a mark. "Could be tomorrow, could be next year."

"Better not be next year," Echo breathes, "I'm too impatient for that. And we're on the road tomorrow."

"Somewhere in the middle, then."

"I want to tell you something, though. I've been thinking about this, and you should know about it before you do propose, whenever that might be." She has a serious tone to her voice, and she pushes my face away from where I've been nuzzling the sweet, lush valley of her cleavage. "Listen, Ben, please?"

I stand up straight and smile at her. "Tell me."

"When we get married, I want to keep my last name. Not because of my father, but because of Mom. It...connects me to her."

I wrap her in my arms and crush her close. "Echo, baby, as long as you're mine, legally, emotionally, mentally, and physically, you can do whatever you want with your name. I love you, and I just want us to be married."

"But you said you're a traditional guy and traditionally, I'd take your last name, or at least hyphenate, but I—"

I touch a finger to her lips, silencing her. "You are Echo Leveaux. It's who you are."

"I'm yours, Ben. I want to be your wife, in every way."

"And that's all that matters."

She grins up at me. "Can't we just call *that* a proposal?"

I shake my head. "No way. I've got a plan. It doesn't count unless I ask you the question and you say yes. That's how it works. Plus there's gotta be a ring involved."

"Do you have a ring picked out?"

I have it in my pocket right now, but I don't breathe a word about it. "Maybe. Maybe not. Now stop asking questions so you can pretend to be surprised when I do ask you."

She lets it go, and kisses me until I'm ready to take her right there against the wall. I manage to hold back, which turns out to be a good thing, since Brayden comes to find us to tell us that there's reservations for us in twenty minutes at a nearby restaurant, and to say that all of us—The Harris Mountain Boys, the Calloways, Oz and Kylie—had better get moving.

Three months later, and the tour is finally over. Echo and the rest of her band are all arriving home today, after three straight months on the road. I've been able to fly out to meet them on the road when my schedule as a graduate assistant coach at Vanderbilt allows. I've put in eighteen months in that position, learning the ropes, and realizing I'm even better on the sidelines than I was on the field playing.

Two weeks ago I had my first official interview with the coaching and management staff of the Tennessee Titans. This morning, I got the phone call.

I am now the youngest person in history to hold a position on the coaching staff of an NFL team. I'm an assistant offensive line coach, thanks in part to my father's influence. He convinced them to watch me at Vanderbilt, to talk to the coaches, and they saw my potential, agreed to an interview, and were duly impressed.

So now I've got a master's degree in management, and a career in coaching. And the ring that's been burning a hole in my pocket for the last four months is about to get put to use.

We're back, comes the text from Echo. *Where are you?*

I haven't seen her in nearly a month, as I haven't been able to make it out to see the show in a while, what with finishing my degree on such an accelerated pace. I've been putting in eighteen-hour days for the last year and half, powering through the master's program as fast as possible, watching hundreds of hours of tape and attending practices and working out, plus spending time with Echo and going to as many of their local gigs as I can.

It's all been worth it though, all part of my plan to be ready to marry the girl I love so much. I just couldn't ask her when I had no direction in my life, or when I had no way to support her, and us. Her music career is taking off, but I wanted to have us covered so she never has to focus on anything else, no matter what happens.

Go home. I left you a note.

That sounds cryptic.

Muahahahaha. *diabolical laugh*

What are you planning?

Just go home and read the note, Echo.

Fine.

Good.

Whatever, weirdo.

I wait for her to find the note instructing her to meet me at Fannie Mae Dees Park.

I'm on the way to the park now. Why are we meeting there? I'm tired. I've been on the road since yesterday morning.

I don't bother answering, because the park is only a couple blocks from her and Bray's apartment—which is where I'm also pretty much living, at this point. I see her approach, and I see the moment when she sees the first votive candle floating in its glass dish of water. Her hand goes to her mouth, and she pauses, glancing down at the candle on the sidewalk. And then she looks up at me, waiting under the gazebo. She follows the path of floating candles, one after another, as they lead to me. I've arranged candles in a circle around the picnic table where we had that breakthrough conversation. The candles leading up the path are all small tea lights, but the candles circling me are all big white cylinders with thick wicks, the biggest candles I could find, a hundred of them. It's dusk, sunlight fading to golden-pink evening, and the lights flicker in the still air.

She stops in front of me, her eyes already wet with unshed tears. And, thank you god, she's wearing the same white dress she wore that night, although this time she has a bra on, and presumably underwear as well.

"Hi," she says, her voice small.

"Hi." I'm wearing a pair of khakis, and a polo shirt with the Titans logo on the left side, with my name embroidered on the right.

Echo takes in my clothing, my shirt, and her brows draw down in thought. "Ben? Does that shirt mean what I think it means?"

She knew I was hoping, and she knew I was waiting for the interview, but she doesn't know I got the interview or the position. Or rather, she didn't know, until now.

I nod. "Yeah, baby. You're looking at the youngest coach in NFL history. Assistant offensive line coach."

She squeals in joy, bounces on her toes, and then leaps into my arms. "BEN! I'm so *so* proud of you! When did you find out?"

"This morning." I let her down onto her feet, and my hands end up cupping her backside. "I had the interview two weeks ago, but I didn't tell you. I wanted to wait until I knew for sure."

She grins up at me and clings to my waist. "That is so cool. You look sexy in coaching gear. Will you get to wear one of those headsets?"

I laugh. "Yeah, I think so."

"Yummy. My man is an NFL coach." She kisses my throat, my chin, and then my lips. "So what's with all the candles?"

I let her continue kissing me as I answer. "I told you I was traditional, right? Well, I've been waiting to do this until I had a job to support us. Now I do."

She breaks away and her brown eyes go apprehensive, hopeful. "Do what, Benji?"

I dig the ring box from my pocket, and open it as I go to one knee. "Echo Leveaux, I love you more than I can even say." I have to swallow past emotion and hunt for the words. "I tried scripting this out, but nothing sounded right. All I know is I love you, and I want to be with you forever. Be my present, and my future, Echo. Will you marry me?"

She lunges at me, sobbing in joy, and we both topple backward to the cement. I cradle her weight on my chest and keep a good hold on the black velvet box. Lying on me, crying, laughing, Echo takes the ring from the box and slides it onto the ring finger of her left hand, and then dips to slant her mouth over mine.

"Yes," she whispers through the kiss, through joyful sobs and laughter, and I taste salt on her lips. "When can we get married?"

I laugh. "Eager much?"

She nods, her face in my neck. "As soon as we can, please?"

I caress her cheek. "Echo, baby, we can do it however you want. I think our family and friends would probably like be there, though, right?"

She shrugs. "Yeah, probably."

"And my mom would like to help you pick out a dress." I say this quietly.

"She would?"

I tilt her face to look at me. "Echo…yes, she would. My mom loves you, and so does my dad.

They've been waiting for me to do this almost as impatiently as me."

"I've been ready for a year and a half, Benji." She gazes down at me.

"Well, like I said, I wanted it to be the right time."

She kisses me again, and then slides off me and gets to her feet. "Come on, let's go home. I want to celebrate."

"And how will we do that?" I ask.

She hikes the hem of her dress up around her waist, revealing that she's not wearing any panties. "Why, naked in our bed, of course." She wiggles her ass at me and then runs, and I chase after her.

She lets me catch her, and we almost don't make it back to the apartment.

Epilogue
Echo
Six months later

WHO KNEW PLANNING A WEDDING COULD BE SO MUCH work? Jeez.

Well, everyone, I guess, except me. I just assumed that because I had no family to invite that it would be easier. Turns out, it's not. We invite everyone we know, everyone from the band and their plus one if they have one, my grandparents, Oz and Kylie, the Harris Mountain Boys—Buddy Helms, Amy Irons, and Gareth Fink, who have become good friends to Ben and me and to the band—as well as Ben's family and the Calloways, Echo the Stars' producers and label owners. That's about it.

And today is the day. I'm nervous, but in an excited sort of way. I'm ready, so ready.

The wedding is going to be amazing. We booked a church and flew Father Mike up here from San Antonio to peform the ceremony for us, with the reception at a hall not far away. It's so perfect. The Calloways and the Dorseys have paid for the entire thing. I argued at first, of course. I mean, Nell and Colt are incredible, but why would they pay for my wedding? I'm just some girl on their label. But then Ben reminded me that Colt and Nell are like second parents to him, that Colt was the one that helped him get his head out of his ass and suggested he leave Nashville for a while, to get some space and time from everything. And once I realized that, I realized that Colt and Nell aren't just great producers and amazing tour-mates, but they're genuinely incredible people. They're warm, and generous, and they're invested in me. Nell and Becca—Ben's mom—helped me pick out my dress, and they took me and Mim out for a spa day as my bachelorette party.

I grew up with no one but Mom and my grand-parents around, never had a lot of friends. And now, suddenly, I'm surrounded by people who seem deter-mined to love me despite myself. Becca and Jason… god, those two have welcomed me into their family as if I've always been a part of it. Becca and I meet for coffee every week, and I just love that woman to pieces.

And the band, they're always there, loving me, investing in me, reminding me that I'm not alone. They keep me accountable when it comes to drinking. I realized pretty early on in the process of recovering from my epic fuckup that the only way to make sure that kind of thing never happens again is to just stay sober full time. It sucks, especially when Bray and the gang want to go out and party after a show. They try to include me, but it's just too hard to be around it and not take part. I would always try to convince myself that I'd be fine, that it was only ever a problem when I had problems. It was Becca who reminded me, over early morning coffee at her kitchen table, that life would always have problems, and that nothing was ever easy and never would be. So I stay sober.

And now, here I am, standing in front of a mirror in a room off the chapel, Becca dabbing under my eyes with a napkin, Nell fussing with my train, Brayden hovering at my side, tall and beautiful in his tux, my man of honor. Kylie is here too, watching with tears in her own eyes. She and I have an odd relationship. It was tense and strained at first, but then we sat down and aired out all the awkwardness, talked it through, and we've become friends. She's Ben's best man, or, as we've joked, his best maid.

"Okay," Becca says, smiling at me as I take a deep breath and compose myself. "You ready?"

I nod. "I'm ready."

I stand by the double door at the back of the chapel, waiting, Grandpa at my side. Grandpa's hand is strong and firm on mine as I hold onto his forearm, and his eyes are warm on mine as we exchange a look.

The doors swing open, and I hear the wedding march played, of course, by my band in true bluegrass/folk glory, Vance sawing at his fiddle, Mim tapping her bass, Will on the banjo, Atticus with a single snare drum. Kylie is standing next to Ben, who has eyes for no one but me. My dress is strapless with an empire waist, a beaded sweetheart neckline, and a loose and floating tulle train. It's molded to me, fitted to my curves. I knew the moment I put it on that this dress was the one, that Ben's eyes would bug out of his head when he saw it. And as I approach Ben, squeezing Grandpa's hand tighter and tighter the closer I get, I see that Ben is having trouble breathing and I'm pretty sure he's barely holding himself back from jumping me right here in the church.

Brayden adjusts the train of my dress as I move to stand facing Ben, and now I'm blinking hard and fast to keep the tears from falling. Ben is grinning ear to ear, and his hands are strong and warm and steady as they engulf mine. I barely hear Father Mike as he talks about love and the sanctity of marriage.

I take a moment to look at the gathered crowd before I read my vows to Ben. I look at Brayden, see the happiness in his eyes for us, but at the same time I notice a heaviness lurking behind it—something that's been there for so long now. I don't know any details, but I make a note to pin him down on it, later.

I glance at Kylie, a knockout in her dove-gray pin-up-style bridesmaid dress, and she offers me a warm smile. Oz is beside her, one of Ben's groomsmen, along with Colt and a couple of the players from the Titans that Ben is close to. God, that arrangement of groomsmen is enough to make a girl swoon, let me tell you. The three football players are massive and gorgeous in a rugged sort of way, and then there's Colt, who is hot as hell for an older guy, his electric blue eyes standing out against his swarthy skin and black hair. Oz is the tallest one in the line-up, standing nearly six-five and pretty built in his own right, although the football players dwarf him in terms of musculature. He's rough and hard looking with tattoos and pierced ears, but he's heartstoppingly attractive as well. And then…there's my soon-to-be husband. And to me, obviously, he's the sexiest of all of them.

He's tall and broad, filling out the tuxedo like he was made for it, his eyes shining as they meet mine.

I draw a deep breath, and then read my vows

from the notecard. "Ben, I have to admit I struggled with what to say to you in these vows. Nothing seems like enough. I could promise you I'd love you and only you forever, but...that's implied in the fact that I'm marrying you at all, I'd say. The first and last time I'll wear white...remember that? I could also promise you I'd be faithful and true, but I could no more betray you than I could tear my own still-beating heart from my chest. I could promise to take care of you in every circumstance life throws at us, but again, taking care of you, being there for you, being your companion and your soul mate and your life partner...that's as much a part of who I am as my music is. So, in the end, all I could think of to say is...I love you. Now and forever, come what may." I swallow hard, and Ben squeezes my hand.

He clears his throat. "Well...I've got even less to say, then. I didn't even write it down, because it's just what's in my heart. I promise to love you and only you with all that I am, for as long we both live, and I promise to love you in whatever lies beyond this life. I promise to be at your side for every adventure and hardship and success that life throws at us. I love you, Echo. You're my everything, now and forever, come what may."

I have to laugh, then, and glance at our family

and friends to explain. "We wrote our vows separately, and didn't share them. So the fact that we both ended our vows the same way?" I'm fighting tears, breathe through it until I can continue. "It just shows you how this is meant to be."

There's one more thing we have to do before we can say I do: there are four white candles on a small, cloth-covered table, a large one in the center, with three smaller ones around it, one to the left, one to the right, and one in front. I light one candle, Ben lights one, and then we each touch the lit wicks of our individual candles and light the third smaller one with both of ours, and then we use that third candle together to light the largest. There's an extra step to this candle ceremony, an extra candle: one for me, one for Ben, and one for Mom. I hold on to the candle that represents Mom for a second, gaze into the flickering flame, and whisper a prayer to her memory. It's a moment just for me. I breathe through the pain of missing her, blink away the tears, and set the candle down beside the largest one that represents my union to Ben.

Father Mike takes my hand, places it in Ben's. "Echo, do you take Ben to be your lawfully wedded husband, for better or for worse, in sickness and in health, till death do you part…now and forever?" He smiles at me as he adds the phrase from our vows.

"I do," I say, my voice strong, my eyes bright.

"And Ben, do you take Echo to be your lawfully wedded wife, for better or for worse, in sickness and in health, till death do you part, now and forever?"

"I do."

"Then by the power vested in me by the State of Texas, and more importantly by our Lord and Savior Jesus Christ, I now pronounce you husband and wife." He turns to our gathered loved ones. "May I be the first to present to you Mr. and Mrs. Benjamin Dorsey!"

It's done. I'm Ben's wife. I feel giddy, over-whelmed with joy, brimming with completion.

Ben and I walk down the aisle together, the band playing "Forever and Always" by Parachute, Mim doing the vocals in that raspy, bluesy voice of hers.

When we reach the front steps of the church, we are overwhelmed by a crowd of loved ones—family and friends—waiting to greet Ben and me.

Colt hugs me, huge, tattooed arms around my shoulders, whispering congratulations, and then Nell is patting my cheek and crying with me, and then there's Jason Dorsey, my father-in-law, already a father to me. And Becca, her deep brown eyes, so like Ben's, on mine and shining with an overflowing wealth of love. Grandma and Grandpa are pulled into the melee by Ben's mom and they are laughing and hugging with everyone, glad to be part of this celebration.

Atticus, Vance, Will, and Mim all hug me in turn, congratulating Ben and me, telling me they love me. And then there's Brayden, and I've got a special hug for him, a long, tearful embrace.

The rain of rice, the cheering of my friends and Ben's family, now my family as well. Everyone is so happy. It all seems like a big, beautiful dream.

A perfect dream. One I never thought would be mine. A family to embrace me. Friends who respect me. And a man to love me. A man who saw something in me I couldn't see in myself. A man who loves me for who I am. A man who will inspire me for my whole life long. I couldn't ask for anything more.

The End

Postscript

That's it. The end.

There will be no more books in The Falling Series. I'm emotional as I write this note. Okay, so maybe I'm crying, just a little. I mean, I had no idea when I wrote *Falling Into You* how deeply rooted into the DNA of my identity as a writer these characters would become. *Falling Into You* is so special to me, being so instrumental in propelling me to where I am today, thanks to all of you, and how much you love these characters. Colt and Nell, Jason and Becca, Oz and Kylie, and now Ben and Echo...they're special people. Their stories are part of the song my stories sing. I'll miss them.

But I have to leave this on a happy note, so let me tell you now that even though there won't be any more Falling books, this isn't the total, final END.

Brayden needs his story after all, doesn't he? I think he does. And so do Atticus, Vance, Mim, and Will (not necessarily in that order).

So…(Drum roll, please):

Look for:

Echo the Stars: Brayden
Coming in 2015

Playlist

I should probably mention that *Falling Away* technically takes place in the theoretical future, some eighteen or twenty years after the events of *Falling Into You* and *Falling Into Us*. But, as this isn't a science fiction novel and I'm not interested in discussing time travel, we're just going to happily ignore that little technicality and pretend that all this music is current and relevant to these characters. I hope you enjoy these songs and the incredible artists who created them as much as I do. Support them. Support art.

"Cowboy Side of You" by Clare Dunn
"Let Her Go" by Passenger
"Better Dig Two" by The Band Perry
"Give Me Back My Hometown" by Eric Church
"What Hurts the Most" by Rascal Flatts
"Whiskey Lullaby" by Brad Paisley and Alison Krauss
"Country Must Be Country Wide" by Brantley Gilbert
"Doing It Our Way" by Gloriana
"More Than Miles" by Brantley Gilbert
"The One that Got Away" by Jake Owen
"Even If It Breaks Your Heart" by the Eli Young Band
"Leave the Pieces" by The Wreckers
"Oh Juliet" by Joel Crouse

"Broussard's Lament" by Sarah Jarosz
"Henry Lee" by Crooked Still
"Undone in Sorrow" by Crooked Still
"Anji" by Simon & Garfunkel
"3 A.M." by Gregory Alan Isakov
"Ebb & Flow" by Brown Bird
"Forever and Always" by Parachute

About the Author

New York Times and *USA Today* bestselling author Jasinda Wilder is a Michigan native with a penchant for titillating tales about sexy men and strong women. When she's not writing, she's probably shopping, baking, or reading. She loves to travel, and some of her favorite vacations spots are Las Vegas, New York City, and Toledo, Ohio. You can often find Jasinda drinking sweet red wine with frozen berries.

To find out more about Jasinda and her other titles, visit her website: www.JasindaWilder.com.

CPSIA information can be obtained at www.ICGtesting.com
Printed in the USA
LVOW07s1511100415

434096LV00005B/466/P